Praise for *Like No Other*, by Una LaMarche

"One of the most poignant and star-crossed love stories since *The Fault in Our Stars.*"

—*Entertainment Weekly*

"Electrifying . . . surprisingly seductive. LaMarche expertly conjures up what high-stakes infatuation feels like.

—*The New York Times Book Review*

"Refreshing tale of forbidden love."

—*People*

"LaMarche tells a truly complex urban story worth telling."

—*Vogue*

★"[T]he dire consequences that threaten this clandestine romance make the novel read like a thriller. . . . Readers will fall for these two love-struck teenagers as easily as they fall for each other."

—*Publishers Weekly*, starred review

"Romantic and wonderful and heartbreaking."

—Slate.com

"You root for Devorah and Jaxon because you remember you were once like them. From our first love or our first rebellion, they are a way for us to relive those strange and exciting days."

—*Boston Herald*

"*Like No Other* is a moving coming-of-age story that will have even adults remembering the burning intensity and insecurities of their first love."

—*VOYA*

"LaMarche alternates between the two perspectives, prefacing each chapter with a date and time stamp, underlining how time expands and contracts in odd ways when one is in love. [Devorah and Jaxon's] time together is forbidden and precious, making each moment simultaneously infinite and too short. Fans of Rainbow Rowell's *Eleanor & Park* . . . will enjoy this story of surprising love."

—*School Library Journal*

"[R]eaders will be fascinated by this peek into a different world, empathetic with the couple's feelings and buoyed by the hopeful ending."

—*Booklist*

"[Devorah's] struggle between tradition and modernity, filial duty and personal fulfillment, is complicated and realistic. . . . This leads to a conclusion that, while bittersweet, is still hopeful."

—*The Horn Book*

Don't Fail Me Now

Don't Fail Me Now

Una LaMarche

razOr bill

An Imprint of Penguin Random House

razOr bill
Penguin.com
Razorbill, an Imprint of Penguin Random House

ISBN: 978-1-59514-817-9

Printed in the United States of America

1 3 5 7 9 10 8 6 4 2

To my parents, Ellen and Gara, who have never failed me . . . and who, therefore, did not inspire this novel in any way. Sorry, guys. I love you.

ONE

Sunday Night/Monday Morning
Baltimore, MD

"Michelle? I'm scared."

Denny's voice cuts through the static that's been building in my brain, a surround-sound symphony of panic made even worse by the digital hiss and spit of the police intercom. My little brother nestles his face into my side, and I lift my half-asleep hand to rest on the soft, tight curls at the nape of his neck.

"It's okay," I say, squeezing him three times in quick succession, which is our family code for *it's going to be okay.* The simple act still soothes me, even though now that I'm grown I can see the irony: A family that needs that kind of a code is not now, and has probably never been, okay. I bend down to kiss the top of his head. "Can you go back to sleep?"

Denny shrugs, burrowing deeper into my T-shirt. "Ina wanu gotslepgin," he mumbles into my armpit.

"Huh?"

He looks up at me with big, watery eyes. "I don't want *you* to go to sleep again," he says.

"Oh, I wasn't sleeping, only . . ." Only paralyzed with anxiety. Not exactly a bedtime story fit for a first grader. "I was just zoning out."

"I want you to stay with me," he whimpers.

They'll try to split you up! I get a flash of my mom, wild-eyed with terror.

"I will, meatball, I promise." I use our family's pet name for him—Denny was the roundest, brownest baby you ever saw—in a cheap attempt to make him feel safe and am rewarded instantly with a teary, hesitant smile that turns into a yawn halfway through, revealing a missing front tooth that—surprise, surprise—the "Tooth Fairy" still owes him for. She tends to save her quarters for other things. I feel another twinge of dread.

Don't let them split you up!

"Hey, do you have any homework we could finish?" I ask, trying to sound like this is a normal, fun activity that siblings often do together when they find themselves stuck in a police precinct at one A.M. on a school night.

Denny nods and leans down, sending the cavernous neck of his men's-size Goodwill T-shirt sliding up over the back of his big mug-handle ears, and pulls his backpack out from under Cass's feet, which causes my sleeping sister to thrash dramatically before burying her face back into her hoodie. The officer at the front desk, a hard-looking Latina with her hair pulled back so tight it gives her cartoon-villain eyebrows, glances up at the commotion and glares at us, and my jaw tenses.

We don't want to be here either.

Fresh shame floods my cheeks as I think back to all of the hushed whispers and pitying glances that greeted us when we got brought in four hours ago, and also to the tall, pasty cop who poked his head out of a door down the hall and made a joke about "crack babies" to whoever was inside.

"Here," Denny says, holding a sheet of paper up in front of me, interrupting my revenge fantasy about punching that ignorant douche right in the center of his big pie-dough face. It's a photocopy of a drawing of a wide, squat tree with two big branches that curl out from the center, making a heart in the middle. Inside the big, fluffy outline of leaves there are four rows of blank boxes. At the top, in a thick, curly font, it says *my family*. "I'm s'posed to fill it in, but I forget how," he says, rubbing his eyes.

I remember this assignment. Denny's in first grade now and has the same teacher I had when I went to his school eleven years ago, Mrs. Mastino. I remember filling out my family tree and having my mother proudly stick it to the fridge with three letter magnets: *M*, *H*, and *D* for my initials. I remember how it stayed up there for two years before she finally ripped it up and threw it away along with all of the other memories of him.

I take the paper from Denny and point to the bottom row of boxes. "You fill it in starting backward," I explain, furrowing my brow, wishing I had a coffee or a soda to aid me in my fake enthusiasm. "This here is us: you, me, and Cass." I point to the next row up. "That's mom and Buck, then above them is—"

"You mean Dad," Denny says, and I trap the tip of my tongue between my teeth, biting down until it goes numb, a coping trick I picked up a long time ago and the reason why I still can't taste some things until they reach the back of my throat.

"Right," I repeat slowly. *"Dad."*

I don't remember when I started calling my father Buck, but it's the only way I can stomach referring to him now. It just makes it easier. "Buck" sounds like a mangy dog or a farm animal too lazy or stupid to find his way home, not like a grown man who walked out on his twenty-two-year-old wife and two kids and never looked back.

Denny, who came later, isn't Buck's son, but for the sake of simplicity we all just pretend he is. I mean, we don't *lie* to Denny—he knows his absent father was different from ours—but it's just easier for everyone to sort of merge them into one deadbeat-dad amalgam. No one except my mom knows who Denny's biological father is, and I would bet money that even she's not 100 percent sure. She was hanging out with a couple of guys around that time, bleary-eyed dudes reeking of skunky cologne she would introduce as "Uncle Trey," or "Cousin Freddy," even though we were old enough by then to know they weren't relatives. I went out of my way not to see them. At the sound of her key in the door, I would drag Cass up the tacky carpeted steps to our room, and we'd play Barbies or Legos and I'd turn on the radio to drown out the voices and clinking bottles downstairs.

But there's no box for "possible fathers" on Denny's worksheet, and our family history is too R-rated to fully explain to a six-year-old.

"You know, maybe we should do something else," I say, but

Denny's already hard at work, a pencil clutched in his little fist, moving slowly across the already-crinkled page on his lap. He proudly holds up the tree, on which he's written *mom*, *dad*, *michel* [sic], *cass*, *max*, and *denny* (with one backward *N*) in crooked capitals. (Max does not exist. Max is Denny's imaginary friend. He surfaced about seven months ago, when mom lost her latest job, showing up sporadically when Denny gets scared, and we can't seem to make him leave, no matter how hard we try. Max is—there's no nice way to put this—kind of a dick.)

"Nice work," I say. "I think your teacher wants full names, though. Here, how 'bout I write them down and you can copy them in."

Denny yawns and passes the paper back to me, letting his head drop against my chest. I glance up at the wall clock and catch Officer Tight Hair giving me a look again. Does she think Denny is my son, that I am some kind of preteen mom, too young and sad to even get my own show on MTV? I guess I can't blame her; it feels like that sometimes. Lately, all the time.

Madison Means Devereaux, I write on the back of the photocopy, trying to make my loose, loopy handwriting clear enough for Denny to read. My mother, Maddie Means, was neither mad nor mean before Buck Devereaux came along. They met in junior high, when Buck transferred schools after his own dad ran out on him (foreshadowing alert!), leaving his mom high and dry and unable to afford the nice suburban neighborhood she had been accustomed to living in. Mom sang in the choir back then, got straight As, and dreamed of going to Juilliard like Nina Simone. She was a pastor's daughter with a dangerous, dormant rebellious streak just waiting for the right trigger.

Speaking of which: *Allen Buckner Devereaux III*, I write,

wanting to roll my eyes hard at the difference between Buck's aristocratic-sounding name and the man himself, a handsome but aimless dropout grifter who couldn't hold a job or, based on the photos I've seen, keep a shirt on for longer than a church service. Right after he left, during her saddest moments, when she would crawl into my bed and curl around me, her sharp, sweet booze breath hot on my neck, Mom used to say that from the day they met it was true love. "I looked in those clear green eyes and saw my future," she'd whisper, hoarse from crying. I have those same green eyes. People always comment on them, so striking against my coppery skin. But I look in the mirror every day, and I can't see any future hiding behind my irises. All I can see in my father's eyes is the past.

Michelle Hope Devereux. I was conceived the same month my mother turned sixteen, which helps to explain why I'm named after Michelle Kwan, who skated her way to Olympic silver that winter while I was doing somersaults under Mom's school uniform. There was a party in the basement of my grandfather's church—Mom has a whole photo album devoted to it—with pink balloons and streamers, lemonade in plastic cups, and a big sheet cake with yellow buttercream frosting and pink letters spelling out *Sweet 16 Maddie Means.* In the pictures, Mom is wearing an orange silk dress with a matching short-sleeved jacket, smiling a coy, closed-lip smile as she poses with her parents and my aunt Sam and an endless parade of friends and relatives who have since cut all ties. Buck and his mother are there, too, loitering awkwardly in the background, beige from head to toe among a sea of black parishioners in their most festive jewel tones. It's the only time I've ever seen a photo of Buck wearing a tie. I wonder if they knew about me yet. I wonder if he was already plotting his escape.

I pause and look down at Denny, whose eyes are fluttering closed against my collarbone, his breath slowing into little waves punctuated by open-mouthed sighs. It's amazing how quickly kids can rebound; he was sobbing all the way to the station, asking me a million times where Mom was and where we were going. I tried to keep calm and reassure him without really answering any of his questions—I'll do anything to protect Denny's innocence, since he's the only one of us who's got any; he doesn't remember the first two times Mom got arrested because he wasn't born yet. Cass and I, on the other hand, we know the drill. We don't cry anymore. We just shut off.

This time, though, I know it's bad. They can't reach Aunt Sam—I've overheard two different officers leave her voicemails—and the next call they make will be to Child Protective Services. That's just what happens when you've got a junkie mother, a deadbeat dad, a missing aunt, and no other known living relatives. I swallow hard and put pencil to paper again, to keep the panic at bay.

Reverend Jeremiah Means and *Cynthia Smith Means*. After I was born, Grandma and Grandpa let Mom stay in the house to raise me, and they paid for all our food and clothes. But they also made it clear that Buck wasn't welcome in their home unless he came on bended knee with a ring, so depending on whom you ask, he either started taking odd jobs or grifting, going around charming people into giving him goods and services he had no intention of paying for, although Mom swears that didn't start until later, when they got really broke. It took him two years, but by the time Mom turned eighteen, the ring—a square quarter carat set in a thin gold band engraved with the letters *BM*, which is appropriate given how quickly things went down the toilet—finally showed up. By all accounts my grandparents were horrified that their bluff had been called, but they gave their blessings anyway. Two months after the ceremony, which Grandpa officiated in the sparse backyard under a near-dead crabapple tree, they got on a church bus headed to a conference in Philadelphia. It was barreling down the highway at sixty-five miles an hour when the front tire blew and the driver lost control, flipped over the median, and hit a tractor-trailer. Everyone on board was killed instantly.

Allen Buckner Devereaux Jr. and *Polly Devereaux.* These two have been AWOL since 1994 and 2000, respectively. They just peaced out. I have no idea if the elder ABD is still alive. Last my mom can recall, Polly moved someplace in the Midwest when Buck decided to go through with the wedding. Apparently she'd been trying to convince Buck to go with her, even saying she'd buy him a new car if he walked away from us, but Buck was young and in love, and besides, he was obsessed with "Goldie," the rusty, Band Aid–colored 1973 Datsun station wagon he'd inherited from *his* deadbeat dad. Incidentally, Polly never met me, but we still drive Goldie. In fact, she's sitting outside right now in the Baltimore Police Department parking lot after having been routinely searched for narcotics. It's like that "Circle of Life" song from *The Lion King,* only way more depressing.

"Shut *uuuuupppp,*" Cass groans, and for a split second I think I must be so fried that I'm saying all this out loud. But then one arm slips down from her face and dangles over the side of the bench, and I can see she's still out cold. Must be dreaming. Something's been bothering her for weeks, and I don't think it has anything to do with Mom's relapse. But every time I've tried to ask her about it, she shuts down. She was always a shy kid—neighbors used to joke they couldn't tell what she looked like since she was permanently plastered to the backs of Mom's knees—but now that she's thirteen, her natural quietness has turned into something more troubling. She's grown cold, even to me. Looking at her face these days, which is still the spitting image of Mom's, and cruelly beautiful despite the onset of puberty, is like watching a storm roll in from a distance while the sun still shines on you, wondering what it's like on the other side.

Cassidy Devereaux. Cass doesn't have a middle name, presumably because all hope had been abandoned by the time she came along when I was four. Mom and Buck were okay for a while, but after Mom's parents died, I think they realized how screwed they were, with a toddler, an old house to maintain, and only one (unreliable) source of income. According to Aunt Sam, that's when the dealing started in earnest. I'm not sure how much I should believe of what she tells me, since she's always resented the fact that Grandma and Grandpa left the house to their younger, helpless, irresponsible child when Sam had been busting her ass to put herself through nursing school *plus* managed to avoid a teen pregnancy. But Mom never had a real job until Buck left, so I have to wonder how they made ends meet for so long. And every time I smell pot in the parking lot at school, or on the late-night customers at the Taco Bell where I work, it's immediately comforting. I guess it must smell like home.

Cass wasn't an accident like me, but she didn't help to save a marriage that was already falling apart. My earliest memories are a collage of conflicting arguments: driving around with my parents singing along to the radio and dancing in their seats at red lights; watching TV with Buck while Mom cries loudly in an adjacent room; licking an ice cream cone at a petting zoo while Mom and Buck giggle and kiss above me; getting tugged in and out of my car seat while they scream at each other. They must have been on one of their highs when they decided to have my sister, not knowing she would come six weeks early on the day after Christmas, stretching their bare-bones insurance to its limit with a stay in the NICU, and sick again by the time she was five months old, underweight and shaking all the time, requiring daily insulin injections that would eventually put them in a debt they would never recover from.

Oh, shit, her insulin. I reach across Denny and pinch Cass's skinny calf through her jeans. "Cass," I say. "Cass, wake up. You need your shot."

She starts and squints at me, sleepy and confused, then looks around and slowly drags herself to a sitting position. Without a word, she unzips the front pocket of her backpack and takes out a Ziploc baggie full of needles and little glass bottles as well as a small foil pack of Wheat Thins. She rips open the crackers with her teeth and pops one into her mouth, then starts to roll up her shirt; Cass is so wiry that her stomach is the only place with enough padding so the shots don't hurt.

"Hey," cries Tight Hair, leaping to her feet. "Stop right there." She turns and yells, "Backup!" and the two arresting officers, one young and barrel-chested, one graying with a potbelly that thunders ahead of him by a good twelve inches, come running down the hall with their hands on their guns. Denny's hand on my waist turns into a viselike claw.

"She's got needles," Tight Hair says. Cass's mahogany eyes grow wide and scared.

"It's *insulin*," I snap, knowing I should watch my tone but unable to mask my anger. Protecting Cass has been my job since she was born. "She's *diabetic*."

"Lemme see," the young cop says, softening his stance. Cass hands him the baggie, and he examines the contents for a long moment. "You got a prescription?" he asks.

With trembling hands, Cass reaches into her backpack again and produces a silver MedicAlert bracelet engraved with her name and condition. She hasn't worn it since she was eight, but at Mom's insistence she always keeps it in her bag. This realization sends even sharper stabs of anger shooting through my veins. Mom was doing so much better. This wasn't supposed to happen again. She swore it wouldn't.

"Okay," the cop says to Cass, attempting a goofy "oops, my bad!" smile. "But you can't do that out here. Come with me, and I'll take you to the ladies' room."

Cass looks at me as if for permission, and I nod. Reluctantly, she follows the officers back down the hall, slouching into her big sweatshirt like it's an invisibility cloak.

"See, she's okay," I whisper into the top of Denny's head. "Everything's okay." I squeeze again, three times. Lie, lie, lie.

"Where's Mom?" he whimpers. "I wanna see Mom."

"Mom . . . has to stay here for the night," I say. "But Aunt Sam is going to pick us up, and we'll have a sleepover at her house." I say "sleepover" like we'll be sleeping on lumpy blankets on the living room floor by choice, as some kind of fun adventure that'll end in ghost stories and s'mores.

"I hate Aunt Sam's," Denny says quietly.

"I know, meatball. It won't be for long this time."

"Max says it will."

Of course he does. Max's contribution to any conversation is usually pessimistic. "Well," I sigh, "tell Max he doesn't know what I know." Turning over the paper where I've been listing the names, I write *Dennis Devereux* inside the heart at the center of the tree. "See?" I say. "You're safe in there." But Denny looks unsure; even little kids know bullshit when they smell it.

"What if Aunt Sam doesn't come?" he asks.

"She's coming," I say.

"When?"

"Soon," I whisper, raising my eyes to the ceiling, repeating it like a prayer even though it's been years and way too many sins since I've seen the inside of a church. "She's coming soon."

An hour later our aunt is still AWOL, but we do have some surprise visitors: a dozen crazy drunk bachelor partiers who tried to sneak out on their tab at Scores. They're so loud and sloppy while the officers try to deal with them that Tight Hair sourly ushers the three of us into a nearby break room so that we don't get trampled or scarred for life hearing all the shouting about some stripper named Nico and the unusual locations of her body piercings. Cass and Denny both brighten when they see the vending machines, so I give them each $3 to buy whatever they want, and as we cluster around a small table eating our snacks and sharing a can of Sprite with a straw pushed through the tab, for a minute things start to feel okay. Normal, even.

"When's your tree thing due, Denny?" I ask between handfuls of carefully curated Skittles combinations.

"I dunno," he shrugs, licking Doritos dust off his thumb.

"Just tell them our family tree burned down," Cass says with a wry smile. "Deforestation."

"Huh?"

"She's kidding," I say, but Denny's already forgotten.

"If we stay here all night, can we stay home from school tomorrow?" he asks hopefully.

"We're *not* staying all night," I say.

"Maybe we are," Cass mumbles.

"Well, even if we do . . ." I don't know how to explain to them that no one's just going to drop us off at our doorstep like we've been on some kind of extra-credit field trip, that we might not get to live in our house or sleep in our beds again for weeks or even months. We might end up with Aunt Sam, or we might get sent to foster care (*Don't let them split you up!*: the last thing Mom yelled as the potbellied cop pushed her head down into the back of the cruiser), but no matter what happens, the one thing we can depend on is that *someone* will make us keep going to school. I realize Cass and Denny are staring at me, waiting for me to finish, so I just shake my head. "We can't get out of school," I say. "I mean, who's going to write our absence notes?"

"Mom can! She was there!" Denny says brightly, starting in on a Three Musketeers bar, and without warning tears spring to my eyes. His trust breaks my heart.

The thing is, Denny doesn't really have a reason not to trust Mom. He forced her to get her shit together—at least as much as shit like hers can be contained (I see it like, most people trip and fall every once in a while, but Mom walked off a cliff when she met Buck and has been falling ever since without realizing it, like one of those Roadrunner cartoons where for a second the dumbass coyote thinks he's just walking on air). The years right before Denny were some of her lowest. She had a string of failed part-time jobs that introduced Cass and me to a rotating roster of strange and wet-eyed babysitters—mostly friends Mom made at the bar—who would use up all our Hi-C making mixed drinks and then either fall asleep on the couch or yell at someone on the phone. She got on unemployment for a while and seemed more stable, but then came her back-to-back arrests for shoplifting and drunk driving, and Aunt Sam moved in with us for a few months. I wish I could say those months were better, but Sam's basically just a mean drunk without the drunk part. As Mom likes to say, she's got a big ol' bug up her ass about us living in "her" house. It's to Mom's credit that even when she was using, she never took my aunt up on her offers to buy the house back, because I don't even want to think about what she could have done to herself with that kind of cash.

"Michelle, you can do Mom's writing, right?" Cass asks. Apparently the conversation's been going on without me, and now the two of them are plotting.

"I'm not doing that," I say flatly. The last thing I need is to be worrying about what those two are doing all day by themselves; school hours—when I can forget about my family for a while, replacing them with Spanish verb conjugations and pointless, empty conversations with the friends I never invite home—are the only times the anxious static subsides.

Cass glowers at me. "You don't even care because you're almost done," she says. "In two months you'll never have to go to school again." She crumples up her Fritos bag and crushes it into the tabletop with her palm. *"Lucky bitch."*

"Hey!" I cry. "Watch it."

Cass rolls her eyes dramatically. "Like Denny's never heard a curse. Doesn't he have Tourette's or something?"

Denny grins, his teeth smeared with chocolate. "Poopy pants!" he cries. It's true that Denny's teachers have complained about him disrupting class, but his outbursts tend to be pretty G-rated. Pee-pee, butt, stupid head, poop: your average first grader's nuggets of comedy gold. I'm not saying it's *great* or anything, but he's not exactly calling someone a stank-ass ho.

"No," I say sharply. "He's fine. And I'm not—" *Lucky*, I want to say. *I'm not lucky.* But instead I say, "I'm not letting you guys cut school."

Cass shrugs and sits back in her chair, but she's chewing furiously on her lower lip—her giveaway since age two that she's trying not to cry.

"Sorry," I mutter.

"Poop, poop, poop," Denny laughs, which are my thoughts exactly. And then there's a knock on the glass behind us.

I turn around to see a short, middle-aged woman with a gray pixie cut and a navy pantsuit standing in the doorway. She's clutching a slim, leather-covered notebook, a pen, and a digital recorder, and she's smiling in that overcompensating way that doctors smile at little kids before giving them a shot. I don't have to look at the ID clipped to her blouse to know she's from Child Protective Services. I stand up, instinctively trying to block Cass and Denny from seeing her, from understanding what she's here for.

"Hi," she says in a condescending, honeyed voice. "Are you Michelle?"

"Our aunt is coming," I blurt in a panic. "She's probably almost here."

They'll try to split you up.

The lady nods even more condescendingly and says, "My

name is Janet. I just need to talk to you for a few minutes. May I sit down?"

I want to say no, to take her fancy notebook, hurl it down the hallway, throw both siblings over one shoulder like I'm Schwarzenegger in *Commando* (Buck's favorite movie, left behind on DVD, and the only thing we have in common besides our eye color), and run until my legs give out. But I know I have no recourse; we're a bunch of unaccompanied minors in a police station in the middle of the night. I step back and lower myself into my plastic bucket chair, folding my hands primly on the table as if somehow weaving my fingers together can contain this phenomenal mess we're in. Cass looks Janet up and down without a word or even so much as a facial twitch. Denny, meanwhile, bounces rhythmically in his seat. I shouldn't have let him have so much sugar all at once.

Janet pulls up a chair between Cass and me and sits with her legs crossed, placing her supplies in a neat row in front of her. She pushes a button on the recorder and then opens the notebook, licking her thumb to turn the pages. I hate that. Seriously, how hard is it to separate two flimsy pieces of paper without smearing your germy saliva all over the place?

"You guys must be tired," she says with a sympathetic frown.

Cass and I say nothing, but Denny, who doesn't know better, chirps, "I took a nap before, and then I had a candy bar." He eyes her notebook. "Can I draw?" This kid will talk to anyone. It must be in his dad's genes, because Cass and I are like Mom, immediately suspicious of strangers until proven otherwise—and maybe even then.

"Sure," Janet says, neatly tearing out a sheet. "I even have an extra pen." She hands Denny one of those thick ones with the four different ink colors that you can change by pushing down the buttons, and Denny beams. I bet she uses that pen exclusively to charm small children.

"So," Janet continues, looking back and forth between the three of us, probably searching for physical signs of abuse she can put in her bullshit report, "I just have a few questions to ask so we can get you out of here as soon as possible." She smiles at Denny. "I'll start with an easy one: How old are you?"

"I'm six," Denny says proudly.

"Thirteen," Cass mutters, barely audible.

"Seventeen," I say, then quickly add, "But I'll be eighteen in July."

Janet raises her eyebrows and writes something down. "Okay," she says. "And you live with your mother, correct?"

"Yes," I say quickly. I don't want my sister and brother to say another word to this woman. I feel familiar tingles climbing up my neck. Ever since I was little I've had episodes—not attacks, exactly, more like tidal waves that I drown in for just a few seconds at a time. It's like I get paralyzed, only it's my brain that shuts down, not my body; my anxiety reaches some max-fill line and overrides the system. I close my eyes and focus on my heart beating, reminding myself that I'm still alive. When I open them again, Cass is being her usual stone-cold self, staring off at a wall poster outlining the steps of the Heimlich maneuver, and Denny is immersed in coloring in the legs on a dinosaur.

"There's no other adult in the home?" Janet asks, not looking up from her notebook.

"No." I splay my fingers out on the tabletop, feeling my weight pressing into the scratched black vinyl, trying to root myself like a tree without soil.

"Is the other biological parent deceased?"

I wish. "No."

"And does your mother have a boyfriend or significant other?"

"No."

"Any living grandparents?"

"Not that I know of."

"But you do have an aunt."

"Yeah, my mom's sister."

Janet licks her thumb again and flips back a few pages, looking for something. "That would be . . . Samara Means?"

"Right."

"And she lives locally?"

"Yes."

Scribble, scribble, scribble.

"Any other aunts or uncles?"

"No."

"And you're all in school full-time?"

"Yes."

"Do you depend on your mother to take you to school?"

"No, she takes the bus and I drive us."

Janet frowns, sending a web of lines running down the sides of her mouth and off of her cheeks like tributaries from a river. "You know," she says, "it's in violation of your provisional license to have other minors in the car without supervision."

Shit. "I . . . um . . ." The truth is, I *am* familiar with that particular passage in Maryland's DMV manual, but what else am I supposed to do? Mom works—well, *worked*, anyway—from seven thirty to six, and we all have to be at three different schools spanning six miles between seven forty-five and eight fifteen, and Denny gets out at two forty-five and then Cass at three ten, and I have to bring both of them to Taco Bell by four for my shift so they can do homework and eat the edible-but-messed-up-looking kitchen errors for free, so we're all screwed unless I take a little creative license with the driving laws.

"Well, I'm sure you can find a suitable alternative for the next month," Janet says with a thin smile.

"I'm sure," I parrot hollowly.

"Would you say your family is . . . isolated?" she asks. I wonder how long this checklist is and whether she has some key at the end that'll tell her where we fall on the spectrum between the Cosbys and the Mansons.

"No, we're right here in the city, over in Berea." Our house is one slightly busted-looking brick row house on a block of dozens. Like most of low-income Baltimore, our street has a few abandoned, boarded-up lots, places you have to stomp by after dark so the rats won't dart out from under the rotting stairs and scare the bejesus out of you. But it's not the boonies by any means.

"Of course," Janet says, a little impatiently. "I mean, do you see friends, have people over?"

"Yes," I say. But the truth is I haven't brought a friend home in years, not since I was a kid. There was this one girl in particular I remember, named Excelyn, who was Mexican and had black braids down to her hips. She would come over after school, and we'd watch cartoons or play with Cass while she bounced in this little chair that hung in the kitchen doorway, and Mom would cut grilled cheese into long strips that she called monkey fingers. There was also a girl named Rosemarie who didn't go to my school but was the daughter of one of my grandpa's parishioners who tried to help Mom for a while after her parents passed. For some reason I don't remember any identifying details about Rosemarie except that in the bathroom at her house, there was a clear, round liquid soap dispenser that matched the seasons. In December it would have a little Santa hat floating in it; in April, a nest of colored eggs; in July, an American flag. At the time, it seemed like an unfathomable luxury item, and later, when things got bad, I sometimes thought of that soap dispenser, convinced that if we were the kind of family who had one, it would have protected us somehow. Made everything perfect.

"So you have a social life outside the home?" Janet presses.

"Yeah," I lie, trying to sound casual, like I don't eat the same fast-food bean burrito for dinner every night in the cramped booth right by the men's room exit, which is the least popular booth due to the pervasive urinal-cake stench, and therefore the only one my manager will let my latchkey siblings park themselves for hours on end.

Janet scribbles in her notebook and then looks up at me, fixing me once again with Meaningful Eye Contact. We're so close I can see the contact lenses glistening on her slate-colored irises.

"Have any of you suffered physical abuse at the hands of your mother or another adult in the home?" She asks this in the same tone of voice that she used when she asked how old we were.

"No," I say, forcing myself to keep calm for Denny's benefit. I glance across the table at Cass and see in her face that she's thinking the exact same thing I am: *We could take her.*

Janet furrows her brow sympathetically. "I know it's a sensitive topic, but this is a standard question in cases where substance abuse is also present." She thinks I'm lying, when for once I'm not. I bite down hard on my tongue.

Denny holds up the drawing he's been working on, oblivious to the tension in the room. "Look!" he cries. "It's a *T. rex* eating a *Brachiosaurus*!" Denny has worn out the red ink cartridge on Janet's bribe pen making spurts of blood shooting out of every possible place on the dinosaur's body, and she smiles at him before jotting something down in her notes. Great.

"No," I say.

Janet nods. "Not even slapping, spanking, that sort of thing?"

I look over at Cass again. Of course Mom handled us rough sometimes when we were mouthing off or misbehaving, but we got it no worse than anyone else we knew. And if anything, the drugs made her seem kind of helpless. She was always much more likely to float through the house like a ghost or lock herself in her bedroom than take anything out on us. For better or worse, she took it all out on herself.

I briefly consider telling the truth but then decide that I'm not going to give this bitch the satisfaction. "Nope," I say.

"But you can confirm that substance abuse is present in the home?" Janet looks at me expectantly, pen poised to write down what she thinks she already knows. And I get that she's just doing her job, and that I probably should be grateful that she's using words Denny can't understand, but I still hate her. I hate her for taking the things that make us ache inside and putting them down on paper, which will turn into some typed report that will turn into a file in some computer database so that anyone can just punch in my name and read about the worst parts of my life anytime they feel like it. I hate her for doing it in front of

Cass and Denny, and I hate her for the way she turns the pages in her shitty little notebook. But mostly I hate her for thinking she can crack me. I take a deep breath and meet her gaze.

"No," I say calmly. "I've never seen her do anything." It's the truth, actually. I've never seen my mother use drugs. Have I found tiny plastic baggies in the bathroom garbage? Does the aluminum foil routinely go missing, only to reappear as charred little strips littering the ground below my mother's bedroom window? Do I notice the heat blisters on her lips and nostrils that she tries to cover with makeup or pass off as cold sores? These are different questions, with different answers. But they're not what Janet asked. If she wants to know if my mom is a drug addict, she can just march her smarmy pantsuited ass down to the evidence room and look at the eight dime bags of heroin the cops caught her with in the Shell station bathroom while we all sat in the car fifty feet away arguing over what movie to watch when we got home.

Janet narrows her eyes at me as if trying to read my face, and for a second I think she's going to press me on it. But then she just writes something down, shuts her notebook, and turns off the recorder.

"All right," she says, standing up. "Thank you. I'll just speak to the officers, and hopefully we can get you out of here and into a shelter as soon as possible."

"Wait, *shelter*?" Cass says, horrified, dropping the deaf-mute act for a minute. "What about Aunt Sam?" She looks at me, wild-eyed with fear, the spitting image of Mom for all the wrong reasons. "She's coming, right?"

"Aunt Sam's not coming?" Denny cries, his big dark eyes instantly brimming with tears.

The panic starts to rise again, and before the dizzying whoosh of blood from my racing heart threatens to render me speechless, I scramble to come up with something, *anything*, I can say to stall whatever's coming next.

"She might not be coming *right now*," I sputter, "but—"

"Oh, like hell I'm not coming," my aunt says sharply from the doorway. I spin around to see her, looking tired and pissed off in her nurse's scrubs and running shoes, like a slightly older, less pretty version of Mom from some alternate universe where time marched on in the boring way it's supposed to. "I'm here, aren't I?" She crosses her arms and looks us over one by one with some mix of pity and annoyance. "Dragged off my shift at two o'clock in the morning, left a man with a half-stapled knife wound, but here I am. And they told me I had to take a cab since she left you with that janky car, too. So you owe me $18." With anyone else, this might be a deadpan joke, but Aunt Sam is serious. She doesn't treat us like her own kids, *mi-casa-es-su-casa* style, or even like the nieces and nephews we are. When we stay at her house, we're lodgers who earn our keep, and she tallies every nickel of what we cost her.

Janet flashes her elementary school art teacher smile at my aunt—*good luck with that*—and holds out her hand. "Mrs. Means," she says, "it's so nice to meet you."

"I'm not a *Mrs.*," Sam snaps. "Who are you?"

"I'm Janet Winters, with Maryland Child Protective Services, and I can't tell you how glad I am that—"

Aunt Sam waves away the attempted handshake. "We don't need you, sister, are you blind? I showed up, didn't I? Now I have to get back to my job, so if you'll excuse me . . ." She claps impatiently. "Come on, let's go, get your stuff."

I hold out my hand to Denny, and he grabs it with a sweaty palm, but not before stuffing his drawings back into his bag along with the four-color pen. (It's probably not on purpose—he's tired and overwhelmed—but in this family you never know.) Cass reluctantly peels herself out of her chair, gazing almost wistfully at the vending machines, knowing that where we're headed won't be nearly this good. Aunt Sam takes off like a race walker, and we rush to catch up, but as I'm stepping out into the hallway, Janet shoots me a look of real sympathy and presses a business card into my palm.

It's not until I'm buckled into Goldie's passenger seat, smelling her signature scent of old tacos and gasoline and looking out her milky windows at the sad, squat, salmon-colored building where we've been trapped for six hours, that I turn the card over in my hand. On the back, Janet has written:

Have you thought about seeking custody of C & D when you turn eighteen? Feel free to call me w/ any questions.

As Aunt Sam peels out of the parking lot, I toss it onto the floor, lean back, and close my eyes. I can't think about that right now—not that I haven't thought about it, agonized over it, since I was too young to even know what it was that I was feeling, that impulse to wake up my sleeping sister and run off into the night. I know what's involved now: the lawyers, the documents, the character assassination of the only person who's ever loved me, no matter how wrong-headedly that love has been expressed at times. But however I spin it, going after custody seems like a sudden-death game that all of us will lose. Because I know I have no future if I stay here. But what kind of future will I condemn my brother and sister to if I leave?

TWO

Monday Afternoon/Monday Night
Baltimore, MD

"You pull an all-nighter or something?" my friend Noemi asks Monday, sliding into the seat next to mine in Mr. Medina's AP physics class. She looks me over with a smirk, pursing her freshly glossed lips. "You look like an extra from *The Walking Dead*. But, you know, in a hot way."

Normally her digs don't really bother me—Noemi's one of those people who thinks true friendship means "being real," aka brutally honest, at all times, which is both annoying and guilt-inducing, considering how much I hide from her—but right now I can't work up the energy to appreciate her level of realness.

"I didn't get a chance to shower," I say, flipping my notebook open. Inside the front cover are columns of handwritten math I spent the night doing and redoing, trying to end up with a number greater than zero. Later today Mom has a hearing to determine her bail, and usually the bondsman will take 10 percent and let you pay the rest on a plan. I have $200 saved, and I get paid again on Friday, but it will make things tight for a while. Well, more than tight, actually. Impossible.

"Okay, but a rubber band?" Noemi laughs, pointing to my DIY hair tie, courtesy of Aunt Sam's junk drawer. "Girl, that's worse than a scrunchie."

I ignore her. We've been friends since ninth-grade Science Club, back when she had braces and bushy eyebrows, and Noemi made me cry laughing when she did a song parody of Lady Gaga's "Poker Face" called "Fetal Pig." But now she's part of a different clique, higher on the food chain. She's invited me to some of their parties, but I can never go, so we're strictly classroom friends at this point. It's just as well. Months back, I stopped telling her any kind of truth about my home life.

Luckily, Mr. Medina stands up and drums his fists on his desk before Noemi can ask any more questions.

"Please put away your textbooks and close your notebooks," he says with a thin smile. "I hope everyone did the assigned reading over the weekend, because it's time for a quiz."

There's a collective groan, and Noemi scowls and curses under her breath. At least I'm not the only one who's going to fail. And how could it possibly even matter if I do? It's April of my senior year, and I'm not exactly waiting around for the mailman to drop off my college-acceptance letters. I was thinking about it a lot last summer, researching financial aid and trying to put aside some money for application fees, but then in September all of the drama happened at Mom's job, and everything fell apart pretty quickly. My higher education was just one of the many things lost in the rubble.

"Good luck," Mr. Medina says cheerfully as he drops a quiz on my desk.

"Thanks," I mumble, self-consciously pulling the rubber band out of my hair.

I stare at the questions for a few seconds, trying to focus through my exhaustion and see if there's any way I can fake my way through, but eventually I give up and just leave it blank. I don't even write my name on it, but hey, Mr. Medina's a scientist. He'll figure it out.

I drift through the rest of the school day until it's time to pick up Denny, half-depressed and half-relieved that no one else has asked me how I'm doing. I skipped my usual lunch date with the Science Clubbers—we officially disbanded as an academic group junior year due to low turnout, and Noemi doesn't come anymore, but me, Manny, and Yi-Lo have stuck together, mostly because as the social stratification gradually solidified, we've all ended up belonging nowhere, to no one particular person or crew. But even though they're great, I didn't feel like facing them, so I napped in a corner of the library. When I want to, I've gotten good at hiding in plain sight at school, skimming along the surface without sticking, like everyone else is water and I'm a drop of oil that got spilled in by accident.

I cross the parking lot and wince when I notice a group of guys standing on the grass smoking cigarettes about ten feet from Goldie's front bumper. Next to all of the unassuming compact cars and sleek SUVs, she looks like a joke prop from a movie set, maybe a comedy about someone's broke 1970s-era grandma who decides to moonlight as a funeral director (Goldie's rear end is so long and boxy, a lot of people assume she's a hearse). The paint, which has faded over the years to the approximate shade of a decaying molar, is peeling around the wheel wells, and dark amber rust coats the back bumper, which is dented in three separate places but doesn't hold a candle to the exhaust pipe, which has detached so far from the muffler that it nearly scrapes the ground. The driver's side door had to get replaced when I was little—Buck left it open after a night of drinking, and it got torn off in a hit-and-run, keys still in the ignition—but the color had been discontinued, so that door is pale and awkward now, like a patch of skin missing pigment. Goldie's namesake golden years—if they ever existed—are long gone now. Even Buck didn't want her anymore—although I guess that's not saying much, considering his track record of ditching things he once supposedly loved.

"Nice ride," one of the boys, a thick football player–type who I vaguely recognize from my sophomore biology lab, shouts as I shove my key into Goldie's temperamental lock, shifting my weight so I can press it all the way left while jiggling the door handle until it finally gives and the button pops.

"Thanks." I toss my bag in the passenger seat.

"We were wondering who drove this," another one in an Orioles jersey says. "We even got a dollar pool going for awhile. I had my money on that janitor with the lazy eye." The rest of them bust out laughing, and I resist the urge to give them the finger.

"Yeah, well, until I win the lottery, this is what I got," I sigh, trying to play along. I get in and slam the door, not even stopping to buckle my seatbelt as I start the ignition and back out of the space.

"Yo, yo!" The football player calls out, motioning for me to roll down the window. I crank it down halfway, and he flashes a grateful smile. "We were just playing. What's your name, beautiful?"

I roll my eyes. "Why do you care?"

He takes a few steps toward the car and shrugs. "We gotta find out who won the bet."

"Since none of you know my name, I don't think anybody won," I say. "Besides, I'm late."

"Come on," he pleads.

If I waste any more time, Denny'll have to wait alone on the curb. "Michelle," I say finally, giving him an *are-you-happy-now?* face. I lean over to roll up my window when I hear another burst of laughter.

"Oh, shit," Orioles Jersey says. "That's her. The one I was telling you about."

I narrow my eyes. I've never talked to this guy before. I've never talked to any of them.

"You work at the Taco Bell, right?" he asks, barely suppressing a smile. "In Ellwood Park?"

I smile tightly. "Yup." Once in a while someone from school recognizes me working a shift, which sadly is pretty much the extent of my post–three P.M. social life.

But Orioles Jersey looks too excited to be scheming a crappy discount on his Doritos Locos taco. He turns back to his friends. "I told you!" he cries. "Her mom got busted at the gas station last night!"

For a second I can't breathe. Time seems to stop, one hand on the window crank, one on the steering wheel, my foot pressed on the brake, the outside of my body frozen while the inside cracks open. *How can they know?* I didn't tell anyone. Even my so-called friends don't know Mom's history. Hell, I've studied as hard as I have mostly just so none of my teachers would ever have a reason to meet her in person. My whole life outside of school is spent dealing with my flesh and blood, but I've built my entire life *in* school around pretending they don't exist. And now, in a heartbeat, in one humiliating night, it's all come undone. If these guys know, I realize with a nauseating chill, Noemi knows, too. Everyone does.

I step on the gas without realizing I'm still in reverse, so I shoot backward and nearly hit another car that's pulling out of a parking spot behind me. That driver leans on their horn, and I frantically shift gears, tearing out of the lot with cruel laughter echoing behind me.

You only have a month left, I remind myself as I stop at a red light a few blocks from the elementary school, gulping air and trying to clear my head. *You can make it one more month.* I know I need my high school diploma to have any hope of doing better than my parents. But even after years of going through the motions, all of a sudden I don't think I can do it for another day, let alone an entire month. I feel like I'm caught in an avalanche, standing still while the rocks pile around me, the window of escape closing in with each passing second.

At Denny's school, Mrs. Mastino meets me at the curb, looking like a bug crawled up her ass and built a two-tiered skyscraper.

"Dennis continues to disrupt class multiple times a day,"

she says brusquely, shoving a piece of official-looking letterhead through the passenger side window. "He's straining our resources to the breaking point, and it simply can't continue."

I skim the letter, which is signed by the principal. *Hyperactive . . . defiant behavior . . . requires medication . . . pursue another institution more suited to his needs . . .*

"Wait, are you kicking him out?" I ask in disbelief, trying to keep my voice down since Denny is loitering a few yards away, throwing rocks at a sapling that's been roped off with a sign reading PLEASE LET ME GROW! I'm still reeling from finding out I'm the hot gossip at my school, and now this. "What did he even *do*?"

"He's just . . . out of control," she sputters. "Shouting, getting out of his seat, fighting, you name it. And don't get me started on the imaginary friend. He needs help he's not getting and we're not equipped for." She grabs on to the window, the fuchsia nails at the ends of her knobby fingers clattering against the glass, and leans in so close I can smell her perfume. "I need to see your mother," she says. "You tell her she needs to return my calls. If I don't hear from her by tomorrow, tell her I'm making a decision without her." Then she turns and walks off in a huff.

"She's mad at me," Denny reports, a little too cheerfully, as he clambers into the backseat a minute later. His T-shirt, which was rumpled already when he put it on yesterday, now bears an enormous grass stain flecked with dirt.

"Wanna tell me why?" I watch him chew on a hangnail in the rearview mirror, those dark doe eyes staring out the window, already distracted.

"Ummmm . . . I dunno."

"Yes you do." I start to merge back into traffic, but I forget to check my blind spot and almost hit a taxi, the driver of which rolls down his window just so he can call me a blind bitch to my face before speeding away. That makes two near accidents in less than fifteen minutes. I need to get some coffee—or better yet, some sleep—before my luck runs out. I take a detour into a Dunkin' Donuts drive-through, figuring I can kill two birds with one stone. After all, a six-year-old's secrets can easily be bought for a chocolate-glazed cruller.

"So," I probe again, slurping down my latte. "What happened at school today?"

"I pushed Jayden," he says matter-of-factly between bites.

I hope to God Jayden is real, and this isn't some weird junior version of *Fight Club* that "Max" is encouraging. "Why would you do that?" I ask.

"He wouldn't give me a dollar."

"And why did you ask him to give you a dollar?" With Denny, a story only comes out sentence by sentence, on a need-to-know basis.

"'Cause I won," he says proudly.

"Won *what*?"

"Our wrestling match."

In a flash I know exactly where this is going, but the big sister in me can't help but hold out a sliver of hope that I'm wrong. "Did this happen in gym class?" I ask.

"No, at recess."

Uh-oh. "Did Jayden *want* to wrestle you?"

"I dunno." I glance in the rearview, hoping to see some trace of shame or guilt, but Denny's happily chowing down on the last few inches of his pastry.

"Well, was he having fun?"

"No," Denny laughs. "He kept squealing, it was so funny."

I let out a deep breath I've been holding for two intersections. It's moments like this when I can see how parenting can really go wrong. Because I know the right thing to do now is to stop the car, sit him down, and explain in no uncertain terms that jumping a classmate at recess, pinning him to the ground, and then demanding money is called "bullying," not "wrestling," and that he will be in serious trouble if I ever hear about it happening again. But in the mood I'm in, with the day I've had and the limited brain function I'm running on, I just don't have the energy to do the right thing. So instead I suck down the sugary dregs of my coffee and drive the rest of the way to the junior high in silence.

For some reason, Cass isn't waiting at our meeting spot when I drive up, even though thanks to our pit stop we're five minutes late. Despite her relatively newfound tween angst, my sister has always been the most punctual member of our family, so it's a little jarring not to see her sitting on the shallow steps outside the gray double doors on McCulloh Street, looking bored and sketching in her journal. (If we had the money for iPhones, Cass would probably be on the five billionth level of Candy Crush by now.)

I dig my phone out of my bag and text Here, flipping on my hazards while we wait. I look for Cass in the crowd of rowdy middle-schoolers spilling out of the main entrance about fifty feet away, but her preferred ensemble of extra-large black hoodie, boot-cut jeans, and black Payless Converse knockoffs is basically urban camouflage. Then my phone buzzes, and I relax a little bit, expecting a text back from Cass, but instead I see I have an unheard voicemail that must have come in while

I was driving. And without even checking the number, I know exactly whom it's from.

"Hi, Michy, it's Mom." Her voice is deep and raspy, like she's been crying or puking—probably both. She'll already be in withdrawal by now. *"I miss my babies so much. So much, you don't even know. And the way things went down . . . it wasn't right. Don't be mad at me, baby. I made a mistake, but I'm gonna make it up to you, all of you—"* She pauses for a coughing fit. *"Listen, I'm at the city detention center, and they set my bond at $4,000. I know it's steep, but the sooner you can post it, the better for all of us, baby. Ask Sam to help. I know she can be a pain in the ass, but she's family."* Mom pauses, as if, like me, she's calculating the unlikely odds that my aunt will decide to morph suddenly from Nurse Ratched into Mother Teresa. "*Tell her I'd do it for her,*" she says, her voice breaking. *"She knows it's true."* Another pause. *"Give my meatball a big kiss from me, okay? I love my babies so much. You know that, right? Okay . . . all right. Bye."*

"I miss Mommy," Denny says loudly before I've even hung up. I whip around, thinking he must have heard the message somehow, but he's just frowning down at his lap, his lower lip quivering.

"Hey. *Hey,*" I reach back and squeeze his leg. "Mommy will be home really soon. In just a few days, okay? I promise." If the bail bondsman will take 10 percent, that means I only have to come up with $400, which means that if I don't spend any money for the next four days, my Taco Bell paycheck will get me there. And if there's one thing I'm good at, it's scavenging. (The potential upside of spending years of scraping by with a parent who drinks or smokes most of her disposable income is that it teaches you some slick MacGyver-style survival skills.)

Denny nods solemnly but then looks out the window and instantly brightens. "There's Cass!" he says, poking a chocolate-covered finger past my cheek. I turn to see my sister sprinting toward the car like she's gunning for an Olympic medal, her backpack—which probably weighs forty pounds, almost half her weight—bouncing behind her. A few yards beyond, a pack of girls who somehow look both menacing and prissy, the kinds who might not be able to throw a punch but who could destroy your life with a single Facebook wall post—dash out of the front doors and start to follow her, stopping only when they see the car.

Cass throws open Goldie's passenger door and jumps in, but before she manages to pull it shut, I hear one of the girls shout, "You better run, *dyke*!"

"Go," Cass pleads. Her face is ashen, and as she tries to buckle her seatbelt her hands tremble.

I peel off as fast as I can, trying to wrap my brain around what I just saw. "What was that about?" I ask, once we're a safe distance away. I glance over at Cass, but she's just sitting there blank faced, clenching and unclenching her shaking fingers. "Wait, is it your blood sugar?" I ask. "Did you run out of insulin?"

"*No*," she says, rolling her eyes. Only a thirteen-year-old could switch gears from mortal terror to bitchiness in two seconds flat.

"Why were those girls chasing you? And why did they call you a—"

"Were you playing tag?" Denny asks excitedly.

Cass crosses her arms. "No," she says. "They're just assho—"

"Mean girls?" I interject.

She nods, looking away. "Just because Erica and I don't wear skirts or care what boys think . . ." she mumbles. Unlike me, Cass has managed to find a best friend, a monosyllabic tomboy named Erica who sometimes comes to our house on her skateboard to do homework and play video games, although I haven't seen her much lately. Erica's mom is a single mom, too, and reportedly lets the girls watch R-rated movies on Netflix. She does Erica's cornrows and offered to do them on Cass, but that's where my mom drew the line. Who knew she had one?

"You should tell the principal," I say. "That word, what they called you—you know what it means, right?"

Cass looks at me like I'm an idiot.

"Okay, well, then you know it's hate speech."

"Whatever," Cass sighs.

"Fine, forget it," I say. And just like with Denny, I give up without a fight, not because I don't care but because it feels like I've spent the last twenty-four hours walking through land mines, and I don't think I can survive setting off another blast.

I don't have work Mondays, so on our way "home," we stop at our real home to pick up clean clothes and toiletries to tide us over for the week. Amazingly, the time spent gathering our stuff is actually pretty relaxed. I think finally being somewhere comfortable for the first time since yesterday morning helps the tension of the day start to diffuse for all of us, and by the time we pile back into Goldie to drive the ten miles to meet our reluctant legal guardian, Cass is talking again, Denny has bathed and is dressed in something that almost fits, and I'm coming close to starting to feel not entirely hopeless.

When we get to the door of Aunt Sam's fourth-floor

walk-up, clutching the pillows and blankets and stuffed animals we've stripped from our beds, she's lying on her ratty chintz couch with her bare feet up on the coffee table, eating egg rolls from a greasy wax bag and watching TV.

"What's all that?" she asks. "This isn't a storage facility."

"Oh, we just figured we'd save you some laundry," I say, forcing a smile.

"Mmmm hmmmm." Sam raises a skeptical eyebrow and returns to her news broadcast. "By the way, I picked up Chinese," she says. "It's on the counter." I was so unconvinced she would remember to feed us that I actually packed instant oatmeal and ramen noodles from our cupboard at home; the prospect of a freshly cooked take-out meal is positively exhilarating. We drop our stuff eagerly and crowd into the dark, narrow kitchen, dividing the two small containers of pork fried rice and chicken lo mein (not enough to feed a family, but I decide to take it as a nice gesture from a notorious cheapskate) onto paper plates.

As we file back into the living room, the TV's still on, but Aunt Sam is slipping into her flip-flops and digging out a crumpled pack of Pall Mall Lights from her purse.

"Michelle, come outside and talk with me a minute." It's not posed as a question, and I feel a pang of despair, not only because whatever my aunt wants to talk to me about can't be good but also because I have to leave my plate of hot food to either slowly congeal or be picked over by my ravenous siblings—probably both.

I follow her out the door and down the stairs to the sidewalk outside her building. Above us, a red-and-white neon sign for the Hung Hing Chinese Restaurant flickers irritably.

"Listen," Aunt Sam says, taking a long drag on her cigarette, her lipstick leaving a wet, pink ring around the paper when she takes it out to exhale. "I want to help you guys. You know I do. You're my flesh and blood. But—" She takes another long drag, blowing the smoke out her nose this time, like a dragon. "I can't have you stay here for nothing. If you're going to be living here, you're going to be contributing, understand?"

I nod. I was expecting her to be a hard-ass, and I've already prepared for this exact conversation. "I can buy all the groceries," I say. "I already know what the kids like to eat, and I'll get whatever you need, too. I'm good at couponing. Plus, I'll do all the dishes and laundry while we're here, and on nights I don't work I can cook."

Aunt Sam looks at me in disbelief, and for a second I wonder if I've overshot and promised too much, even more than she was expecting. I'm really not looking forward to playing Cinderella for the next four days, but at least no harm can come from getting on her good side.

"Honey," she finally says, in a tone that strips the word of its endearment, "that's nice, but what I mean is I need some rent money. I can barely afford this place, and I'm not going to pay to give up what little privacy I have."

Now it's *my* turn to stare in disbelief. My aunt's apartment is a tiny one-bedroom with water-stained walls and holes in the floor that are covered with duct tape. I don't know how much nurses make, but Aunt Sam is pushing forty. There's no way she can't afford the rent on this shithole.

"How much?" I ask, mentally calculating the maximum I can possibly afford and still make Mom's bail. If I have $200 in the bank and my biweekly paycheck is $279.34, like usual, I can pay Aunt Sam $79 this week . . . if I somehow avoid stopping for gas. But there's no way she could ask me for that much a week—that would be over $300 a month, which would be insane, even for her.

"Six hundred a month," she says flatly.

I'm too shocked to control my anger. "What?!" I shout. "That's crazy. I don't even make that much!" Mom asks me for $250 a month to split the gas and electric bills and help with groceries, which leaves me more than half of my paycheck to use however I want. I try to put money aside (for college, I tell myself on good days; for the next time she needs bail, on bad ones), but lately I've been too embarrassed to wear the ill-fitting hand-me-downs and tag-sale stuff she gets for me, so I spend most of my extra cash on clothes. I look down guiltily at my skinny jeans and Nine West boots. I should have been saving more money. I knew something like this would happen again. I wanted to believe her, but deep in my bones, I knew.

Aunt Sam takes another drag of her smoke and shrugs. "Can't you pick up more shifts?" she asks.

"I'd have to almost double my hours." I wouldn't have time to do my homework except on the weekends. Cass and Denny would have to spend five or six nights a week loitering at Taco Bell, instead of just three.

"Hard work builds character," she says, tapping a long, gray piece of ash onto the sidewalk, where it scatters onto my scuffed toes. I decide to try a more practical appeal.

"My mom left me a voicemail this afternoon." That gets her attention. "If I can post her bail, she can get out, and you won't have to deal with us. I'll have enough money at the end of the week, so if you can just wait, we'll be out of your hair and I can still pay you $75 for the four nights." I'm not, as my mother suggested, going to ask my aunt for any of the bail money. I'm pretty sure that would end with me getting cursed out.

Aunt Sam presses her lips together and looks down at the ground. "She'll never learn," she says.

"What?"

"Your mother," she says, louder now, her eyes tired and angry. "Every time she gets herself in trouble, someone's there to fix it. Get knocked up in high school? Here—have a townhouse! Arrested? No problem! Three times? Still no problem!" She tosses her cigarette butt on the ground, stomping on it like a cockroach. "I know you think you're doing the right thing, but believe me, if you get her out she's just going to do it again. And again, and again, and again. She's been doing it her whole life, and she's not going to stop now."

"*Someone* has to help her," I say.

"Why?"

"Because . . ." I filter through potential reasons in my head, all of which boil down to unconditional love. Because you help people you care about. No matter what. You just *do.* But I know my aunt and I are at an impasse when it comes to the definition of love, so I go with my mother's suggestion from her voicemail. "Because she'd do it for you," I say.

"If you believe that, you don't know her very well," Aunt Sam says, lighting another cigarette. "Did you know when Grandma and Grandpa died they left a safe in the attic? Inside there was some jewelry, old stuff, from a few generations back, that Mama never wore because it was too flashy. She used to let me try it on. Just me, never Maddie, 'cause even then she had sticky fingers. She even left it to me in the will. But when it came time to collect, guess what? It was gone."

"The safe was gone?" I ask.

"Oh no, she's too smart for that," Aunt Sam says. "The safe was there, lock intact, but it was empty. 'Mama must have decided to sell it off,' Maddie said. I can't believe she kept a straight face."

I frown into the smoke. Mom complains often about Aunt Sam's resentment, but I never once entertained the notion that it might be deserved.

"Then there was the time I asked her to take in my mail and water my plants while I went on vacation," my aunt continues. "You know I never asked her for any money all those times I took you in. All those things I paid for. I just asked for a *one-time* favor, and when I came home my bonsai was dead and three of my packages had gone missing."

"Oh." I don't know what else to say.

"So, no, if I was in jail I don't believe she would bail me out," Aunt Sam sighs, throwing her half-finished second cigarette on the pavement, still burning. "I believe she would tell me how hard she was trying to come up with the money, and then she'd disappear for days, only to come back looking like she got run over by a truck with some story about some terrible something that happened that managed to drain whatever she'd managed to save."

Mom's bad luck is a running joke between Cass and me. She's always losing her wallet, getting duped into signing up for memberships she doesn't want, and bitching about bills for things that never seem to actually get fixed, like the light in our front hall, which has been out since the upstairs toilet overflowed four years ago. I know I can't always believe what she says, but that doesn't change the fact that she raised me and that, unlike some people in our family, I won't give up on her.

"I still want to help," I say.

Aunt Sam looks me straight in the eyes. "I don't care," she snaps. "I won't let you."

"You can't tell me what to do," I say, regretting the next sentence before it's even out of my mouth but unable to stop myself. "You're not my mother."

"Tell that to Miss Child Protective Services," she cries. "If it weren't for me, you'd be in some group home right now." I bite down on my tongue so hard I taste blood. "I want a $300 down payment tomorrow night," she continues, "and if I don't get it, I will be more than happy to escort you back to the police station and let them put you wherever they see fit. Understand?"

I nod silently, fighting back tears. She's probably bluffing, just taking out her anger at Mom on me, but I can't afford to find out. Despite everything we've already been through, Cass, Denny, and I still have each other. It's the only thing we have left, and I won't risk losing it, even if it means letting Mom sit in jail for another few weeks until I can figure out a new plan.

"Good," Aunt Sam says with a self-satisfied smile. "In that case, welcome home, Michelle."

THREE

Tuesday Night, Part 1
Baltimore, MD

Today at school I learned that whispers, which don't even pass through the vocal chords, can be deafening. And the whispers were by far the nicest of it; three different guys thought it would be hilarious and original to make a big show of asking me if my mom could score for them. My friends were barely better. I can't decide which is worse: Yi-Lo hugging me and confessing that her dad had recently struggled with quitting smoking, or Noemi over-apologizing for being mean about my hair, adding, "Seriously . . . that's some Lifetime Original Movie shit."

After my last class ends at two twenty, I practically sprint through the parking lot, desperate for the comfort of the closest thing I have to a home now, also known as Baltimore's inner-city outpost of the country's sixth-most popular fast-food chain, modeled to look like some kind of southwestern adobe hacienda by way of Legoland. It would be depressing under any other circumstances, but right now the Ellwood Park Taco Bell, which sits on a slow stretch of highway between an auto-body shop and a much more popular McDonald's, feels like a five-star spa (or at least what I fantasize a five-star spa must feel like, which is getting a foot rub while lying on a bed made out of marshmallows).

I've been working here since I turned sixteen, doing everything from stocking napkins to washing floors to filling burritos to working the registers, and I got promoted to shift leader about eight months ago, which means I get to boss around the newer people and micromanage the soda machine so the Coke comes out perfect, not too watery or syrupy. Even though we're in a bad neighborhood, we've got some good Yelp reviews going, and my manager, Yvonne, gets really competitive about beating the Taco Bell down in Lakeland. She was a high school track star back before her brother got shot and she had to start working full time to help pay for his medical bills. Apparently he's still in a wheelchair. I've never seen him, but she takes home a bag of food for him every night. That's probably why she's so cool about me having Cass and Denny around while I work. Yvonne knows what it's like to have people depend on you.

My shifts at this point are comfortingly predictable. From four to five we get a lot of kids, either high school age or younger ones who stop in for an after-school snack with a parent. This is by far the loudest hour, and food gets thrown on a regular basis. Afterward there is always at least one urinal full of broken taco shells, but one of the perks of being shift leader is that I can make someone else scoop them out. Then from five to six it's Early Bird Hour, which means a lot of old people who come in alone and eat slowly while staring out the window. This overlaps somewhat with Family Circus, which goes from five thirty to seven and is mostly four- to six-person groups with your standard mom, dad, and assortment of children ranging in age from infants to teenagers. By that time the dinner rush is busy enough that I need to be on a register, and so I get to spend ninety minutes staring out at people who have the kind of life I want. You'd think families that eat dinner at a Taco Bell instead of sitting around a table at home like some Norman Rockwell painting would be kind of sad, but actually most of the ones that come in are really happy and playful. It's a treat for them. The moms don't freak out when a drink spills, and the dads make nachos into airplanes or show their kids how to drip water onto straw wrappers to make them wriggle like snakes. I always try to time my breaks so they happen during Family Circus. I can only take so much at a time.

After I get food for Cass and Denny, I go out back in the parking lot and sit on the curb. I've been stressing all day about how to come up with the extra hundred bucks for Aunt Sam, and all I can think of, short of robbery or selling Goldie for scrap metal, is to ask for an advance on my paycheck. In fact, I've been avoiding Yvonne for two straight hours because I'm so ashamed to have to ask for a handout. I start to listen to Mom's voicemail again to psych myself up, but then Yvonne bangs through the kitchen exit dragging two handfuls of garbage bags, and I know I have to seize the moment.

"Hey!" I call, shoving the phone into my back pocket. It's

a warm spring night, and a soft breeze—trash-scented, but still kind of nice—blows through my hair. "Need some help?"

Yvonne drops the bags at the foot of the big gray dumpster we've affectionately nicknamed Hellmouth and shakes out her arms. "You know it," she sighs. "My shot put skills aren't what they used to be." Together, we heave the heavy trash up over the four-foot lip. On the last bag, runny cheese sauce drips down onto our forearms, and Yvonne dashes back into the kitchen for some napkins, cursing in Spanish.

"Nasty," she squeals as we wipe ourselves down. "This job should come with a hot water bonus, 'cause you know I need two showers just to get the smell off me after."

"I know," I laugh.

Yvonne examines her clothes for stains. "Would you believe my mom keeps asking me why I don't have a boyfriend?" she asks, rolling her eyes. Yvonne is twenty-five and still lives at home. By her own calculation she's gained forty pounds since she quit school, stopped hurdling, and started eating free fried food three meals a day. "And I'm like, *Mama*, you see any man who likes a woman who smells like day-old ground beef, you send him my way." She laughs bitterly. "At least I'm not in high school, though. I don't know how you do it, those guys can be such dicks."

"It's not just the guys," I say, flushing with shame as I relive the highlights of my day. I don't ever want to go back.

My mental state must show on my face, because Yvonne stops laughing and puts a hand on my arm.

"Hey, you okay?" she asks. "You've been kind of out of it today."

"Yeah, sorry." I know the more I tell my boss about what happened, the more sympathetic she'll be, but I don't think I can bring myself to say the actual facts out loud. "I just had a bad weekend."

"You wanna talk about it?" She smiles warmly. "I'm not above making a ten-minute trash dump, and I'm starved for gossip."

"It's not the fun kind," I sigh.

Yvonne's heavily lined brown eyes scrunch in concern, and I try to screw up my courage. "It's just my mom . . . has some health problems," I say (technically not lying). "And there are some . . . unforeseen costs." I feel like an asshole using what I know about Yvonne's brother to manipulate her sympathies, but I don't know what else to do.

"So you need money," she says. Her tone's not judgmental, but hearing the words makes me feel like a beggar. And one of the first rules Mom taught me is that we Devereaux don't beg. We plan, we find, we take, we earn, but we do. Not. Beg.

"Yeah, but not like a loan or anything," I say quickly. "I was just wondering if there was any way to get paid sooner than Friday."

She frowns. "Corporate doesn't let us give advances on checks, but—"

"It's fine, forget about it," I say, trying to smile like it's no big deal.

"Let me finish!" she says. "*But* I know how hard you work, and I know you got those kids to take care of, so if you need cash, I could loan it to you."

"No, I couldn't take your money." I wish I could rewind time ten seconds and just not bring it up. Yvonne is the closest thing I have to a regular friend, and I'm getting dangerously close to making her pity me.

"Don't worry, I wouldn't give it to you for free," she laughs. "But I can spare a couple hundred for the next few days, and then you can just sign over your check to me." She leans in conspiratorially. "I'm secretly loaded," she whispers and then cracks herself up laughing.

I relax a little bit. "Thanks," I say. "But you know, now that I'm thinking about it, I don't really need it till Friday anyway."

"You sure?"

"Yeah." I force a smile and lie through my teeth. "Just making a big deal out of nothing."

"All right, if you say so." Yvonne shoots me a suspicious side-eye and starts trudging back toward the kitchen. I shove my hands in the pockets of my loose black uniform pants and look up at the sky. There's one of those perfect half moons tonight, like a black-and-white cookie missing the chocolate part. I remember being freaked out as a kid that someone was eating away at the moon when it wasn't a full circle. But then Buck told me about the shadow of the earth and how the moon is always whole, it just doesn't always look it. He even taught me a rhyme to track the phases:

If you see the moon at the end of the day
A bright full moon is on its way.
If you see the moon in the early dawn
Look real quick, it will soon be gone.

"Hey," Yvonne calls, and I look over to see her standing in the doorway, silhouetted by the garish restaurant lights. "There's gonna be an assistant manager job opening up this summer. It's salaried and everything, like $30K with benefits.

If you want it, it's yours. Could solve some of your problems." She lets the door slam shut, and I hang my head, feeling heavy all over.

I should be happy. She's right: Money like that would solve a lot of problems. If I took that job, I could pay for everything. I wouldn't even need Mom . . . because for all intents and purposes, I would *be* Mom.

But I want more than that. I want more than a crappy service job and a house full of ghosts. I want more than the kitchen scraps. I want more than half the moon.

I don't know what it is I want, exactly, but I know I want more than that.

Doing math at the register helps me calm down. Numbers soothe me, the way they play by the rules, always bending to my control, adding up the same every time, neat and easy. Even though I know the prices of everything by heart and can do the totals in my head, we also have a digitized screen that makes my job as easy as punching a button with the item name. So after a bit of therapeutic quesadilla equations, I let my brain drift and start doing other, more urgent tallies.

By some act of God, Goldie still runs, but the sum of her parts can't be more than a few hundred bucks at this point—enough to buy me time with Aunt Sam, sure, but then what? Without a car, I'd still have to buy bus passes for the three of us, and the delicate balance of drop-off and pick-up times would be shot. It wouldn't be worth it, especially since I really only need the money for three days. I wrack my brain for anything else I could pawn. Mom doesn't have any decent jewelry she hasn't already sold off, but we do have a good-sized TV and a lot of old furniture in okay shape that might sell on Craigslist for fifty bucks a pop. Of course, I wouldn't be able to sell it tonight, but I could cut school tomorrow, which would be a relief, and probably get it done in a few hours if our ancient desktop—which loads web pages at the approximate speed of an octogenarian eating a plate of churros—cooperates.

I'm so busy mentally pricing family heirlooms that it takes me ten seconds to realize there's a customer standing in front of me who's just staring.

"I'm so sorry for the wait, sir," I say with as much sincerity as I can muster. This guy can't be much older than me, but he's white and blond, and I've had enough experience with disgruntled customers to know when to play it safe and suck up to them, especially on a night like tonight when I'm phoning it in. I part my lips in some semblance of a friendly smile. "Welcome to Taco Bell. May I take your order?"

"Uh . . ." He looks up at the backlit menu that runs across the wall above my head. Great. One of those. It's called fast food for a reason, people. If you don't know what you want, please don't get in line and waste my time.

"Sir," I say, trying and failing to hold my faceful of fake cheer. "If you're not ready to order, I'll help the next customer, and when you decide, you just let me know." The dinner rush is peaking now, with all three registers at least five people deep. I start to beckon the next person, an Asian woman who looks about eleven months pregnant, when Blondie holds up his hands.

"Wait, please," he says. "I'm actually—"

I cock my head.

"I'm actually looking for someone," he says. "Is Michelle Devereaux working tonight?"

"Who wants to know?" I've heard that line used by Mafia toughs in a whole bunch of movies and always wondered if it worked. Plus, this dude is starting to piss me off. And after Mr. Orioles yesterday, I can't be too careful.

"Um, I do?" He laughs nervously.

I point to my enormous nametag, and his face turns even whiter than it already is, if that's possible.

"*You're* Michelle Devereaux?"

I nod, a little taken aback that he looks so shocked. Who *is* this guy? I don't think he goes to my school, but whatever he wants, it can't be good. Not with my luck the past few days.

"Are you going to order?" the pregnant lady asks loudly.

"Sir, if you're not going to order, please step aside so I can help the other customers," I say.

He takes a deep breath and leans in, sweat beading on his forehead, damp honey-colored locks of hair hanging in his eyes. "Okay, look, I'm really sorry to surprise you like this," he says, keeping his voice low. "But my name is Tim—Tim Harper—and I think my stepsister, Leah, is related to you."

"What?" I ask, shaking my head. "Listen, I don't know what you want, but unless it's a taco, I really need you to step aside. Other people are wai—"

"Her father's name was Buck Devereaux," he says quickly, his blue eyes darting nervously between my face and the napkin dispenser next to the register. "I mean, *is* Buck Devereaux. But he's dying. And he asked her to find you, so I looked you up on Facebook—"

"I don't even update my Facebook," I snap. This is the part of the sentence I'm choosing to focus on, because everything that came before it has the makings of a tidal wave, and I can't get dragged under right now. I used to pray for my father to come back, to show up on our doorstep begging forgiveness or magically appear in the parking lot at school, leaning on Goldie with graying temples and a sad smile and offering to take me out for a beer so he could explain everything. But some preppy kid showing up out of the blue during Family Circus on the worst week of my life and dropping the bomb that Buck is dying? That shit I did not sign up for. I look Tim straight in the eyes. "You can either order some food or you can get out of my face right now," I whisper.

"I'm sorry," he sputters. "This was a mistake."

"*Next!*" I yell, louder than necessary, and the pregnant lady pushes past a stricken-looking Tim to get her chalupa fix. My heart racing, my tongue going numb, I punch in her order and then call in a trainee to take over for me, nearly falling onto a hot stove in my rush to get to the back door before my knees buckle.

Outside, I stumble over to Hellmouth and crumple at its graffiti-covered base, taking in desperate lungsful of warm, pungent air. It's not news that Buck has another daughter. I already knew that part, although since I didn't know her name or where she lived, the sudden fact of her actual existence and proximity is shocking. This girl—*Leah*—she's the reason he left. Or that Mom kicked him out. I was never really clear on the specifics. I just know Buck was caught, Jerry Springer–style, with a secret family and that for whatever reason, he chose them over us. What bothers me is that Mom always made it sound like they moved away. But if this girl—*Leah*—is from around here, does that mean Buck is here, too? That he's been here all these years, close enough for me to pass him on the highway or stand next to him at a grocery store without even knowing? That's the part that feels like a sucker punch. I can deal with him dying, but I can't handle the thought that he might have been living right around the corner all these years.

I hear footsteps on the asphalt and look up to see Tim coming around the corner of the building. He's in a flannel shirt, jeans, and some brown shoes that look like a nerdy version of Timberlands—not as preppy as I first pegged him. A little more hipster but with a conservative haircut and a clean shave. Not that this makes me loathe him any less.

"Leave me alone," I say, jumping to my feet. "I'm still on shift. I was just getting some air."

"Please just give me one minute," he says, taking a hesitant step toward me. "I should never have ambushed you like that. I'm really sorry, I was just afraid that if I didn't talk to you in there, I wouldn't get another chance."

"Look, I don't care who your sister is," I say. "Buck left a long time ago, and as far as I'm concerned he's already dead. So, you know, go ahead and make the funeral arrangements without me." I know it sounds cold, but it's true. I've moved past the point of wanting closure with my father. He obviously never wanted it with me. What could I possibly owe him now? A bunch of stiff, ugly orchids to stick in some sad funeral home? *Sorry you sucked so much as a father, but here is $80 worth of flowers that will wither and die even faster than our relationship!*

"It's not about arrangements," Tim says, shifting uncomfortably. "It's . . . he says he wants to see you."

"Fuck you." The words come out so blunt and angry that Tim takes a step back like I might try to hit him. I look down at the pavement, feeling guilty but livid at the same time.

"I don't blame you for shooting the messenger," Tim says. "But he says he has something for you. Some heirloom."

I lift my eyes up to the half moon, breathing hard out my nostrils, trying to parse what's happening into some kind of sense. What kind of sick cosmic joke is this that on the day I hit financial rock bottom, Buck reappears on his deathbed with a surprise windfall? That's the kind of shit that happens to some perky actress in some stupid romantic comedy, not to me, in real life, next to a Taco Bell dumpster.

"What is it?" I ask, hating myself a little bit for even caring.

"I don't know," Tim says. "But according to Karen, he says it's worth a lot."

Worth a lot. Right. Unlike Buck's word. And who the hell is Karen? I narrow my eyes at Tim.

"Is this some kind of scam?" I ask. "I thought you said her name was—" *Leah.* But before I can say them, the two syllables get stuck in the back of my throat, blocking my windpipe. "*Different*," I cough. It's only just now dawning on me that this guy could be crazy, some random stalker. Aren't most serial killers nice-looking white boys? I take a step toward the kitchen door, deciding that if he comes any closer I'm going to book it.

But he stays put, frowning apologetically. "Sorry," he says. "I should have explained. Karen is my stepmom, Leah's mom. She married my dad three years ago."

It's still not adding up. "Why didn't Leah"—her name is coppery in my mouth like a new penny—"just call me?" I ask.

Tim shoves his hands in his back pockets and stares off into the highway traffic, avoiding my eyes. "She doesn't know I'm here," he says. "But I know—I mean, I think—" He clears his throat, another telltale sign that he's about to feed me a lie. "I just think if it was my mom I'd want to know in person. I wanted to do the right thing."

"Nope, try again." I cross my arms and stare him down.

"What?" He still won't look at me.

"You don't care that I won the Dying-Dad Lottery," I say. "You could have Facebook messaged me for that. Saved yourself the trouble. So do you want to tell me why you're really here, or can I go back to work now?"

"Okay, fine," Tim says with a sigh. "I guess I just need your help. Leah's been really messed up about it. She was the one who picked up the phone, and I guess . . . it didn't really go well."

"No shit," I say under my breath.

"Anyway," he says, "Karen thinks maybe she should go visit him before, you know, before he passes."

"Look," I say, softening my tone slightly. "I'm sorry she's having a hard time, but I still don't get what this has to do with me."

Tim shrugs. "I thought maybe you could talk to her, convince her that it's in her best interest . . ."

"Why would she listen to me?" I ask. "She doesn't need me. You said yourself she doesn't even know you came."

"Right," Tim says—but not in throwaway agreement, more like he's reminding himself to stick to his story. And sure enough, within seconds his eyes dart over to an SUV parked in the back corner of the lot, in the shadow between two streetlamps. Even in the dark I can see there's someone in the car, hunched in the front passenger seat.

"So she's here." The words sound hollow coming out, the opposite of the nauseating maelstrom of excitement and fear flooding my veins. "What, is she waiting for a formal invitation?" I try to laugh, but no sound comes out.

"She got scared," Tim says.

"Poor baby," I snap.

"Hey." For the first time I see anger flash across his face. "She's been through a lot, too."

"Well, get her out. We can compare notes." I can see Yvonne peering through the kitchen door, making a *what-the-hell?* face at me. If this gets me in trouble, I swear I'll go Schwarzenegger on Tim's J. Crew ass.

"She's not ready now," he says. "But she will be. I know you can help her."

"I doubt it."

"Michelle—" Tim pleads, but I cut him off.

"You know what? Stop saying my name like you know me," I say. "You don't the first *thing* about me or my family. You don't know what *I've* been through. You want me to say I'm sorry Buck ran out on your sister?" I turn toward the car and shout, "Yeah, I'm sorry!" Tim cringes. "I know what that feels like," I continue, my anger rising steadily. "But she's not *my* sister. And Buck's not my father. Not anymore. And if you're capable of coming all the way to my job just to tell me all this shit, I'm pretty damn sure you can escort Princess Leah of the Minivan down to Johns Hopkins to visit her beloved *daddy* before he croaks." By the end of my rant, I'm out of breath, and

Tim looks so taken aback that I almost feel bad for yelling at him. Almost.

"He's not at Johns Hopkins," Tim says quietly. "He's at some hospice. In California."

I laugh bitterly. It figures Buck ended up three thousand miles away, as far as he could possibly get from us without hopping a continent. "Well, then you should take her out there, make a little vacation for yourselves," I say. I gesture to the car, which it's just now dawning on me must be one of two or maybe even three they own, if the kids are allowed to take it out for joyrides. "I'm sure you can afford it."

Tim nods down at the pavement. "Yeah, well. Maybe we will."

"Great," I say sarcastically by way of goodbye. I turn to walk back to the kitchen, but as my rage fades, a gnawing shame replaces it. I used to think all the time about meeting Buck's other daughter. I pictured how it might go down, but it was never anything close to this. Leah might have hidden in the car, but I didn't behave much better. And if there's one thing I pride myself on, it's being a good big sister. Someone who's not like my parents. Someone who doesn't walk away.

"Hey," I say, looking back over my shoulder. "I'm sorry I lost my temper. I'm not having the best day."

Tim nods and pulls a slip of paper out of his pocket. "I get it," he says, "but if you change your mind, I think you guys could help each other." He approaches me tentatively, with his hands up in mock surrender, and holds out the paper. "It's my number," he explains. "And my receipt. I finally ordered a burrito."

"Congratulations." I take the slip and close my fist, crumpling it in my hand.

"It was the least I could do," he says, offering me an apologetic half smile.

No, the least you could have done was leave me out of this, I think. But I don't have to tell him that; I'm pretty sure my shouting got that point across. I make a show of putting the balled-up receipt into my pocket as some sort of peace offering—like I would even consider calling, like I need to add a dubious far-off inheritance and a mystery half sister with anxiety issues as bad as mine into the mix of what I'm dealing with right now. I step across the threshold into the steamy, grease-tinged air of the kitchen and try to regain my composure. I might not ever be able to close the door on Buck metaphorically, but at least right now I can let it slam literally, with a satisfying *thwack*, in Tim's face.

FOUR

Tuesday Night, Part 2
Baltimore, MD

"What's wrong with you?" Denny asks on the car ride back to Aunt Sam's.

"Nothing," I say. I turn up the radio, which is playing "Daddy's Home," by Usher. Of course it is.

"You look weird," Denny insists.

"That's just her face," Cass says.

Fifteen feet ahead, the light turns yellow, and I have to make a split-second decision whether to speed up or slam on the brakes. I choose brakes. We screech to a halt.

I was seven when I found out Leah existed. It wasn't that Mom tried to keep it from me for a year, it was just that it took her that long to say it plainly instead of using grown-up code I couldn't understand. "Knocked up" sounded violent, which confused me even more, because despite his many failings, Buck didn't hit us. (He was even big into Gandhi for a while and interpreted passive resistance as a good excuse not to get a job.) I didn't ask questions because back then, when it was still new, anything could make her crumble. I knew he'd left, and I knew he wasn't coming back, and I poured all of my anxiety into making sure I didn't do anything to make my mother cry.

One day, in late summer, we were sitting on the stoop in the early evening, trying to cool off, because somehow it was hotter in the house than outside no matter how many fans we had running. I remember I was blowing bubbles, barefoot, as Cass tried to catch them between her palms before they burst against the pavement. Mom was leaning against the house, talking to one of our neighbors and smoking a cigarette, when a four-year-old girl whizzed by, topless, on a scooter. Mom turned after her and stared.

"What is it?" the neighbor asked.

"Buck's other daughter would be about that age," Mom said, shaking her head. "Every time I see one, I just . . ." She shuddered.

I had just released an enormous bubble when she said it and can still remember seeing the world reflected upside down in its shimmering skin as it bobbed lazily down toward the weeds lining the basement wall.

I got up the courage to ask her later, while I was brushing my teeth and she was struggling to give Cass her nightly injection. "Why did you tell Mrs. Wilson that Daddy has another daughter?"

"Because he does." She finally landed the needle, and Cass howled.

"Is she my sister then?"

"No," Mom said softly, kissing the top of Cass's head. "Don't worry about her. She's nobody."

Back at the house, I take a much-needed shower while the kids watch one of those cooking-nightmare shows on TV. Aunt Sam's working a late shift, so I stand under the spray for fifteen minutes, ignoring the Post-It on the door reminding us that hot water isn't cheap. Despite her stinginess, though, the shower caddy is packed full of upscale shampoos, scrubs, and body washes (mostly for "mature skin," or "color-treated hair," but whatever—Devereaux rule #2: Free is free), and I use a tiny bit of everything, luxuriating in the sweet botanical smells as they wash down my body in a sudsy waterfall. What is it about water that's so healing? I remember reading in a magazine that some women have their babies in tubs and that even though it seems like they would drown, they know not to breathe until they break through the surface. Mom says when I was a toddler, I would lie on my back in the bath and let the water cover my face. She said it didn't scare me. She said I could smile and hold my breath at the same time—which is funny, because that's still what I do every single day.

I'm tugging some leggings over my still-damp thighs when I hear the TV go off and feel a pang of guilt. I've barely spoken to my siblings all day, aside from some grunts in the car. And while I know I need to tell them about what happened, I just don't know how. They've been through enough in the past forty-eight hours, and I can't stand seeing them hurt again.

Besides, I don't even know if Buck's really dying. All I have to go on is what Tim said, and he flat-out lied about Leah not being there with him. Before I do anything else, I should make sure that's true, at least.

I tiptoe across the hall into Aunt Sam's room, which I usually avoid both because I fear her wrath and because of the *Hoarders*-level foot-high layer of wrinkled clothes and romance paperbacks littering the floor. Luckily her laptop is partially visible under a towel on the unmade bed. Hunched and hovering, trying to keep my wet curls from dripping any evidence of my presence onto the duvet, I turn it on and open a Google search box.

"Buck Devereaux California," I type quickly, keeping an ear open for the sound of a key in the front lock. No matches. Just a listing for Charles Buck in Georgia (work on your reading comprehension, Google), a Wikipedia entry about some old MLB player with our last name, and a reddit thread about the Milwaukee Bucks.

"Allen Devereaux California" gets one legitimate hit, but when I follow the White Pages link, it turns out that guy is sixty-four years old. Try again.

"Devereaux California dying" is a stretch and gives me nothing but unrelated obituaries and funeral homes. I even type in "hospice California," thinking maybe I can call around to places and ask if he's there, but without a city to filter by, there are enough listings that I'd be glued to my phone for a month straight.

Then I remember what Tim said about finding me on Facebook, open a new window, and sign in to my account. Ironically, I only created it in the first place to search for Buck, when I was twelve. Now I have a couple hundred "friends," but no one my age really updates. The top story in my feed is from one of Mom's weird junkie pals/ex-babysitters named Violetta.

Buck didn't have a Facebook page five years ago, but I type his name into the search bar anyway, holding my breath. Nothing. I don't even bother looking under Allen, since he would sooner show up at our door with confetti and one of those giant TV checks for eleven years' worth of child support than identify himself by his given name on anything but government paperwork.

"Leah Devereaux," I type instead, holding my breath. Three profiles pop up, but two are way too old, and the last, very promising one, a super cute black teen with glasses, lives in Ontario. "Tim Harper," I try, and even though I get eight names this time, I recognize him immediately. First of all, he's listed as "Timothy," which definitely fits with his wannabe-yuppie vibe, and he's the only one who's wearing something other than a wifebeater or suit and tie. I click on his photo, in which he's leaning on a wooden fence with some kind of livestock in the background, and scan his page. His posts and all but his profile and cover photo are private, but he's listed as a student at McDonogh, which is a swanky private school outside the city. And under "Family" there are three people: Jeff Harper, Karen Harper, and . . . Leah D. Harper. Bingo.

I click on my long-lost half sister's face, feeling what I know is a very modern sense of dread. A century ago, you could probably have a secret sibling and never know about it as long as they didn't live next door or write you some kind of confessional letter while they were dying of polio. Now the news never turns off, the Internet is forever, and anyone under the age of seventy is probably in your face on at least four separate types of social media. I never looked for Leah because I didn't know her name until today, but a part of me knew it was only a matter of time before one of us found the other.

Immediately, two things become clear: one, that Leah D. Harper has abandoned her Facebook page—the last update is from 2013—and two, that she's . . . white. Really white. The-color-of-tracing-paper white, with blonde hair even lighter than Tim's. I don't know why this is such a shock, considering that we share the same sperm donor, who is also white, but it is. It shatters the image of her I've had in my head all these years. I always pictured her looking like me.

Leah is white because Karen, her mother and the woman Buck left us for, is also white. That much is obvious from Leah's publicly available cover photo, a family portrait set in front of a big (also white) clapboard house. Everyone is wearing pastel and smiling toothpaste-commercial smiles. Polly Devereaux would have approved. Maybe she even had a hand in it, offering her son something more than a new car this time in a final push to rid her family tree of its thorny branch of jungle fever.

My chest feels tight, and I realize I'm not breathing. *Stop it*, I think, as I coax the stale, ash-scented air back into my lungs. But it's too late; I'm desperate for more, needing to scratch this scab until it bleeds. I open a new browser window and pull up Instagram, searching for her name. There are more profiles to wade through this time, but now that I know what she looks like, I find her pretty quickly, under the username *leah__butterfly*. By a huge stroke of dumb luck and lax parental controls, the account is public, and I click through the most recent photos, each one a cruel funhouse mirror image of a life I never stood a chance of having: "mall trip with mom!!!!" (Leah and Karen—a plump, pretty redhead—clinking milkshake glasses); "<3 <3 <3 love my besties!!! xoxoxox" (Leah, looking like a Barbie doll flanked by two swarthier friends, all three with matching pink streaks in their hair); "spring break J J yessss finally lol!!!!!" (fuchsia-painted toes anchoring a tropical beach panorama). Her social media presence on this site is the opposite of hiding in a car, and I suddenly realize that if I'm shocked she's white, she might be shocked I'm not. Tim certainly seemed surprised that I was me, at first. I cringe retroactively at his wide-eyed stare back at the Taco Bell counter.

When I was ten and Cass was six, during the scary times before Denny was conceived, we started making up stories about our third sister, taking turns imagining her out loud as we drifted off to sleep—where she lived (Florida), what she looked like (like us, but also like Beyoncé), the nonsensical adventures she had that always ended in the three of us joining forces to fight off villains and save the day. A few years later I found out that this storytelling technique—taking turns to craft something whole—is called exquisite corpse, which gave me chills not only because that's a creepy-ass game name but also because that's *exactly* what Leah was: a nameless, faceless, exquisite corpse that we felt safe animating only because we were convinced she would never come to life on her own. Until now.

I land on a photo labeled "bro time" with four different emoji. It's a selfie with Tim in which Leah's sticking out her tongue Miley Cyrus–style, but he thinks it's a normal photo. His lack of pretense, compared to her posturing, is weirdly endearing. *But he's not your real brother,* I think, swallowing a sudden swell of jealousy, sharp as a shard of glass. *He's not your blood. I am.*

"What are you doing?"

I spin around to find Cass standing in the doorway, hands shoved in the pockets of her hoodie, Mom's old purple sweatpants—a wearable security blanket we've passed back and forth over the years—almost covering her toes.

"You scared me," I say, closing the laptop in a deliberately slow way that I hope comes off as casual. "I thought you were—"

"Auntie Dearest?" Cass deadpans. "Nah, don't worry, she's still at the hospital terrorizing sick people."

I shake my head. "Ugh, can you imagine what it's like to be one of her patients?" And seamlessly, Cass juts out a hip and cocks an eyebrow, curling her lip into a surly sneer.

"What do you want, grandma? I just *changed* your damn bandage last *week*!" she barks in a near-perfect imitation of Aunt Sam's weary growl.

I start cracking up, and she saunters over waving a finger, not breaking character.

"You tell those bedsores ain't nobody got *time* for them, some of us need to go get our *chins* waxed!" (During one of their bitterer fights, Mom called Aunt Sam The Bearded Lady, and ever since that day we have jumped on every possible opportunity to bring it up.) We double over, trying not to let our cackling wake Denny.

"Stop it, I'm gonna die," I gasp, my diaphragm spasming.

"Sorry," Cass giggles. Within seconds, her features settle back into impenetrable neutrality, the sparkle in her eyes fading to a bored stare. It's startling to watch, like getting a door slammed in your face. "When do you think we'll get out of here?" she asks.

"It'll be a while," I say. "I have to save up."

"What about the money from Yvonne?" Cass asks. "Didn't Denny give it to you?" I must look confused, because she sighs and mumbles, "The little thief." She darts out of the bedroom and returns a minute later with a roll of bills held together by a hair elastic. "Here," she says, holding it out. "She said not to give it to you until we left. I guess she thought you might not take it otherwise."

I unwrap the cash slowly, gritting my teeth to keep from crying, and count out five twenty-dollar bills, three tens, a five, and twelve ones. With the $200 I emptied from my checking account this morning, this gives me enough to pay Aunt Sam plus $47 left for gas. It's not much of a cushion, but it's something. It'll buy us another couple of days, at least.

I'm so focused on the tallies in my head that I don't even notice Cass opening the computer, and by the time I look over, it's too late. Leah's dimpled smile (*Dimples. Those are Buck's. Cass has them, too, she just hasn't smiled in . . . what, years now?*) fills the screen, a sheaf of golden hair covering one of her give-away green eyes, a pool of amber-flecked jade, just like mine.

"Who is that?" Cass asks, giving me an odd, suspicious look. She's perched on the bed, all taut angles, like a runner on the starting block.

I briefly consider lying, but my brain is too fried. "That's her," I say.

"Her who?" I give Cass a look and watch as the realization tenses her features one by one: the full lips thinning, the small nose scrunching, the straight eyebrows knitting together into a shallow *V.* She squints at the screen. "*That's* her?"

"Yup."

"Damn," Cass says, "I always pictured her as more Willow Smith than Taylor Swift."

"Me too."

"How'd you find her?" Cass asks, shaking her head, clicking through the photos. "I thought I'd looked at every Devereaux on here." She looks at me expectantly, and even though I want nothing more than to avoid this conversation, I can't work up the necessary energy.

"She doesn't use it," I say. "She goes by Harper. Her stepdad's name."

"Leah Harper," Cass whispers, and I know her brain is working overtime all of a sudden, struggling to fit a new name and face to the specter we've been building in our heads since we were kids. "How did you figure it out?" she asks, her facial muscles as usual not betraying anything beneath the surface.

"Her brother came in tonight," I say, rerolling the bills from Yvonne's loan to avoid eye contact. "He was looking for me."

As if on cue, Cass lands on the photo of Leah and Tim. "Oh yeah, I saw that guy," she says. "I knew *something* freaked you out. What did he want?"

"Nothing," I say before I can stop myself. "He was just curious."

She shoots me a skeptical side-eye. "Come on. Why would he be curious about you?"

"Um, thanks?" I shove her.

"You know what I mean. He's not even related to us. Why would he care?"

"It's . . . complicated," I hedge.

"*What?*" she asks, getting annoyed.

Cass and I have an amateur telepathy thing going where I can usually communicate basic messages just using my eyes. When we were kids, it was stuff like, *Go upstairs. It's okay. Don't be scared.* But right now I'm just pleading with her, *Let it go. You don't want to know. Trust me.*

"Tell me," she says.

"Not now, okay?"

"Shut up and just tell me, Michelle," she says, her voice getting loud. "You're freaking me out!"

"Fine." I look her straight in the eyes and take a breath. "Buck is dying."

"Oh," she says, with the surprise of someone who was expecting a different, much worse, answer. I wonder if she thought something had happened to Leah. Better to lose a confirmed piece-of-shit father than a perfect imaginary sister, I guess. Cass thinks for a few seconds and then asks, "What's he dying of?"

"I don't know."

"You didn't even *ask*?"

I didn't care, I want to say, but I don't want to transfer my bitterness over Buck onto my sister. She was only two when he left, so she doesn't even remember him. She basically grew up without a dad, like Denny. I think Buck is a little bit like a cartoon villain to Cass: a one-dimensional bad guy who let us down that time, long ago. But I remember. He was *there*; he was my father—until he wasn't. And I will never, ever forgive him.

"How bad is it?" she asks. "Like . . . how soon is he . . ."

I shrug. "It's enough for me to know he's on his way out,"

I say. "I'm not really sweating the details." Actually, of course I want to know. I'm kicking myself for being too mad to ask Tim for more information when I had the chance. But Buck clearly didn't care about my life, so I'm trying hard not to let myself care about his death. So far, as evidenced by my recent Google searches, it's not working out so well.

"God, do you know *anything*?" Cass groans.

"I know he's leaving us something," I say defensively. "I know he's in California."

"What's he leaving us? *Where* in California?"

"I . . . don't know," I admit, and Cass rolls her eyes so hard she could knock over a set of bowling pins. "But apparently Leah's having a rough time with it all, and this guy, her brother or stepbrother or whatever, Tim, wants me to go talk to her."

"Seriously?" Cass asks. "*She's* having a rough time?" My sister stares down at the carpet for a minute and then says, "Cry me a fucking river."

"Cass—"

"Don't tell me not to curse," she snaps. "You don't get to play mom right now. Everything's too screwed up."

I bite my tongue—only figuratively—this time. She has a point. "See, this is why I didn't want to tell you," I say.

"Are you gonna talk to her?" she asks.

"No," I say. "Of course not."

Cass nods and seems to relax a little bit but closes the web browser and shuts the laptop. She shoves her hands back into her hoodie. "I pretend he's dead sometimes," she says.

"Yeah," I say. "Me too."

"When I imagine it, he gets shot in a holdup. Like at a liquor store or something."

"That's kind of violent," I laugh. In my version, he just sort of evaporates out of existence, kind of like I'm ordering an execution with a pencil eraser instead of a lethal injection.

Cass shrugs. "What other way is there?" she asks.

"I think maybe you've been watching too much *CSI*," I say. "And we should probably go to sleep before we give ourselves nightmares." I reach out to hug her, but she swivels out of the way and leaps to her feet.

"He left them, too, right?" Cass asks. The sweatpants pool around her ankles, making her look like she's disappearing into the floor.

"Yes."

She sucks her bottom lip into her mouth and chews on it a minute, visibly relaxing, before letting it go. "Is it bad that that makes me feel better?"

"No."

"Do you know how long he . . ." She pauses in the doorway and shakes her head. "Never mind."

"How long he has left? I don't know. Not long, I guess."

"No," Cass says. "I was gonna ask how long he stayed. With them."

"I don't know that either."

"Forget it," she says and slips out the door as quickly as she came in.

A few minutes later, after a little more Instagram stalking, I return everything in my aunt's bedroom to the way I found it and then pad down the hall in bare feet, feeling around in the dark for my spot on the floor but finding either warm bodies or sharp pieces of furniture taking up all the prime real estate. So even though I know Sam will find some reason to give me shit about it, I crawl onto the couch and nestle my still-damp head into the well-worn, tobacco-scented cushions.

He left them, too.

The thought *is* comforting, although after seeing those pictures, it's a hard scenario to imagine. How did Buck ever fit into, let alone abandon, that happy, normal, magazine-shiny family I just glimpsed? He's the same color, but that's where the similarities seem to end. The Buck I remember, the long-haired, allergic-to-dress-shirts, raucous, laughing, mercurial drunk who drove a car that even in its prime looked like it was destined for a junkyard, could never have posed believably in front of a white picket fence.

Then again, neither could I. Neither could any of us. No matter what shade of sea foam you dressed us in or how you straightened and smoothed out our hair, our untrusting eyes and our closed-mouth smiles would give us away in a second.

We'll never be a part of that kind of family. We'll never be our sister's sisters, not outside of a DNA lab. That fantasy is just a silly game best kept in the past.

FIVE

Wednesday Morning, Part 1
Baltimore, MD

I wake up unable to breathe and start to panic thinking I'm paralyzed again—it always happens more when I'm stressed; it's actually kind of amazing I'm not in a coma by now—but then Denny peers into my face, and I realize he's straddling my chest like a wrestler, a wriggly, fifty-pound bundle of sharp elbows and knees.

"Max and I are hungry," he whimpers.

"Then go get some food," I groan, struggling to push him off with the minimal strength in my sleepy spaghetti arms. "You know how."

"She doesn't have anything," he whines, sliding down onto

the tangle of blankets on the floor. "Just some weird cheese and mom juice." Mom juice. That's what he calls booze.

"Okay, okay." I sit up and blink into the still-dark room. The thin strip of visible sky outside is peach-colored, and my phone alarm hasn't gone off, so it must be just after sunrise. Aunt Sam's door is shut, but her purse is hanging on the chair by the door, so she must be home. There is one thing conspicuously missing, though. "Where's Cass?" I ask.

"Doing her shot, I think," Denny says, punching all of the buttons on the remote in an attempt to turn on the TV. A black screen appears with the words CONNECTION NOT DETECTED.

I poke around in the cupboards until I find a box of Special K stashed next to an empty carton of cigarettes over the stove. I pour some into a bowl and look for milk, but Denny was right—there's no liquid in the fridge except for a bottle of white wine and a few hard ciders. When I close the door, I notice that Aunt Sam's only magnet reads, GET BEHIND ME, SATAN—AND DON'T PUSH! *Right.*

"You'll have to eat this dry," I say, sticking a spoon into the pile of cereal and setting it in front of him on the coffee table. I grab the remote and fix the input, scrolling until I find a Ninja Turtles cartoon and then lowering the volume until it's barely audible. "We don't want to wake the beast," I whisper, ruffling his hair.

"But I already woke you up." Denny grins, flake shards shooting through his lips onto the carpet.

"Smartass." I flop back down on the couch and check my phone. It's six fifty-five. If we hurry we can probably get out the door before Aunt Sam even remembers we're here. I pull a rumpled sheet around me (not that Denny would ever take his eyes off a screen, unless—and maybe not even if—the house went up in flames) and shimmy out of my gym shorts and into some jeans. The tank top I slept in has no visible stains and still smells like coconut oil conditioner, so I leave it on. Devereaux rule #6: No stains, no smells, no problem.

I know how scarce and precious private bathroom time is these days, but after ten minutes of folding up the makeshift bedding and playing solitaire on my phone waiting for Cass to emerge, I start to get impatient.

"Hey," I whisper through the door, drumming my fingers on the hollow, white-painted wood. "You almost ready?" I hear shuffling and the blast of sink faucets. A few seconds later, Cass comes out with a mumbled, "All yours." Her face is dripping wet, but not enough to distract me from her bloodshot eyes and puffy lids. She's been crying.

I shut myself in and stare at my reflection in the mirror, my self-loathing steadily rising. I should never have let Cass see Leah's photos. I should never have told her about Buck. My sister acts so tough that I sometimes forget how young she is. She's thirteen. *Thirteen.* Her armor's just starting to grow. And she's already been through more than a lot of people twice her age. She has to stick herself with needles just to stay alive, not to mention survive the basic soul-suck of adolescence, which apparently includes some posse of mean girls gay-bashing her at school—and she's not even gay. Or maybe she is. I don't know. Would she even tell me? Either way, on top of all that, she definitely didn't need another thing to worry about.

I wash my face and brush my teeth, but as penance for my

misjudgment I decide to leave my hair in its natural state, which might best be described as "Solange Knowles after falling on an electrified fence."

I turn to leave the bathroom and come face-to-face with Aunt Sam, the only person I know who can manage to look intimidating in a Hello Kitty kimono.

"Good morning, sunshine," she says, putting a hand up on the doorframe. "You got something for me?"

"Um . . ." The wad of bills is safe in my bag in the living room, stuffed into a pair of ankle socks. It's all there, and handing it over would make her happy and get her off my back—for the time being, anyway. But for some reason, I can't bring myself to part with my entire life savings just yet. "I got it," I say, thinking on my feet. "But since I worked late and deposited my paycheck after eight, it won't post until tomorrow."

"Don't lie," she says, clicking her tongue. "You think I don't know a liar, you must have forgotten who my sister is."

Mom lies because she's an addict, I want to say. *Which is better than being a sad, lonely old bitch like you.* But instead I try to look shocked. "I'm not lying!" I say. "I swear, you can come with me to an ATM right now. I've got it all, $347 and change. We can even go talk to the bank manager and see if they can make an exception." I crinkle my forehead and swallow hard. If I actually let all the heartache I've been bottling up for the past decade show on my face, I'm afraid I might crack for good, so instead I just give her a fake bootleg version. "Please don't kick us out," I whisper, pressing my lips together and chattering my teeth to make my chin tremble. "Just give me one more day."

My aunt purses her lips and steps back, looking me up and down with her hands on her hips. "Fine," she says finally.

"You're lucky I haven't had my coffee yet." She sweeps back into her bedroom and kicks the door closed with one slippered foot.

Today's ride to school is even more chaotic than usual. It takes me three tries to get Goldie to start, and when she does there's a rattling sound that doesn't stop even when I press on the brake. Great. Then when I start to pull out into the street, Denny screams, "STOP!" at the top of his lungs because apparently I have almost run over Max, and I have to resist the urge to shrug and keep going. Then Denny has to get out of his seatbelt to let Max in the car, and *then* Max somehow manages to kick the back of Cass's seat even though he has no legs. ("He does have legs, and he's wearing cowboy boots," Denny informs us.) Cass, meanwhile, won't look at or speak to any of us. She's even more robotic than usual, and I only last five minutes before I resort to shameless bribery to clear my conscience.

"Who wants a doughnut?" I sing as I veer into the drive-through.

"We do!" Denny cries. "I want coconut, Max wants chocolate frosted."

"You and Max have to share," I say.

"*No!*" Max kicks the back of my seat this time.

"Denny!" I yell in my best warning voice. "I'm doing something nice. You can either say thank you or forget it."

There's silence for a few seconds and then a grumbled, "Thank you." My eyes fall on the letter from Denny's school, still sitting on top of the dashboard. I haven't even thought about it since Monday. I guess I could tell Mrs. Mastino that Mom's in jail and buy a few weeks of pity overtime, but I know it won't change anything in the long run. Denny has attention problems and behavior issues. He can be a sweet kid, but she's right—he's not getting what he needs to thrive, not at school and not at home. It's just a matter of time before they kick him out, and unless we can afford a special school, he'll just bounce around disrupting more classes and shoving more kids, getting yelled at by every adult in his life until he gets immune to it. I've seen those boys in the back of my classrooms, the ones who slump over their desks like they're asleep with their eyes open, staring angrily down at the ground and quietly doing their time. Teachers either ignore them or pick on them, rubbing their inadequacy in their faces. They're failing out of school, yes, but they're also being failed by the system. I can't let that be my brother's fate.

I get a couple of doughnuts and a large iced coffee and then pull into a parking space so we can eat without getting it all over ourselves—not that a fresh dusting of crumbs would even be visible amid the crap rolling around on Goldie's floor. I hand Denny his chocolate-coconut compromise, and he temporarily kicks Max to the curb so he can shove the entire thing in his mouth. But when I hand Cass a raspberry jelly—her favorite—she turns away.

"Come on, take it," I prod. "You haven't eaten anything."

Silence.

"You're *diabetic*," I say, still holding it out inches from her face. "You're not allowed to not eat."

She looks at me quickly and shakes her head, chewing on her lip.

"Just take it for later," I say, and Cass bursts into tears.

"I said I *don't want it*!" she sobs.

It's been so long since I've seen my sister cry that instead of trying to hug or comfort her I just freeze in place staring like I'm rubbernecking at a roadside accident, the jelly doughnut getting warm and soft in my increasingly tight grip. Cass buries her face in her sleeve, her narrow shoulders shaking, and we sit in silence for a minute until Denny pulls his head up over the seatback and tugs three times on her hood with a coconut-crusted fist.

"Max is really sorry he kicked you," he says, his voice high and sweet, and Cass quiets, wiping snot from her nose with the back of one hand.

"It's not that," I say. "It's something I did."

"No it isn't," Cass sniffs.

"You don't have to pretend for his sake," I say. "I should never have told you about Buck like that, out of nowhere. I should have sat you down and—"

"It's not about him," she says, more forcefully.

"About who?" Denny asks. "Dad?" I hand him the jelly doughnut as a distraction.

"Then *what*?" I ask Cass. She looks down into her lap, while Goldie's rattle vibrates under us like a volcano about to erupt. "Is it school?" I press on. "Those girls—did they do something? Are people messing with you? Do you . . . have anything you want to tell me?"

Fresh tears spring to Cass's eyes, and she wipes them away with the already-damp cuff of her hoodie.

"You have to talk to me," I say. "If you tell me what's going on, I can help. I can—"

"What?" she snaps. "What can you do? Tell them to stop? Tell them my mom's locked up and my dad's about to bite it, so they should give me a break?" Cass sucks in her cheeks and straightens her back. "Just forget it," she says.

I shift into reverse and back slowly out of the parking space, trying to give myself time to think. After what just happened, I can't drop my sister off at school like it's no big deal. Maybe I *should* put my forgery skills to good use, write an absence note, and let them play hooky for a day; blow all my cash at a theme park or an arcade, live it up for one last hurrah before we all get carted off to foster care. Because that's what will happen, eventually. We're running out of options. We can't stay with Aunt Sam anymore. She may be our blood, but she's not our family—real family doesn't hold you for ransom. And even if I could stick it out long enough to post bail for Mom, what then? Court dates and sentencing and probably jail time. If not now, then someday in the not-too-distant future. We don't have anyone we can depend on to take care of us, I'm doing a shitty job, and even if I *did* take the CPS lady's advice and decide to throw everything away to become a legal guardian, we'd be screwed for five more weeks, and right now it feels like we won't make it five *days*. If this was a video game, the three of us would be falling off a cliff to sad trombone music while the words GAME OVER flashed on the screen.

I brake for a stoplight, and Goldie's rattle gets even louder. I have no idea what to do. We're less than a mile from Denny's school. I pick up my watery iced coffee just to have something to do with my hands instead of anxiously tapping the wheel, and a damp receipt falls off the bottom of the plastic cup. I look down at the handwritten black ink numbers starting to bleed together. *Tim.* He must be on his way to school now, too, him and Leah, in their swanky SUV—in the light of day this time—listening to Top 40 hits instead of the death knell of their junky car, smiling their Crest Whitestrips smiles and wearing their wrinkle-free clothes that probably smell like fabric softener and freshly mowed grass. The jealousy hits me in the gut just as the light turns green.

"Who did Dad bite?" Denny pipes up from the backseat.

"He didn't bite anyone," I sigh, merging into the slow lane, trying to decide where to go. "It's just an expression."

"I don't get it," he says. I look to Cass, hoping she'll jump in with one of her perfectly timed punch lines to shut down the line of questioning, but she's leaning against the window, gnawing anxiously on a thumbnail.

"It means he's . . . sick," I say after some consideration. "Buck is sick." I don't think Denny will be as calm as Cass and me when he finds out Buck is dying. I'm planning on putting off that conversation for as long as humanly possible.

"How'd he get sick?" Denny asks.

"I don't know," I say, rubbing my right temple with one hand, hoping for once that Max steps in to pull one of his douchey stunts. "He probably did something he wasn't supposed to do." Buck would only be in his midthirties, so it has to be drugs, or maybe cancer. Something slow and awful, which I wouldn't wish even on my worst enemy . . . who also happens to be my father.

"Is he in a time-out?" Denny asks. I'm losing my patience.

"No," I say wearily. "He's in a place called California. Now, please—"

"Can we go there?" I glance in the rearview mirror to see Denny bouncing excitedly on the ripped imitation-leather seat. "Can we go?" he repeats. And all of a sudden, something clicks.

We have no life here. I'm about to graduate high school with no prospects but Taco Bell middle management, Cass is getting bullied, Denny *is* the bully, Aunt Sam has Satan behind her, pushing hard, and Mom is sweating out her heroin habit in an eight-by-six cell. The only thing I can think of that can even begin to solve our problems is money, and the only person who might have something for us that could give us a new lease on life (and on a new car, because I'm half-convinced this one is going to kill us) is the person whose stellar decision-making skills got us here in the first place. In a twist so ironic it actually turns my stomach, Allen Buckner Devereaux III now stands as our last shot at keeping this family together.

But hey, at least someone saved something for us. At least someone wants to say they're sorry. And right now, I'll take anyone as that someone. I'll even take Buck.

Ten feet before the turnoff for Denny's school, I pull a screeching U-turn that leaves about five cars leaning on their horns in my wake. The adrenaline hits my system like a lightning bolt, kicking Dunkin' Donuts' ass by a country mile.

"What the hell?" Cass asks, bracing herself against the glove compartment.

"Sorry," I say, "there's been a slight change of plans." I watch Goldie's odometer click over to 97,678 miles and say a silent prayer that she's up to the task I'm about to give her.

SIX

Wednesday Morning, Part 2
Baltimore, MD

In the parking lot of a strip mall Family Dollar store, I make a list of what we'll need for our trip, my hands still shaking from the rush of abruptly veering off course.

Toothbrushes

Toothpaste

Baby wipes (aka "insta-baths," not to be confused with the more thorough "ghetto baths" we'll be enjoying in gas station sinks)

Underwear

Nonperishable snacks

"Can't we just go home for that stuff?" Cass asks, peering over my shoulder. "And what about clothes?"

"We already took everything that was clean to Aunt Sam's,"

I remind her. "Besides, you wear the same thing every day anyway. I think you'll live, as long as you have enough insulin for another week." Devereaux rule #8: The less you need, the farther you'll get.

"Yup," she says.

"Are you sure? Because I really don't want to have to hold up a pharmacy."

"I'm suuuure," she groans, but the corners of her lips turn up in a faint smile. Her mood has markedly improved since we did a one-eighty, going from impenetrable fortress of angst and despair to impenetrable fortress of slightly less angst and despair. But I'll take it. Even the most minuscule positive changes slow the intestinal spasms about the decision I've just made.

"How long does it take to get to California?" Denny asks. He's so blissfully ignorant about the real reason we're going, and what's at stake, that it's all I can do to restrain myself from dragging him to the nearest wishing well to try to force a *Freaky Friday*–style brain swap.

"About four days, maybe." I don't have GPS on my phone, but I've already done the math in my head: If we start at nine A.M. and I do sixty on the highway, which is about as fast as Goldie can take, we'll log 650 miles a day over twelve to thirteen hours, allowing time for bathroom and meal stops. That should get us across the country by Saturday night—Sunday morning at the latest.

He pokes his head in between the front seats and grabs the straw from my empty coffee with his teeth. "Where will we sleep?"

"We'll camp," I say.

"Like in tents?"

"More like in car," Cass quips, but Denny's enthusiasm can't be deterred.

"Cool!" he cries, the straw spewing melted-ice water onto the dashboard. "Dibs on the trunk!" If only Child Protective Services could see us now . . .

I glance around the parking lot, growing more paranoid by the second. I wonder if this is how it felt for Mom in the Shell station, if she felt this same sick thrill at knowing before anyone else does that you're about to do something wrong. I'm pretty sure this little road trip is five different kinds of illegal, considering I'm underage with a provisional license, taking minors out of state without their parents' knowledge, and—since Goldie's not registered to me—probably also *technically* stealing a car.

I'd like to think that I'm owed this one transgression after so many years of playing by my mom's hypocritical rules, especially since my motives are mostly pure . . . but another part of me can't help but wonder if I'm just finally fulfilling my genetic legacy, as if a criminal mind is inherited like schizophrenia or Parkinson's—something that hides in your DNA for years, only to show up one day out of nowhere and ruin your whole life. And I have to admit that it does feel good, the prospect of leaving all my responsibilities behind. Maybe I have more in common with Buck than I thought.

"So . . . what do we need for all this, like, ten bucks?" Cass asks, perusing my list again. But then a cop car passes by behind us, and I suddenly lose the ability to speak.

"Sorry," I stammer once it pulls out onto the highway. "Let me see." I tick off the items, counting out loud. "Four toothbrushes, one toothpaste, maybe two packs of wipes—"

"Three toothbrushes, Einstein," Cass interrupts.

"Yeah, *Einstein,*" Denny parrots, giggling at what he thinks is a bad word.

"No," I say slowly. "We need four." There's still one major detail to discuss, something I knew I had to do the minute I turned the car around, and I watch the muscles in Cass's neck gather into tense little ropes as she realizes what I'm about to say. "I'm inviting her, too."

Cass is silent, and after a few seconds of stillness I let myself hope that she's okay with it, but then the door flies open and slams shut as a black blur that vaguely resembles my sister storms off across the asphalt.

"Who's *her*?" Denny asks, gripping my upper arm. His eyes are big and anxious again, like they were in the police station that first night, and I feel a sharp pang of guilt for bursting whatever safe little bubble he's managed to crawl into in the interim.

"A relative," I say, giving him a reassuring smile. "She's about the same age as Cass. A year older, actually." Buck's affair had already become a full-fledged family when my sister made her premature, dramatic entrance into the world, a tiny three-and-a-half-pound thing who my mother says never even cried and who the NICU nurses had to massage to get circulation going because she moved so little at first. It's like Cass already sensed there was no space for her and just decided to play dead from the start.

I leave Denny in the car with the windows rolled down and strict instructions not to let Max touch the gearshift, and I jog after Cass, who's made a left at the Family Dollar and is angrily stomping past a RadioShack a few stores down.

"Hey!" I call. "Come on, just listen!" I'm taller and have longer legs, so I'm starting to close the distance. Cass speeds up her walking without turning around. "She's the one he called," I yell, panting a little. "She's the only one who knows where he is."

"Then call her," Cass snaps, spinning around. "Facebook message her. Just *ask*. She doesn't have to come with us. She didn't even have the guts to talk to you face-to-face."

"She was there," I say. "She stayed in the car."

"That's even worse!"

"I know, but what am I supposed to do?" I ask. "Call and say, 'Hey, we're driving to visit our dying father—who's also *your* dying father, condolences b-t-dubs—and we just need the address. Good luck with your closure!'?"

Cass shrugs, like *why not?*

"Look, the only reason we even know about him is because of her," I say. "She tried to do the right thing. We owe it to her to at least invite her. She probably won't even come."

"We don't owe her anything," Cass spits. Her anger surprises me; she hardly seemed fazed last night when she saw Leah's photos.

"Maybe you're right," I sigh. "But she's still his daughter. She still deserves the chance to see him."

Cass broods, cursing under her breath for a minute, before finally walking toward me with her arms crossed tight against her chest.

"Fine," she says, giving me a look that says it is most definitely not even remotely close to approaching fine. "But no *way* she gets her own toothbrush. She can use her finger. Or get cavities."

"That's big of you," I say, only half joking. Under the circumstances, I don't feel like meeting Leah either, let alone being trapped in a car with her for a week. But as far as I can tell, she's our only way to get to Buck, unless we feel like driving aimlessly around the country's third-largest state, randomly accosting handsome sick people. I don't even know what he would look like now. He could be pudgy or graying, even balding. But nah, if Buck started losing his hair he'd be that guy who shaves it all off and makes it seem like a lifestyle choice. Everything is a facade with him. I have to be careful not to pin too much hope on him this time around . . . which is going to be pretty hard, considering he's basically the only hope we've got left.

Before I can dwell too much on my father's track record of broken promises, I run back to the car to rescue the receipt with Tim's number on it before it disintegrates or Cass changes her mind, whichever comes first. Denny is in the driver's seat, pretending to drag race, so I lean through the open window, fish the slip out of the cup holder, and dial before I have a chance to second-guess this decision, too.

He picks up on the fourth ring and sounds pleasantly surprised—if a little suspicious—to hear from me.

"Does Leah still want to meet?" I ask.

"Um . . . yeah," he says in a very low voice that lets me know she's in earshot. "I think so. I mean, I know she would. Yes."

"Can she be in the parking lot of your school in half an hour?"

There's a pause, and his voice drops to a whisper. "Do you even know where our school is?"

"You're not the only one who can use the Internet," I say, the anxiety making me snippier than usual. "So can she meet me or what?"

"I don't know . . . that's in the middle of first period." Suddenly a female voice asks him something in the background, and Tim says, "Just my physics partner. We have to finish a lab before class." I smile to myself. He's not a great liar, but with those altar-boy looks, he probably doesn't need to be.

"It's important," I say. "You said so yourself."

He starts talking too loudly now, trying to cover his ass. "Okay, no problem," he shouts. "I'll be there."

"Just make sure *she's* there," I say and hang up.

Twenty-five minutes, twenty-two bucks, one map, two bribery sodas, and three off-brand toothbrushes later, we're turning off the highway onto a leafy suburban road that's only nineteen miles from the city but feels worlds apart from the streets we call home. The houses here are all set way back from the curb, some so far you can't even really see them through the trees. And that's another thing: the trees. They're everywhere. It's greener than the city parks.

The houses I *can* see are well-manicured one-stories, not that showy but still sort of grand, with bright red brick, painted shutters, and bushes carved into rounded rectangles. In a row, they look sort of like those fake presents that department stores line their windows with at Christmas: evenly spaced, gleaming little boxes that hold the promise of the perfect gift inside, that one elusive thing that you're convinced might make your life different if only you could have it.

"Where *are* we?" Denny asks, gluing his face to the window, and the innocent question sums up my feelings so exactly that I don't know quite what to tell him.

"We're almost there," I say distractedly, staring at a woman who's literally on her knees by a flower bed pruning roses, like she got hired by central casting just to be there while we drove by: *Show the urban youth with the negligent parents what they've been missing, Ruth! Make sure to polish your shears in advance, and bring the gardening gloves with the pink grosgrain trim. Oh, and wear clogs. Not Crocs, real wooden clogs—you know, the kind people never actually walk in and the Dutch use for Christmas stockings.*

"We're almost in California?" Denny says excitedly.

"Yeah," Cass mumbles, still—and maybe eternally—pissed off at me. "Welcome to Beverly Hills."

I ignore her and squint down at the map in my lap. I'm so used to driving the same pattern every day without even thinking about it that navigating new territory is hurting my brain. I would get a GPS except, for one thing, Goldie's way too old to be compatible with most of them, and also they start at, like, $100 and I've already spent almost 10 percent of our meager funds on doughnuts and toiletries. I'm not sure I'll even be able to afford gas for all four days, let alone food, so I hope the sandwich crackers and mixed nuts we stocked up on at Family Dollar can keep us alive until we get there. Or that Leah's wallet is lined with hundred-dollar bills.

Luckily, there's a big sign with the school name on it at the turnoff, which is marked by two stone columns.

"It's like Hogwarts up in here," Cass says, peering at the long, winding path that leads to a big, intimidating, city hall–looking main building about a mile uphill.

"I want to go home," Denny says.

I'm gathering the energy for a reassuring speech when I notice a kiosk in the middle of the road a couple hundred yards up. There's a dude in a gray uniform standing beside it, speaking into a walkie-talkie. I brake and redial Tim.

"You didn't tell me your school has a bouncer," I say. Cass rolls her eyes.

"Did they stop you?" he asks, genuinely confused in the way only a privileged white boy could be.

"Not yet, but I don't want to give them a chance," I say. "Can you come down the road?"

"I don't think so," he says with a nervous laugh. "It's probably harder for us to get out than for you to get in. Listen, I'll call and put you on the list. I'll tell them you're dropping off Leah's math textbook—they hardly ever question academic stuff."

"Okay," I say, acid churning in my stomach.

"Also, what does your car look like?" he asks. "They'll want an approximate make and model."

"Tell them it looks like it doesn't belong here," I say. "Just like us."

"I'm serious," he says.

"So am I. It's a 1973 Datsun that looks like shit run over twice. I'm pretty sure they'll know it."

Somehow we make it past security, like Annie's grubby orphan friends sneaking into Daddy Warbucks's mansion, and drive up to the main campus, which looks like one of those Ivy League schools on the college brochures I may or may not like to page through in my school's library on low days.

Tim and Leah are standing in a handicapped parking spot under a big maple tree, having what looks like a heated conversation. Leah is willowy and almost as tall as Tim, with long, skinny legs that my mom would call a symptom of TTDT—Thighs That Don't Touch—Disease. They're both in polo shirts and khakis (him, pants; her, skirt) that look so aggressively matched they've got to be uniforms. As we pull up, they stop fighting and turn to stare at Goldie. Leah says something to Tim and then stays put, staring down at the toes of her black Mary Janes, as he walks up to the car. He taps on Cass's window, but she doesn't react, so I put the car in park and get out to meet him. The breeze smells fresh and a little bit sweet, like someone sprinkled it with cinnamon.

"Hey," he says, grimacing a little. I look past him to Leah, who refuses to break eye contact with her shoes.

"She wasn't in on this one, huh?"

"No. Well, she knew you might call, but she didn't expect—it's all just a lot for her, I think."

I take a few lungsful of this real-life Yankee Candle air and weigh my options. I could make everyone's life easier and just leave her out of it, get the details for the hospice like Cass wanted and then split. But for some reason I can't shake a nagging feeling not only that we need her but that she needs us. Why else would she have made Tim drive her out to a Taco Bell in a bad part of town? Also, as far as I know, we've only got four living blood relatives, a number that will soon shrink by a full 25 percent. And she's one of them. I push past Tim and walk straight up to her.

"I'm Michelle," I say, forcing my hands to stay at my sides and not hug my chest defensively like they want to. Leah glances up at me, taking in my hair, my face, my slept-in shirt and well-worn jeans. I clench my fists, not out of anger but because

I don't want her to see my nails, chewed down to the quick—another coping mechanism I've relied too much on lately.

"Hi," she says, avoiding eye contact and crossing her arms. She reminds me a lot of Cass already.

"Look," I say. "I know we've never met, and this is a weird way to do it, but I feel like I should tell you that we're going to California. To see Buck."

Leah knits her thin blonde brows and looks over my shoulder at Tim.

"You didn't tell me that," she says.

"I didn't know!" Tim appears at her side, and now I have *two* Children of the Corn staring me down. "You're *driving* to California?" he asks incredulously.

"Yup."

"In . . . *that*?" Leah asks, nodding her head at Goldie. I look back and see Denny watching us through the back window. He's got a finger up his nose. I turn to Leah and offer a thin smile.

"Yup." Tim and Leah exchange perplexed looks. They don't understand why I'm here. They've never had to live with an escape route constantly evolving in the back of their minds. "I *heard*," I say, looking pointedly at Tim, "that you might want to try to see him before he . . . you know." Leah bites her lip. "So I figured I should come and ask if you want to come with us."

"What?" Leah says, shock replacing her frown of confusion. "Drive cross-country? Like, *today*?"

Tim grabs my arm and pulls me a few feet to the left. "I thought you were going to talk to her," he whispers.

"We *are* talking," I shoot back, yanking my arm away. Behind me, I hear the car door open and know without even looking that Cass is standing on the curb now, ready to have my back if

I need her. *That's what real sisters do*, I think, watching Leah pout. But then it dawns on me that if Cass saw enough commotion to break her mime act and come to my defense, there might be people inside the school—people with a lot more power—ready to come to Leah's. We have to get out of here soon.

"If you don't wanna come, don't come," I say, holding up my hands. "But *you're* the one who found *me*. I figured I should at least ask."

"It's really nice of you," Tim says. But Leah looks like she's slowly imploding.

"What about school?" she asks, her face getting pink. "I can't just *leave*. And what about Mom and Jeff?" She lets out a laugh of disbelief. "Don't your parents even care where you are?"

"*Leah*," Tim says.

"And you want me to get in that falling-apart car right now and just *go*?" she continues. "I don't have clothes. I don't have a suitcase. I . . . I don't even have my retainer!"

"Neither do we," I shrug.

"So you're just wearing *that* for a week?" she asks, barely able to mask her horror.

"We didn't exactly have time to pack," I say. "And we don't have time now, so if you don't want to come, just tell us where his hospice is, and we'll get going."

I want her to take the bait at this point. She might be spoiled, but based on all of the emoticons on her Facebook, I expected that she'd at least be happier. What does she even have to be that pissed about (dying loser dad aside, obviously)? She has the life that everyone's supposed to want—pretty, thin, white, blonde, popular, family just screwed up enough for her to have a legitimate claim on teen angst but not so much that she turns tragic and starts to scare off the ripped lifeguards at the country club pool. I'm working myself up now, starting to get angry. We're risking everything to go on this trip, and she's sulking because she won't be able to bring her *retainer*?

"Well?" I ask impatiently.

"He . . . didn't tell me the address," she says, tucking her hair behind her ears. "He sounded kind of out of it."

"So you don't even know where it is?"

"He said Venice Beach, right?" Tim jumps in, putting a hand on Leah's shoulder. She nods.

"The Golden . . . something," she says and then sighs heavily. "I guess I could map it on my phone for you."

"Don't bother," I say. "I'm sure we can find it." I give them a wave and turn to head back to the car. I know I should probably thank her, but I'm afraid if I talk any more I might crumble; I don't know if it's disappointment that she's not what I wanted her to be, or shame for dragging myself and my siblings through this crappy Disneyland detour of Things We'll Never Have, or just the anxiety of what lies ahead for us, but I'm suddenly on the verge of tears.

"Wait!" I hear Tim call, but I can't turn around until I get myself under control, so instead I lean against the car on my elbows and pretend to check my phone.

"You should go," I hear him say. "You know you won't have another chance. And this is something you could regret for the rest of your life, Lee, I'm serious."

"I don't even *know* them," she stage-whispers, her voice high and unstable. "And Mom would freak."

"She wants you to go, it was her idea."

"Yeah, on a plane or something. With *her*." There's a long

pause. "I'm not going anywhere by myself with them. And seriously, that car—"

"What if I go with you?" Tim says. "What if I come, too?"

I freeze. That was not part of the plan. I like Tim more than Leah at the moment, but that's not really saying much. And it's another mouth to feed—or to have to listen to. For twelve hours a day. Plus, I'm not even sure the middle seatbelt in the back works. I spin around.

"We have to go," I say. "So whatever's happening, it needs to happen now."

Leah scrunches up her face like she might cry. "I don't *know*," she squeals, looking desperately at Tim.

"What do you have to lose?" he asks. "A few days of school, maybe a few weeks of being grounded. But this is your *dad*. I know if it was my mom . . ." he trails off and tries to compose himself. It's the same line he used on me in the parking lot last night. I hope he really does have a sick mom, because if not, he might be kind of a sociopath.

Leah looks back and forth between her school and Goldie a few times, as if weighing the potential costs of such an enormous social downgrade against the chance to reconcile with her biological father. "Okay," she finally says, squeezing Tim's hand. "I'll go if you go."

Tim hugs her tight, and I have to look away. Something about their obvious closeness and how much he cares about her makes me irrationally jealous. They've only been steps for, what, three years, he said? I can't remember the last time I hugged my real sister that way. Maybe that's the problem. Maybe I'm the one creating the distance.

"We're in," Tim says, walking toward me with Leah

following/being dragged behind him. I hear a tapping on the car window and turn to see Cass looking at me with murderous eyes.

"*We?*" she mouths. All I can do is break eye contact and suck in my cheeks.

"So what now?" Tim asks.

"Now get in the car," I say.

Tim blanches. "We'll need early dismissal notes to get past security," he says.

"Not if they can't see you," I say, annoyed that he's only just realizing this roadblock. Devereaux rule #4: Identify your obstacles in advance. I knew the minute I saw the guard station that I'd need a way to get Leah out, if she said yes. I open the trunk hatch, shove aside the boxes of ramen and the random bags of Mom's stuff, and gesture to the space in between.

"No way," Leah says. "No. Effing. Way."

"Got a better idea?" I put my hands on my hips and give them my best I-suffer-no-fools face, a dominant gene mutation inherited from my mother.

"I just don't think we'll both fit," Tim says hesitantly.

"It's not for both of you. One can go on the floor in the backseat next to Denny. We've got plenty of clothes and a few sheets we can cover you with."

"It's like riding in steerage on the *Titanic*!" Leah whimpers.

"Only to the bottom of the hill," I say through clenched teeth. "Then some prime first-class seating will open up. Our amenities include seatbelts and all the Golden Grahams you can find embedded in the cushions."

A few minutes later, our reluctant cargo loaded and concealed, I walk shakily around to the driver's side door and slide back into my seat, Goldie's furious rattle matching the rising panic in my chest. Whatever I started this morning is growing, fast, and threatening to spiral out of control. I've got two extra runaways now, who come with a lot of extra baggage. And if we get caught, I know there'll be no cozy stopover at Aunt Sam's this time, no chance any CPS agent would grant me custody. They'll split us up. I'll lose Cass and Denny, which means I'll lose everything.

I ease the gearshift into drive and roll slowly out of the parking lot. There's no going back now.

SEVEN

Wednesday Afternoon
I-40, Near Cumberland, MD

Usually I love highway driving. That steady thrum of engine, white noise of rotating tires, and the blur you catch if you look out the side windows, like life just turned into a watercolor. But these past two hours in the car have been tense. As soon as she sat down, Leah got chocolate frosting on her butt, which led to a stream of delighted poop jokes from Denny that almost made her cry. Then Tim's knees were digging into my back through the seat, and I asked Cass to switch with him, and she gave me the finger. When we finally stopped for gas and Tim clambered into the passenger seat, he asked me where the USB cord was so he could charge his iPhone, and then he proceeded to try to diagnose Goldie's rattle for twenty miles. Meanwhile, Leah and

Cass were concentrating on totally ignoring each other while Denny updated us all on the status of a booger he was slowly excavating from his left nostril.

But then, as if by magic—or intense boredom—three of them fell asleep. Unfortunately for me, though, the chattiest one is still conscious.

"Could it be a loose wheel bearing?" Tim asks, straining his seatbelt as he leans forward to reach an ear toward the front of the car. He peers over the dashboard like he might be able to see what it is using X-ray vision if he just concentrates enough. "Maybe it's the lower shock mount, or the heat riser or heat shield on the exhaust pipe," he mutters.

"It's fine," I say for maybe the thirteenth time. "If it bothers you so much, you can look under the hood when we stop for the night."

Tim shuts up for a minute, and I hear the faint tapping of his finger on a screen. "How far do you think we'll make it today?" he asks. "I can hit up Yelp for hotels and make a reservation."

I'm already regretting bringing them along. I spent so much time worrying about how we'd fit in with them that I never considered the fact that they might not fit in with us. There's no way they're going to be able to hack three nights of sleeping in a car and taking "showers" in fast-food sinks. "Why don't you worry about your parents," I say, changing the subject. "You need to make sure they're cool with this."

"'Cool' is not a word I'd use to describe my dad," Tim says with a laugh.

"Well, your school then. Aren't they gonna call someone when they realize you guys disappeared?" For once in my life

I'm thankful that no one cares where we are. It makes running away a lot easier.

"Crap, you're right," he says. "Don't talk for a minute." I hear the tapping again, and Tim clears his throat. "Hi there, this is Jeff Harper," he says in a slightly deeper voice. "I sent a family friend to pick up Tim and Leah this morning. Unfortunately there's been a death in our family, and I need to take them out of school for a few days." He pauses. "My mother. Yes, thank you. I appreciate that." I grip the wheel tighter. I hope he knows what he's doing, because it sounds like he's just quoting *Ferris Bueller's Day Off.* Tim coughs nervously, a dead giveaway. "Yes, of course," he says. "If you, uh, send the form to my email address I can fill it out and fax it right back. Yup, it's jharper71 at Yahoo. Okay, thank you so much. Take care."

"What was that?" I ask. "Now your dad's getting an email from the school, genius. And where are we supposed to find a fax machine?"

"Relax, I know his password," Tim says. "He never checks his personal account until he gets home from work. I'll just download the form and delete the email. And then we can just go to a Kinko's or Staples."

I purse my lips in reluctant agreement. "Only if you can find something on the way. I'm not taking some crazy detour through the backwoods of Ohio just so you can use the latest cutting-edge technology from 1992." I glance over to see Tim smirking at me.

"You're the boss," he says. We drive in silence for a few minutes, and I stare at the back of the car in front of us, a powder blue Prius with the bumper sticker NOT A LIBERAL. I wish more people would be up-front about things that might not meet the eye.

"That was pretty cold, killing off your grandma," I say finally. "It's bad juju."

"Juju?"

"It's like a superstition," I explain. "Bad luck, or a bad omen." I'm not sure of the exact definition, but my mom says it all the time—which is ironic, considering where her own juju landed her.

"Well, she's already dead," Tim says. "So I don't think it counts."

"She's rolling in her grave then."

"She was cremated."

I swallow back a smile. Tim is quicker and more resourceful than I gave him credit for, but I'm still a long way from trusting him.

"What about your schools?" he asks. "Want me to call them?"

"Nah, they won't care," I say, flipping on my signal to pass the dick in the Prius. "They're used to us being gone for no reason. My mom's not exactly on the PTA."

"I can't believe she's okay with you guys driving to California by yourselves," he says. "That's so awesome."

I blink into the harsh late-morning sunlight, trying on this new image of my mother like a dress a few sizes too big, this blithe free spirit who probably sells handmade dream-catchers at craft fairs and treats fevers with essential oils and who trusts her kids to live their own lives and explore the world, sending them off to find peace with the father who left them. It's a prettier picture, but still all kinds of negligent.

"Yeah, she's . . . hands-off," I say. "What's Karen like?" It's an innocent enough segue that I hope Tim can't tell that the answer to this question will unlock a Pandora's box I've been dying to open for years. When I was younger I thought more about Leah, but recently, when I lie in bed at night imagining what might have been if Mom and Buck had worked it out, gotten clean, and turned into normal parents, I focus more on Karen. My mom has her issues, but back then she was young and bright and beautiful. What did this other woman have that Mom didn't? What made him pick her over us?

"She's great," he says. I wait for more but instead hear the tapping of Tim on his iPhone again. I guess I shouldn't have expected more from a guy.

"Does she work?" I ask, trying to sound bored with my own question, like I'm just making conversation to keep from falling asleep at the wheel.

"Yeah, she's a real estate agent." *Tap, tap, tap.*

"Did she always? Or was she, like, a stay-at-home mom before?"

"I think always." *Tap, tap.* That battery's gotta die sooner or later.

"But she was young when she had Leah, right? Not even out of college?"

"I guess, yeah," he says distractedly. "I don't know what she did then."

I decide to change my tack. What I really want to know is if Karen was wild when she was young—a junkie or a drunk or at least a rebel. I need to know if Buck was trading up or just hopping from one disaster to another.

"Does she have any tattoos?" I blurt. I don't realize how random and strange it sounds until the words come out.

Tim laughs. "Um, yeah, actually. How did you know?"

I shrug, keeping my eyes on the road, both for safety and because I know they'd give me away. "Just a guess. I mean, I know she married Buck, so . . ."

"Right, he was covered in them."

"You met him?" I also need to know when Buck left Karen. He wouldn't have overlapped with Tim unless he was still around three years ago, and that—I can't even think about that.

"No," Tim says, sending my pulse back down to normal. "But I've seen pictures. Leah has a framed one in her room of the day he got hers."

"He got *Leah* a tattoo?"

"No, the one of her name."

The tidal wave I didn't see coming hits me full-force, so hard that I have to make a conscious effort to keep control of the car. I stare at the white slashes on the black tar ahead of me as blood rushes to my head so fast that dots start flashing in front of my eyes.

"Woah, are you okay?" Tim asks, putting a hand on my arm.

"Don't touch me," I say. "I'll be fine, just—" I take a gulp of air, which makes things a little better. "Just please don't touch me."

"Sorry. Do you need to pull over?"

I shake my head. What I need is to unhear that last sentence. I need to unlearn the fact that Buck spent money to tattoo Leah's name on his body but could never seem to find the means to pay child support for us.

"You know," Tim says, "my dad left my mom, too. And she wasn't that different from—"

"*Stop*," I say. If I wanted any more of Tim's pity, I could have just told him the truth about Mom.

"I just want you to know that I understand—"

"No, you don't," I snap. "You do *not* understand."

"Maybe not exactly, but—"

"There's no but," I say, my voice rising. "You don't know, and you can't know, and I can't listen to how hard your cushy life is right now, okay?"

Tim goes quiet for a minute. Not even a tap.

"You know, you invited us," he finally says. I shoot him an angry side-eye. "Okay, *her*," he corrects himself. "But so far you've acted like you hate us."

I seethe silently at the road. "I don't hate you," I say, unconvincingly.

"Well, you've got a chip on your shoulder about something."

"Just drop it, okay?" I look over at Tim, who's staring ahead, squinting with worry or hurt, I'm not sure which. I know I need to stop taking out my anger on him when it's really for Buck. And Mom. And Karen. And everyone else who made it so I'm sitting in the dying old car of a dying old man (okay, not *old* old, but midthirties, which is kind of old) with the half sister I never wanted and the non-brother I can't seem to shake. But there's just too much of it, and it keeps spilling out. I decide the best thing is just to not talk at all for a while.

Tim Google-maps a Kinko's just off the highway in Cumberland, and I pull into a strip mall that looks almost exactly like the one we left from this morning. It's funny—and sad—how so much effort must have gone into making every place in the country look basically the same, all of those architects and builders just slapping up the same crap from Tampa to Tacoma. I guess all this boxy plastic and glass and cement is supposed to feel comforting.

But I wonder if anyone ever tried to tell them that familiar isn't always comforting. Sometimes it's what you're running from.

While Tim goes in to print his fake absence note, I send a quick text to Yvonne, who's the only person I care about disappointing.

Have to take the rest of the week off, I type. So sorry, family drama. I hit send before I remember to thank her for the money and then overcompensate in a second text with all caps and smiley faces. Part of me hopes she'll let this truancy slide, but there's also a shameful sliver of hope that I've filled my last burrito. If whatever Buck has for me is as valuable as he thinks it is, maybe it could float me for a while as I figure things out.

"Where are we?" Leah suddenly cries shrilly from the backseat. "Where's Tim?" She sits up looking absolutely horrified, like she's woken to discover she's in the middle of a carjacking. This wakes Cass and Denny up, too. Cass takes one look at Leah and hops out of the car, and then Denny shoves her, yelling, "You're sitting on Max!" As her lower lips starts quivering, I almost start to feel bad for Leah. *Almost.*

"Relax, I didn't throw him out of the moving car," I say. "He's in the Kinko's faxing a form to your school."

"Oh." Leah looks down at her lap and taps on her own iPhone, which I didn't notice has been clenched in her hand this whole time, possibly to keep it from falling into Denny's eager, sticky grasp. "I guess I should text my mom."

"Don't tell her where you are yet," I say, frowning down at the dashboard and feeling more and more like a criminal. "Just . . . say you're staying over at a friend's house. Will she buy that?"

"I don't know," she says.

"I'm hungry," Denny announces, and I reach down into the plastic bag to get him a package of crackers.

"Well, you have to *make* her buy it." I shoot Leah a serious look in the rearview mirror.

Leah sighs heavily, annoyed. "She's gonna know I'm gone eventually. I can't stay over for a week."

"I know," I snap. I'm angrier at myself than at her—how could I not have thought about this before? Tim and Leah aren't like us. They can't just skip town without anyone asking questions. It's not a relief to anyone when *they* disappear. I take a deep breath and try to change my tone. "I just need time to come up with something else."

"You could say we're on a spaceship!" Denny offers, neon orange crumbs dropping onto the floor of the car.

"Thanks, buddy, but I don't think that's very believable."

"A *red* spaceship," he says, as if that changes everything.

"Fine, I'll just tell her I'm going to my friend Hannah's," Leah grumbles and carefully opens the door Cass just bolted from, stepping her long, porcelain legs over the seat cushions to keep skin-to-garbage contact at a minimum.

"Can we leave her here?" Denny asks once the door slams shut, licking peanut butter from a deconstructed cracker sandwich. "Max doesn't like her." I smile in spite of myself. I've noticed "Max" likes to say things Denny thinks are too mean to pin on himself.

"Tell Max for once I agree with him," I say, turning around to grab a cracker. "But we can't leave her. She's . . ." I chew the cracker into a few sharp pieces and force them down my throat. "She's family," I finish, nearly choking on both the food and the words.

Denny considers this, his little brow furrowing. I wonder how all these pieces connect in his brain and whether they make any sense to him yet. "Aunt Sam's family, and she sucks," he says.

"You've got a point," I laugh.

"I just want you and Cass and Mom as my family," he says, giving the back of my seat a hard kick for emphasis.

Shit, Cass. I have no idea where she went. "Stay here for a sec," I tell Denny, getting out of the car and surveying the overwhelmingly beige suburban landscape. Leah is standing in the middle of an empty parking spot a few feet away, staring intently at her phone. The lot is about half-full, and people amble from their cars toward the shaded strip that houses, in addition to the Kinko's and RadioShack, a sad-looking gym, an Edible Arrangements, and a Mexican restaurant called Burrito Allegre.

I lean against the hood, dial Cass, and try not to panic as it rings and rings. I don't think she would actually try to ditch us—this is still the girl who, now that my mom's legs aren't long enough to hide her, darts around corners to avoid talking to strangers—but she's not above laying low for an hour or two and making me sweat it out as punishment.

"Cass, please come back to the car," I beg after that Stepford female robot voice tells me to leave a message at the tone. "I know today has been crazy, but you're only making it worse by hiding."

"Who's hiding?"

I turn to see Cass standing by the rear bumper, holding her backpack by one frayed strap.

"I was just doing my shot," she says. "The gym let me use their bathroom." She leans in conspiratorially and gives me a little smile. "I could've even taken a shower, they didn't care. For future reference."

"Thanks," I say slowly, shutting off my phone. My sister is acting downright chipper . . . which happens about as often as a Halley's Comet sighting these days. I'm thrown by the quicksilver change in mood, but hey, I'll take it. Since we don't have enough cash to get us all the way to Venice, we might have to rely on our sparkling personalities.

Speaking of which, Tim has materialized with a triumphant grin and is chaperoning a reluctant Leah back to the car.

"I got us some food," he says, holding up a greasy paper bag. "Figured we could have a parking lot picnic." I watch as Tim doles out tacos to the kids, calling the girls "m'lady" and goofing around with Denny—even offering food to Max. Having another person around to play grown-up might not be so bad after all.

"And for you, I got a burrito," he says, turning to me with a smile. "For old time's sake." He's clearly very pleased with himself, and although I try to fight a reflexive smile, I can feel it starting to show.

"What, I'm not worth a bouquet of cantaloupe?" I ask, putting my hands on my hips and nodding toward the Edible Arrangements.

"Next time," he says, "I'll buy you a dozen long-stemmed honeydews. But for now: truce?"

I take the foil sleeve and examine its contents. "What kind?" I ask, poking a finger under the wrapper.

"Just bean and cheese," he says. "I didn't know if you were a vegetarian."

"Sour cream and guac?" I like to douse my food in more

condiments than a normal human should consume in one sitting.

"Yes and yes," he says. "I decided to go for it."

The smile breaks through, despite my best efforts. "Thanks," I say.

Tim looks relieved. "So we're good?"

I cock my head and think for a minute. "Maybe just one more thing?"

A few minutes later, Tim is punching Aunt Sam's number into his phone, and I'm holding up a cue card made from the back of a Chinese take-out menu I found on the floor in the backseat. I'm 99 percent sure Aunt Sam won't pick up a random call from an unknown number, but I bite my tongue nervously until Tim gives me a thumbs-up sign.

"Hi, Mrs. Means," he says, dropping his voice again. "This is Agent Yusuk from CPS. I'm calling to let you know we picked up your nieces and nephew and will be holding them for a few days to ask them some further questions. We'll be sending you a check for your trouble. Take care." He hangs up and shakes his head, laughing. "I don't get it."

"You don't have to," I say. "Just know you got back some good juju." Hopefully that message will keep Aunt Sam from reporting us missing or saying something to Mom, at least for a while. And I love picturing her checking the mailbox every day, resplendent in her kimono, for a nonexistent payoff.

"Phew," he says with a playful grin. "I guess things are looking up."

I take a bite of my burrito and look up at the bright, cloudless sky. I'm not convinced yet, but I have to admit, it's a nice thought.

EIGHT

Wednesday Night
I-70 W, Near Terre Haute, IN

Almost nine P.M. and the Indiana highway is dark and quiet, with streetlamps only at intersections, so in between all we can see are the headlights of other cars flashing past like fireflies. In the past ten hours, we've been through four states. Pennsylvania was a breeze, just a quick shortcut across the southwestern corner (which took us right through a town named, ironically, California), but then Ohio was a long, flat slog punctuated by passive-aggressive fighting between Leah and Cass—who literally could not agree on a radio station to save their own lives—and Denny either complaining about being bored or having to use the bathroom. (An impromptu song consisting only of the lyrics "I HAVE TO POOP!" serenaded us through downtown Columbus.)

Tim and I have spent most of our time hashing out a decent cover story. I have more experience crafting lies of omission, but it turns out that he, in addition to singing lead tenor in an all-boys a cappella group called the SkeleTone Crew, is co-captain of the McDonogh debate team, which means he always has to have the last word. So for now, we're at an impasse.

"I just don't think it's *believable* that I would borrow a friend's car and then drive it three thousand miles on a whim," he says. We've been trying to come up with an alternate vehicle for them to be riding in, since everyone agrees it's best that Tim and Leah's parents don't know they're with us.

"Could you hitchhike?" I ask.

"Ew, no way," Leah says.

"Yeah," Tim says. "That would completely freak them out. They'd have our pictures on some national news site in about five minutes." He sighs. "Missing kids drive page views like crazy."

"Depends on the kids," I say, changing lanes. "What about . . . do you have a girlfriend?"

Leah snorts, and Tim reaches back to swat her. "Why is that so funny?" he asks. To me, he says, "Uh, not currently."

"Damn."

"Sorry to disappoint you. Believe me, I wish I did."

"It'd be a good cover for a car," I shrug.

"Do you have a boyfriend?"

I feel color rising in my cheeks but hope it's too dark for him to notice. "Not relevant," I say. "I'm not driving with you, remember?"

"Right," Tim says. "I forgot."

"You can't forget that part!" I say. "I don't want the cops chasing *me*."

"They wouldn't *actually* call the cops," he says at the same time Denny announces, "Michelle *doesn't* have a boyfriend."

"Thanks, Den!" I say, hoping to cut him off there. I guess I don't mind Tim and Leah knowing I don't have a boyfriend—this trip means we'll have to start getting to know each other, piece by piece—but I don't want them to know I've *never* had one. The sad truth is that I've only been kissed once, in sixth grade, on a dare during a brief and regrettable period when I was trying to make friends with the popular girls in middle school. His name was Ernest Hudson, and we faced off on the basketball court like it was high noon, slowly moving closer and closer and then connecting almost violently, as if we were two magnets held apart and then let suddenly go. His potato chip–flavored tongue thrashed around in my mouth for exactly four seconds. I know because I counted, because I just stood there, squeezing my eyes shut, listening to the catcalls swelling around me in surround sound, thinking, *Is this how it's supposed to feel?* I still don't know, because I never tried it again.

"What about that weird Russian guy in your grade who looks like he's forty-five?" Leah asks. "Doesn't he drive to school?"

"Yeah, but I've never even spoken to him," Tim says.

"Then he's perfect," I say. "So here's what you tell them: Leah was going to sleep over at Hannah's house, but then during English, the teacher mentions *As I Lay Dying* or something, and it makes her think about Buck, and she freaks out in the middle of class, so you decide to take her off campus to calm her down, and she starts begging you to take her to see him."

"We have a counselor at school," Leah says. "Even if I did lose it in public—which I wouldn't—I'd get sent to her office."

"Maybe she was at lunch," I sigh. "It doesn't matter. The point is, Tim is worried enough that he asks his Good Samaritan buddy Vladimir or whatever to borrow his car."

"His name's Dmitri," Tim says.

"And security would never let us leave," Leah adds. "You can't hide under a set of *Toy Story* sheets if you're the one driving."

"Just say you forged it," I say. "This doesn't have to be airtight. You just have to make it pathetic enough so they won't focus on the details."

"It's definitely pathetic enough," Cass says.

"You got something better?" I expect her to retreat back into the hood of her sweatshirt, but instead my sister speaks up.

"Well, I just don't think she should snap all of a sudden. I think it should be premeditated."

"Why?" Leah asks.

"It's just more serious or something. You thought it out. You knew what you were doing." Cass leans back, the vinyl squeaking against her jeans. "It's better than being powerless."

"I think they'd be even madder if they knew we planned something," Tim says. "But man, how do you *accidentally* drive across the country?"

Desperation, I want to say, but I bite my tongue. And after a few long seconds our collective exhaustion syncs up and everyone falls silent for a while, until there's no noise but the whirring tires on the Indiana highway. And, of course, the ever-present death rattle.

"I'm going to look for a place to stay," I announce, trying to sound pumped for the kids' sake.

"Thank God," Leah says. "I can't be in this car anymore. I think my butt fell asleep." Denny guffaws, and I hear the soft shifting of cotton on pleather that tells me Cass is probably throwing her some serious side-eye before tucking her face back into her sleeve.

Instinctively, I want to side with my sister and hate on Leah for pretty much everything she says. But I can't begrudge her wanting to sleep in a real bed. I want that so badly it literally hurts—there's a mad ache in my joints that I know can only be soothed by sinking into a mattress and letting my body rest, even if my brain can't. So it's with genuine sympathy that I break the bad news to her.

"About that," I say. "The thing is, we have to sleep in the car."

"WHAT?"

"We can't afford hotels," I shrug apologetically.

"Yes we can," she cries. "Tim, don't you have, like, $4,000?"

I look at Tim expectantly, holding my breath. I haven't asked him outright about money yet because I don't want him to feel like I did when Aunt Sam cornered me . . . but if he's loaded, that will solve a lot of problems, and fast.

"No," he says, grimacing in the glow of his phone screen. "Those are savings bonds from my grandpa, Lee. They don't mature until I'm twenty-one."

"So . . . we have to wear the same clothes every day for a

week without showering?" Leah says in disbelief, her voice rising with every syllable. "We have to *sleep* in here, all *five* of us? Like *homeless* people?"

"Dibs on the trunk!" Denny says again, and I have to bite my lip to keep from laughing.

"It's *not* like being homeless," Tim says.

"Yeah, we're not going to an alley behind a Walmart, we're going to find a campground," I explain. "Tim, can you search for free camp sites near . . ." I squint up at the green road sign flashing past in the glare of our headlights. "Terre Haute?"

"Wait, camping? We're camping?" Leah says, leaning forward. "Do we at least get tents?"

"I want a tent!" Denny says. Great, the Gospel of Leah is spreading.

I shake my head. "Unless it's raining, some of us can just sleep outside. We've got blankets."

"No!" Leah says. "I can't—I mean, we *have* to stay in a hotel. I never would have come if I knew we weren't going to have basic stuff like clothes and beds. That's *so* ghetto."

"Shut. Up," Cass snaps.

"She does have a point," Tim says. "It's going to be pretty rough. Maybe we could just find a cheap motel, something really low-end."

"Sure," I say. "If you want to spend the rest of the week illegally siphoning gas with your mouth, then by all means, let's spring for a hotel room."

"Ohhhh-kay," he exhales. "Exactly how much money do we have?"

I bristle. "*We* don't have money," I say. "*I* have $276." I signal right and take the exit ramp. "How much cash do *you* have?"

"Maybe ten bucks," Tim says sheepishly, quickly adding, "but I bought lunch."

"No one asked you to."

"I didn't hear you complaining."

"You're right, 'cause I was too busy trying to figure out how to cover your asses."

"You guys!" Leah cries from the backseat.

"We wouldn't have to cover anything if you hadn't showed up at our school and begged us to come with you," Tim says.

"You *guys,*" Leah repeats.

"Please just *shut up,*" Cass moans. But I can't drop it.

"I don't remember begging *you* to come anywhere," I say.

"Well, I guess we both made mistakes," Tim says.

"I wanna go home," Denny whimpers.

"Guys!" Leah shouts. "Just be quiet, I know what to do." I hear rustling and then a magnetic snap. In the rearview mirror, I see Leah proudly pull a shiny gold credit card from a pink leather wallet. "I have Jeff's AmEx!" she cries gleefully.

"We can't use that," Tim sighs. "It's supposed to be for emergencies."

"This *is* an emergency," she says, totally serious. And I guess, technically, dictionary definition–wise, she's right. This *is* an unexpected, urgent, and possibly dangerous situation. Especially since at this juncture we're all ready to smack each other senseless.

"Won't they get the bill?" I ask, hating myself a little for how much I want to cave and let her use her magical plastic get-out-of-anything-free card.

"Yeah, but not till next month," she says. "It'll be too late for them to do anything about it." She turns to Denny. "Wouldn't you rather have cable TV and a big down comforter than sleep next to old gas cans in the trunk?"

"They have TV?" Denny perks up at this. He's never been to a hotel. None of us have, except for the one time we visited Mom during the years that she worked at an Embassy Suites.

"Don't get too excited," I say. "Even if that card can pay for it, nobody's gonna rent a room to five underage kids with no parents."

"It's not like they'll arrest us," Leah groans. "We might as well try."

"Maybe we should," Tim says. "I mean, we'll never know otherwise, right?"

"It's the law," I say. "That's how we know." Devereaux rule #3: Keep your head down. Don't go looking for trouble that can't find you on its own.

"Come on," Leah says. "Please?"

"Yeah, please?" Denny whines.

"Cass, could you back me up here?" I ask, but the hoodied lump just shrugs. "Okay, fine," I say testily, looking out at a glowing Comfort Inn sign half a mile down the road. "But don't say I didn't warn you."

The front desk is manned by a skinny red-haired guy who can't be more than a few years older than me, with a lumpy Adam's apple and a wide, greasy forehead that reflects the yellow-tinged fluorescent lights above his desk. He's wearing a blue button-down and a nametag that says QUENTIN. He looks like a pretty easy mark, as far as corporate types go, but if I had any money I would still bet it all on Quentin kicking us merrily to the curb.

Tim and Leah walk up first, with me, Cass, and Denny trailing by a few feet. I clutch Cass's backpack—stuffed with ramen packets and dollar-store underpants—in a weak attempt at legitimacy, but I'm sure my face gives away my anxiety. Now that the adrenaline rush is gone, the reality of what I've done is sinking in. And not just running away, or missing school, or ditching Mom without bail or Yvonne without a shift manager—all of which are shameful on their own. But Tim is right: It was my idea to take them with us, and now I have two extra pieces of baggage in my car, newbies who don't worry about the things I need to worry about all the time.

"Hi, sir," Tim says in his fake parent voice, looking like a slightly rumpled Boy Scout. "We're, um, checking in."

"Can I see some ID?" Quentin looks directly at me, even though I'm not the one at the counter.

"Sure." Tim pulls out his wallet, and even though I want him to get humiliated (if for no other reason than to prove me right), I have to give him credit for having the balls to keep going.

"Her, too," he says, nodding at me. Clenching my jaw and holding my head up, I walk over to the desk and slide my license across the slick, fake marble. Quentin looks back and forth from the picture to me, a few more times than necessary.

"We only rent to eighteen and up," he says curtly. Which is funny, since Tim's birth date didn't seem to bother him. I smack my palm back over my ID.

"Thank you," I say in a *fuck-you* voice.

"We have the money," Tim says. "You can charge it up front, if you're worried about contract enforcement." He smiles self-consciously. "My dad's a lawyer."

This nugget of information seems to relax Quentin. "It's really liability," he says, sounding almost apologetic. "Some people"—he glances at Cass and Denny—"don't know how to behave."

"We can take care of ourselves," I say, knowing I should keep quiet but unable to help myself. "That won't be a problem."

"It's policy," Quentin says to Tim, deleting me from his field of vision.

"Thanks anyway," Tim says. *Finally.* I can't beat a hasty enough retreat. But before I can make it to the door, I hear Leah pipe up.

"Hi, *Quentin*," she says. I spin around to see her leaning on the desk with both elbows. "See, the thing is, our dad is a criminal litigator with Buckman Farrell in Baltimore, and he's working over at the courthouse all night on this crazy murder case. We had to come with him because this is his week with us, and our school is closed for a stupid teacher's retreat, and he figured it was just easier to drop us off because he has to get back to work, and we're super tired and otherwise we'll just be, like, sleeping on benches at the courthouse. And my sister has diabetes," she adds, gesturing to Cass.

"You guys are all siblings?" Quentin asks incredulously. I want to kick him.

"Um, yeah, interracial families exist, haven't you seen that Cheerios commercial?" Leah says breezily, not missing a beat. "Look, I have my dad's credit card, it's in both of our names, and I can give you my school ID, and like my brother said, you can even precharge the card if you want. But Dad already left, so if you can't accommodate us I'll just call him and ask him to take us to the Ramada, where I'm sure they'll be more understanding." She pushes the gold AmEx across the counter like a pro. She might have adjusted to the Harper lifestyle, but there's no mistaking it: That girl's got Buck Devereaux in her blood.

"That was impressive," I tell her once we're safely in the elevator, clutching our keycards to room 413. I still hate the idea of the hotel, and not just because of the obvious racial profiling, but I know I can't turn down a free room for the night out of pride. Not when the alternative is five people sleeping in a single car.

Leah smiles self-consciously down at the toes of her Mary Janes. "I wanted to help," she says, and for the first time all day there's not a trace of irony in her voice.

The room, I'll admit, looks like heaven—if heaven were upholstered exclusively in quilted yellow fabric. I even hear Cass say, "Sweet!" under her breath when we step inside. There are two beds, a loveseat, TV, a desk with a vase of stiff fake flowers, and a brightly lit bathroom full of origami towels from which I instinctively swipe all of the mini shampoo and conditioner bottles before anyone even has a chance to shower. Hotels are such a racket—you wouldn't take someone's used mattress off the street, so why would you pay a hundred bucks to sleep on it in a tiny room under a piece of bad abstract art?—and I have a special hatred for them ever since Mom lost her job last year, which led to the seemingly terminal unemployment that led to her starting to use again, but I keep my mouth shut so I don't ruin it for everybody else.

As I run water for Denny's bath, I try to wrap my sluggish brain around the fact that twenty-four hours ago the most rebellious thing I was doing was testing my aunt's beauty products. I hadn't even found Leah's Instagram, and now she's in the next room, trying to sell Cass on watching a *Pretty Little Liars* marathon instead of *Iron Chef.*

"Ow!" Denny cries suddenly. I'm spacing out, and I let the water get too hot.

"Sorry, meatball." I adjust the temperature and fight the urge to rub his hair. I probably shouldn't even hang out while he bathes at this age, but it seems like he wants the company, plus I don't really know what to say to any of the others right now. First-grade-level conversation is exactly what I need.

"Can I have more bubbles?" Denny asks, and I nod, letting him squeeze the little complimentary container of lavender body wash until it wheezes and crumples in on itself. I'm relieved I can afford not to be stingy about this one simple luxury when it feels like all I've said this week is no.

"Hey, are you doing okay?" I ask, drawing my knees up under my chin so I'm perched on the toilet like a gargoyle. I look away from Denny's naked torso and catch a glimpse of myself in a magnified makeup mirror, my eyes puffy and red, my chin starting to break out in gravelly little bumps. One of my mother's favorite self-esteem boosters—"If you can't feel good, you might as well *look* good!"—runs through my head, and I hide my face in my jeans, feeling tears climb the back of my throat. I'm so tired of being so worried about everything. I'm so tired of being so angry at her that she left me to deal with the mess of her life.

"Are *you* doing okay?" I look up to see Denny staring at me nervously, a beard of bubbles clinging to his chin.

"Yeah, sorry." I swallow hard and force a smile, because Denny already has enough caretakers in his life who can't keep their shit together. "I'm just tired."

"No you're not; you're sad," he says. "And mad." He turns the faucet up so high the water thunders down into the tub, splashing droplets onto the floor. At home I'd yell at him for that, but here I decide to let it go, even though I cringe inwardly knowing that someone is going to have to come in here tomorrow and pick up the sopping wet bathmat, clean up after us for the promise of a crappy, crumpled one-dollar tip.

"Sometimes being really tired can make me act mad, but I'm not mad at *you*," I say.

"Max says you're mad at Mom."

"I didn't realize Max was in the bath with you."

Denny rolls his eyes. "He's over there," he says, pointing to the sink like I'm blind. "Shaving."

"Max has a beard?" I ask, raising an eyebrow. Denny ignores me.

"I miss Mom," he says. "Why don't you miss her? Why are you mad at her?"

"I do miss her." I miss half of her, anyway, the half that'd suddenly wake us up with kisses and scrambled eggs when for the past twenty-four hours she'd been an empty shell, like she'd had to go away for a while but left her body with us so she could move more freely. I clear my throat, shoving the tears back down. "You can miss someone and be mad at them, too," I say.

"Yeah," Denny says, like he already knows. Maybe he's not as naive as I like to think he is.

"You know, she's coming back," I say. "When we get back from California we'll get her out, and then everything will be . . ." I can't bring myself to say "fine," so I settle for "back to normal," which is probably true and really, really depressing.

"I wanna watch TV," Denny says, abruptly switching his own channel. I leave so that he can towel off and put his clothes back on, and I bump into Tim, who's hovering on the other side of the door.

He puts a finger to his lips and nods at Cass and Leah, who are lying on their stomachs side by side on the far bed, propped up on their elbows.

"That's Aria," Leah says, as a pretty actress's face fills the screen. "In season one, she was dating her English teacher, but then his son got kidnapped by the people covering up her friend's murder."

"Damn," Cass says, watching with rapt attention.

Tim raises his eyebrows. "Should we hold our breaths?" he whispers.

"Knowing Cass? Probably not."

"Yeah, knowing Leah, same," he says. "Still, you have to admit this is better than the car."

"Of *course* it's better," I say. "I just don't think it's smart. There's a difference." His face falls, and I instantly feel bad. This is an act of kindness, after all, no matter how self-serving. So I force a smile. "It's really nice, though." To underscore my point, a half-naked Denny shoots between us and leaps headfirst onto the nearest bed.

"Hey," Tim says, "why don't you let me do some of the driving tomorrow, to give you a rest?"

"Nah, that's okay."

"Please? I really want to." He gives me an apologetic smile, and I notice for the first time an almost imperceptible sprinkling of freckles across his nose. "Listen, you're still the captain," he says. "I'll just be your deputy."

I smirk. "I think you mean first mate."

"I don't know," he laughs. "That sounds pretty intimate for someone I just met yesterday."

My skin feels tight as I suddenly realize how close we're standing, so close I can feel warmth coming off his skin like a space heater, sending wafts of citrusy deodorant and tangy sweat into my lungs.

"Sure, you can drive," I mumble and walk hastily over to the edge of the bed where the girls and Denny are now watching a bunch of teens in short, tight funeral outfits freak out while staring into their phones. I pretend to look interested, but out of the corner of my eyes I'm watching Tim as he carefully empties five packets of chicken-flavored ramen noodles into paper cups, fiddling with the dinky coffee-machine buttons to get the hot water to dispense.

Despite his annoying tendency to second-guess everything I say, there's something about Tim that's so sturdy and even and just kind of . . . *good.* It's like watching a different species through binoculars, trying to figure out what it's gonna do next. Buck was definitely never like that. I remember him being affectionate and fun sometimes, but even as a kid I got the sense I couldn't really count on him, or Mom. They both seemed like—I didn't have a word for it then, but unstable, I guess, like the atoms we learned about in physics that can turn radioactive, vibrating and contorting while they try to balance out but can't. I wonder if some people are just born that way.

"Dinnertime!" Tim calls, arranging the steaming cups in a row on the desk, and Cass, Denny, and I spring up like the scavengers we are, hardwired to eat whatever is offered before anyone else can get it.

I slurp down the hot, salty broth with a hunger I didn't even realize was there. And later, when the TV is off and everyone but me is asleep and the only light in the room is the moonlight peeking through a gap in the heavy yellow drapes, I watch Tim's chest rise and fall in the next bed and wonder if I'm more like him or more like my parents. Can I steady myself and find a way to be the rock my family needs, or will I be cursed, too, with a life spent freewheeling through the universe, desperately reaching out for something, anything, to hold me down?

NINE

Thursday Morning
Terre Haute, IN

I have two vivid dreams, one after the other. In the first, I'm driving down a dark, rural road, so groggy I can't really see, so I keep running the car into trees, which send me spinning backward with a gentle, rubbery bump. In the second, I'm looking for Mom in the empty halls of a jail, but every time I turn a corner, sure that I'll find her on the other side, there's a crumbling brick wall.

Knock, knock.

Mom? I yell in my dream voice, which annoyingly comes out like a whisper no matter how hard I strain. I put my palms on the bricks and find that they're loose, so I pull them out one by one as the knocking gets louder.

Mom, I'm coming!

"It's the manager."

I stop pulling bricks and try to peer through the hole.

Mom, is there someone with you?

"Please open the door, it's the manager."

I seize out of the dream and into a pool of bright sunlight. Cass is huddled under the covers next to me, and Denny is sprawled across us, making a sloppy *H.* I realize two things at the same time: (1) The knocking is real, and (2) I'm not wearing pants.

But then Tim is up, his shirtless back wide and pale and smooth, his hair knocked out of its Hardy Boy tidiness and into soft curls and peaks from the pillow. He stumbles as he pulls khakis on over his boxer shorts and steps over the remnants of our noodle cups to get to the door. I lean back and stare at the ceiling, my heart pounding, as I hear the locks click open. This can't be good.

"Can I help you?" Tim asks groggily.

"Yes," I hear a stern male voice say. "You can come with me. Get your friends and get your things."

"Why?" Tim asks. "What is this about?"

"I'll explain downstairs. For now, just get everyone and everything out of the room."

Ten minutes later, we ride down three floors with the extremely pissy-looking hotel manager, who wears his jet-black hair in a mushroom cut—a bold move for a middle-aged man the height of a hobbit. It's barely seven A.M. Denny is clinging to my arm, and I don't think Cass has even woken up yet, but I can't tell because she's got sunglasses on indoors, like a movie star, or a drunk. Tim and Leah look gray and nervous;

Mushroom won't answer any of their questions. I've decided to keep my mouth shut, both because I don't want it to get me in trouble and because I'm a little bit afraid I might throw up.

This feeling only intensifies when the elevator doors open into the lobby and I see two uniformed cops waiting at the front desk. I get hit with a panic attack that's like a FIFA World Cup player kicking me in the chest at close range. *This cannot be happening.* We're in the middle of Indiana with only a half tank of gas and a family-size bag of Skittles to our name. I dig my nails into Denny's palm so hard he yowls.

"Your credit card was declined," Mushroom says as we reach the cops. The front desk faces the continental breakfast buffet, and a sunburned family of four tries not to look like they're eavesdropping while they eat their Corn Flakes and stale pastries. "Early this morning we received a call from Jeffrey Harper," he continues, "the *cardholder*, who told me directly that he did not authorize the charge."

"But that's my dad," Tim says, keeping his voice low. "You didn't need to call the cops."

"If we suspect a stolen credit card is being used, police involvement is standard procedure," Mushroom says stiffly.

"It's not stolen!" Leah pipes up. "It's *mine*."

"I'm guessing you don't pay the bill, though." Mushroom treats us all to a condescending smile, and Tim and Leah exchange terrified looks. They've probably never been in any real trouble and have no idea how to handle this. Leah might have talked us into the hotel, but talking us out is gonna be up to me.

"Could you call him back?" I ask as calmly as I can manage. "I'm sure he doesn't want to press charges."

"Yeah," Tim says, "can I talk to him?"

"I'll see what I can do," Mushroom says and goes behind the desk to the phone. The cops look bored, and I let myself relax a little. We're not getting arrested. Not if Tim's dad is anything like him.

Mushroom gets Jeff Harper on the phone and, after some stony small talk, hands the receiver across the counter to Tim.

"Hi, Dad, it's me," he says, looking stricken, running a hand through his bedhead. "Listen, I'm so sorry . . ." He gets quiet for a minute, and I can hear his dad yelling even from ten feet away. "Indiana somewhere," Tim finally says. "I know. I *know,* okay? I swear I was just trying to do something good for Leah . . . yeah, she's fine. We just didn't think it through . . ." Another pause. "I know that, but could you at least let this charge go through? We don't have any money, and—" He closes his eyes and grimaces. "Well, could you at least tell the manager to send the *police officers* away? . . . Yes, I understand. Okay, Dad . . . Bye."

Tim hands the phone back to Mushroom and walks over to me. "He's not pressing charges, but he's not paying for the room either," he says. "We're going to have to use your money."

"*What?*" I whisper. "No! That's, like, half of what I have left!"

Tim shakes his head helplessly, his eyes still sleep-swollen. "I'm sorry," he says. "I don't know what else we can do."

"I knew this would happen." I'm saying it almost more to myself than to him. I knew we had to stay off the grid, but I let them sway me. These oblivious kids with their emergency credit card and their blithe confidence that the world would give them everything they needed.

"I'll pay you back," he says.

"Great, I'll just buy gas from the future then."

"Come on," Tim pleads, starting to get that anxious eye glaze I know only too well. "What do you want me to say?"

"You could have told your dad our story, for starters!" I know I'm talking too loud; I can feel both the cops and the sunburned family staring. "You barely said two words. You didn't explain anything!"

"You're mad because I went off script?"

"No, I'm mad because you're ruining everything, and so is she." It's harsher than I meant it to come out, but it still feels true. Tim looks away, and I stalk back over to the desk to pay the room charge of $109.99, plus tax. I count out the bills slowly, feeling a fresh twinge of anger each time I slide one across the desk. We were already stretched beyond our means, and now it's a bad joke. Have you heard this one: *How did the kids in the beat-up station wagon cross the country? They didn't, because they ran out of money halfway! Ba dum bum, ching.*

Mushroom dismisses the cops, and we lug our bags back out to the parking lot, where we form a rough semicircle around Goldie's mismatched front door. From the looks on everyone's faces, all of the tentative goodwill of last night has come undone. Even Denny looks miserable.

"What did he say?" Leah asks.

"That I should be ashamed of myself," Tim says softly, scuffing the toe of his loafer against the gravel. "That we have to turn around and come home right away, or he'll call the cops on us for real."

"Do you think he'd do it?" I ask, squinting into the sun

rising over the highway. We're about ten hours from home, which means we've only got another ten before the Harpers realize their kids aren't coming back. That would still leave us with two days of travel left to go—way too long to be dodging police.

"I don't think so," Tim says, frowning. "He sounded more scared than mad. But I don't know. And, I mean, I can't get arrested. I just got in to Johns Hopkins."

"You're not getting arrested," I say. "It's your dad sending a rescue team. Plus, you'd have to do a lot worse than run away."

"How do you know?" Leah asks, crossing her arms defensively. I take pleasure in noting that there's a beige ramen stain on the right boob of her white polo.

"'Cause I *know*."

"Have *you* been arrested?" she asks. "I bet you have."

"Stop it," Cass says, stepping out from her hiding place behind the rear bumper.

"No," I say, "but I know people who have. And they look a lot more like me than like you."

Leah scowls. "Well, now I can't say anything," she says.

"Yeah, white privilege is a bitch."

"Hey," Tim says, putting a protective hand on Leah's shoulder. "She's just scared. We're risking a lot, too."

"You're not risking *anything*," I shout. "That's what you don't get. There are no consequences for you. None."

"That's not true!" Leah cries.

"What, you might lose Instagram privileges for a day? I could lose—" *my entire family.* The words are right there, acid letters burning my throat, but I swallow them. I don't think I could stand their pity. "A lot more than that," I choke out. I feel

Denny's weight press into the backs of my legs, a squirmy sandbag anchoring my resolve. "If we keep going," I say, "you have to do what I tell you. No hotels, no frills, no paper trail . . . and no phones."

Leah turns to Tim. "I don't want to be here," she says.

"Believe me, the feeling is mutual," I mutter.

She spins around, her eyes narrowing. "Why are you so mean?"

"Why are you so spoiled? I know you don't get it from your daddy." We're almost chest-to-chest now, and even though she's got a few inches on me, I know I can take her.

"Guys, *stop*," Tim says, shoving his arms between us. "Remember, you're sisters."

"Unfortunately," I say under my breath at the same time Leah snaps, "I hardly *know* her."

Like boxers ending a bout, we retreat to separate ends of the car, her with Tim and me with Cass and Denny.

"Okay," I say, rubbing my eyes with my palms, "I don't know what they're doing, but do you guys want to keep going? Or do you want to go back?"

"Can we see Mom if we go back?" Denny asks, and I shake my head. "Then keep going, I guess," he says sadly.

"Yeah," Cass says with a shrug. "This sucks, but it's better than school."

Monday afternoon comes rushing back like a sucker punch—*You better run, dyke!* Cass's been even more withdrawn than usual, and I've been so busy worrying about logistics and money and so distracted dealing with Tim and Leah that I've been kind of relieved that my sister likes to stay so self-contained. But it's the quiet storms you have to keep an eye on.

"Hey," says Tim, walking up to us with a teary-eyed Leah under his arm. "If it's okay with you, we'd like to stay."

"Are you sure?" I ask. "*Both* of you?"

"Yeah," Leah whispers, wiping her nose with the back of her wrist. "I want to see him."

Him. Buck. Sometimes I forget he's the pot of gold at the end of this crappy-ass rainbow. I've gotten so used to pretending he doesn't exist that he's a fiction at this point; we might as well say we're going to see Mickey Mouse, or the Easter Bunny. I don't know if I'll want to see him when we get there, but I decide to keep that particular doubt to myself for the moment. "What will you tell your dad?" I ask. If Tim's dad is even halfway serious about involving the police, I know I should just leave them here. I was so shortsighted not to see how this would play out. I guess Leah's not the only one who can't imagine a different world outside her bubble.

"I'll figure something out," Tim says. But I see the look on his face. It's the same look I see every time I pass a mirror. He has no idea what he's going to do next.

TEN

Thursday Afternoon/Thursday Night
Indiana-Illinois Border → Bristow, OK

Goldie's noise is getting worse and worse. She starts okay but sounds like a vacuum cleaner sucking up quarters once she gets going. Tim frowns at the dashboard approximately every sixty seconds, trying to diagnose the problem. I took him up on his offer to drive, and I'm trying really hard to focus on watching the trees whoosh by as we pass into Illinois. But ironically, the silence in the car is making it hard to relax.

Remember, you're sisters, Tim said. Like I could ever forget. I've been holding on to Leah since I was seven years old—the idea of her, anyway. I always fantasized I would know her if I saw her someplace random, like she'd shine in a way only I could see. Then we'd walk slowly toward each other and hug, instantly bonding over the shared pain brought on by our lowest common denominator. In my head it was always us versus Buck, us versus the world. It never even occurred to me it might be me versus her.

"Hey, Tim?" Denny pipes up from the backseat. "You said your sister . . . was my sister's . . . sister." He speaks in a slow, probing way that makes me realize he's been trying to figure it out since we left the hotel. Leave it to this kid to be a lightning rod for the tension on everybody's mind.

"Yeah," Tim says.

"We're *half* sisters," Leah says pointedly with her face turned to the window.

"What does that mean?" Denny asks.

"We have half of the same parents," Cass says. "The same dad but not the same mom."

"You and Michelle and Leah?"

"Yup," she sighs.

"But if you guys are sisters, then is she my sister, too? Can she go on my tree?"

"What's he talking about?" Leah asks.

"He's making a family tree for school," I say.

"Yeah," Cass deadpans, "this trip is for extra credit."

"So *are* you my sister?" Denny asks.

"No," Leah says. "You have to have at least one of the same parent to be siblings."

"Hey," Tim says, feigning injury.

"So you're her brother . . ." Denny says, starting to piece his puzzle together again.

"Stepbrother," Tim corrects. "My dad married her mom."

"Do you and I have the same dad?" Denny asks hopefully.

"No," Tim says with a smile. "I wish."

"Oh." Denny thinks for a minute. "But if *they* have the same dad, why does *she* have a different mom?"

"You wanna take this one?" I ask Tim with a smirk.

"No, ma'am," he laughs. "All yours."

"Well, our dad kind of . . . switched moms," I say. It sounds silly reduced to first-grade vocabulary, but I know it's still a trigger subject for Cass, so I glance back to check on her. Amazingly, both she and Leah are smiling a little bit, staring out their respective windows.

"You're allowed to do that?" Denny asks incredulously, and Tim stifles a laugh.

"If you're a jackass," Cass mutters.

"So he switched from our mom to her mom?"

"Yup," I say, biting my own lip to keep from grinning. I really don't know why it all seems so funny coming out of Denny's mouth, but I'm grateful for the levity.

"And then her mom switched from our dad to his dad?"

"You got it, buddy," Tim says, barely holding it together.

"Was our mom mad?" Denny asks. Now even Cass is laughing.

"I think she's *still* mad," I say, and Denny gives me a big, one-front-toothless grin. And I know it's really not funny, but for some reason a surge of laughter I've been holding in for the last few minutes—days, months, years, who's counting?—finally comes, and I throw my head back and let it wash over me like a new kind of tidal wave, breaking me open, shaking my whole body like it's trying to set me free.

We drive for hours under the vast sky of Illinois, fat clouds drifting lazily overhead, past the lush forests and rock faces of

Missouri, breezing through the northwest corner of Arkansas straight into the plains of Oklahoma right as the sun decides to set in all kinds of sherbet colors in front of us like a drive-in movie. All of our phones are turned off (Devereaux rule #1,000,001: When on the lam, technology is your enemy. Submitted to the official rulebook by M. H. Devereaux, April 27th), so there's nothing to do but talk or listen to the radio, and we do some of both, blasting whatever half-decent station is coming through with the least amount of static, catching pockets of Pharrell or Taylor Swift or twangy country ballads that I see Tim lip-synching along to. When the radio craps out or somebody rejects the available music, we start to talk, the conversation forced at first but then finding its legs, starting to flow. We find out that Leah plays clarinet and only got her braces off two months ago; that Tim led the SkeleTone Crew to a Northeast Regional Championship with an a cappella arrangement of "All About That Bass"; that they have a Labrador named Nemo; that Jeff and Karen aren't home much and that most nights, Tim and Leah eat microwave burritos and watch TV by themselves. So much for the magic of the white picket fence. Leah mostly wants to know if we see a lot of shootings in our neighborhood like on *The Wire*, and what's really in the ground beef at Taco Bell, but Tim asks more about our schools and home life, and while I try not to go into the details, I do get Cass to do some of her Aunt Sam impression, which gets us all cracking up again.

There's real terror, of course, lurking below the surface. I know we're in uncharted waters now and that all of the things that were worst-case scenarios yesterday—running out of cash, begging for food—are now best-case scenarios, replaced by the new and infinitely more chilling worst-case scenario of being arrested and charged with grand theft auto and child endangerment and watching my siblings retreat into specks from the back of a police cruiser. *They'll try to split you up! Don't let them split you up!*

But the more miles we put between us and the hotel parking lot, and the more the general mood in the car improves, the more I'm able to push that fear down. In a fit of denial, I even make Tim stop at a Walmart in Tulsa so I can get a little $15 five-by-five dome tent and a couple of cheap polyester blankets for the kids to sleep on. I'm down to $101.87. There's no amount of math that can make that stretch till Sunday.

"It's better than the trunk," I say as I pass my gifts around, and Leah actually squeals with glee.

We follow signs to a free campsite in Bristow, pulling up to the edge of Lake Massena just as the last of the purplish dusk gives way to night. It's basically a beach, with a grassy area and a picnic table but otherwise just endless pebbly sand up to the lake, and so while Tim sets up the tent on the grass and Cass gives herself her shot, Denny, Leah, and I kick off our shoes and run down to the water's edge to stick our toes in the cold black waves that are lapping at the shore under the light of a full, yellowy moon.

"This is better than the hotel," Denny says, and I rustle his hair and let him splash algae onto my jeans with his overexcited stomps.

Since we have no way to get hot water, dinner tonight is an assortment of cheese and peanut butter crackers washed down with the last of a half gallon of grape Gatorade from Family Dollar. We eat sitting pretzel-legged on the beach, knee-to-knee in a tight circle to keep the wind from blowing sand onto our meager feast.

"We'll get better food tomorrow," I say, wiping my mouth with my wrist. "We're not far from Oklahoma City, and they've got to have a mall."

"Why do we have to go to the mall?" Leah asks, perking up.

"The food court," I say. "You can get all kinds of stuff from the trays people leave behind."

Leah wrinkles her nose. "So we're, like, stealing people's leftovers?"

"We have to eat," Tim says.

"What about going to a Whole Foods and just eating the free samples?" Leah asks.

"We can do that, too," I say. "Good thinking." She smiles.

"They have free cookies at church!" Denny says. "But you have to sit through the boring part first."

"Come Sunday, if we still need food, we'll get some church cookies," I promise.

"What day is it now?" Denny flops back onto his elbows and stares up at the moon, his eyelids starting to droop.

"Thursday," Cass says.

"What do you think Mom and Jeff are doing now?" Leah asks softly, drawing her knees up to her chin, her question punctuated by a reedy chorus of literal crickets. With her hair tucked behind her sticking-out ears, she looks especially vulnerable. Just like Cass, she puts up such a tough front that it's easy to forget she's still a child.

Tim shakes his head. "I don't know."

"We should call them," she says. "I don't want them to worry."

"I think it's too late for that." Tim's jaw tenses, and he swigs the dregs of the Gatorade and then tosses the bottle like a football back onto the grass.

I wonder if Mom's worrying about us, for reasons other than the bail money. I wonder if Aunt Sam will even tell her we're gone. If I could call my mom in jail to tell her we were okay, would I? Or would I let her sweat it out, give her a taste of what it feels like to think the one person you're supposed to count on might not be coming back?

"You can call them," I say, standing up and rubbing the gooseflesh on my arms. "Be vague, but let them know you're alive. Try to stall." I actually feel sort of bad for the Harpers, alone in their giant house, their fancy home alarm blinking away, oblivious that any sense of security they had has been shattered.

I kiss Denny goodnight, promising that Cass will tuck him in and sing him to sleep with our "safe" song, Mom's favorite oldie, the one she still has on vinyl tacked up to the living room wall years after she sold her parents' record player, by the band with the impossibly ironic name the Mamas and the Papas. I try to hug Cass, but she darts out from under me before I can touch her. Typical.

Even though I've been acting like it's no big deal, I'm not looking forward to sleeping in the car. I've never done an overnight before, just occasional naps between classes or back when I was much younger and Mom and Buck would take us on long, circuitous drives that featured lots of random stops but no identifiable destination. The vinyl upholstery on the backseat is ripped in three places; two are patched with curling silver duct tape, plus the surface of the seats are ribbed in this weird way that makes your butt hurt if you sit on them for too long. I never sleep well anyway, but this is a new low. I pull a sweatshirt off the floor, give it a sniff test (old French fries and body odor, check), and roll it into a makeshift pillow, then lie back and try to let the sound of giggling from inside the tent help me feel right again—as right as I can feel, anyway. Does anyone ever feel really great, or is that just a lie we all agreed to keep telling as a species?

There's a knock on the window, and I look up to see Tim standing with a toothbrush jutting out of his mouth. I bet Denny gave it to him. That kid never met a cootie he didn't like.

The front door handle lurches up and down a few times before Goldie finally lets him in with a metallic squeak.

"Hey," he says, dropping the toothbrush in the cup holder, and then just kind of stands there frozen, bent awkwardly at the waist, half-in and half-out of the car. After a few seconds I realize I'm watching *him* realize that we're basically sleeping on top of one another. Unless he folds himself into the trunk, which would require the removal of a number of ribs, he'll have to recline the front seat so that his head is separated from my waist by just a few inches. Gasoline smell aside, a twin bed might be less intimate.

"It's okay," I say. "I know it's tight, but if it's any consolation, the sleep will be terrible."

Tim's face reddens as he breaks into a bashful grin. "Great," he says. "Whenever I travel cross-country to see an estranged invalid, I like to arrive as unrefreshed as possible." He sits down and slowly cranks himself to a semi-horizontal angle. "Sorry," he says, looking over his right shoulder so he has the most flattering possible view of my chin and nostrils. "I know I don't have any right to talk about him like that."

"'Estranged invalid' isn't trash talk; it's a fact," I say.

"I guess." He puts his hands behind his head, his elbows spreading out like tetrahedrons. "It just feels weird to rag on a guy I never met."

"I could rag on your dad," I say. "I hear he's so old, he was a waiter at the Last Supper."

Tim laughs. "He's only forty-four, but I could see that."

We shift in the darkness for a few minutes. I can see the moon upside down through the window, a waxing gibbous. I hate that every time I see it, I think of him. It's really inconvenient. Couldn't he have pointed out some star that would eventually explode, like everything else he touched?

"Hey, I'm sorry about this morning," Tim says. "That was really embarrassing."

"Don't worry about it."

"I was serious when I said I'll pay you back."

"I said don't worry about it."

"Don't make me come back to Taco Bell and put it in the tip jar," he says.

"There is no tip jar, and please don't ever come back," I groan. I think of what Yvonne would have to say about Tim if she met him. I think of what she probably has to say about me right about now. "Plus, I probably don't work there anymore."

"You quit?" He says this kind of breezily, like hocking nachos was just a hobby of mine I did for fun.

"No," I say. "But this isn't exactly approved vacation time."

"Wait—you didn't tell them?"

"That I was going on a vision quest to find my sperm donor? No thanks."

"Isn't it more than that?" he asks.

"Maybe for her," I say. "Not for me."

"But didn't he live with you when you were a kid?"

"I was six when he left."

"So you must remember him."

"Of course I remember him, but that doesn't mean he deserves my sympathy."

"Michelle," Tim says, really serious all of a sudden. "He's *dying.*"

"I *know,*" I say, mocking his tone. "Everybody dies."

"Come on, you can't be that cynical."

"It's a biological certainty," I say. "You can't argue with science."

"But he's your biological father."

"You keep saying that like it means something," I say. "Like that makes him important. But just because *your* dad shits rainbows in between monitoring his gold card statements doesn't mean all dads are inherently awesome."

"I guess I just don't understand why you're still so angry," he says.

"You don't understand why I'm *angry*? Do you need a bulleted list?"

"No, no," he says. "That came out wrong. I meant . . . if you were really ambivalent, he couldn't make you so angry. I know he deserves it, I'm just saying you don't have to pretend you don't care. Not with me, anyway."

"You sound like a shrink," I say.

"Sorry. I guess five years of therapy rubs off on you."

I bite my tongue, literally and figuratively. I'm not sure what to say to that. The first thing I feel is more anger—it seems so bougie and frivolous to dump your problems in some doctor's lap instead of handling them on your own. But maybe that's just my jealously showing. Because I also can't help but think about what might have happened if Mom had been able to afford real, extended care instead of the quickie court-ordered one-offs that judges threw at her almost as an afterthought: *Here, this will look good on your record. Talk to someone for an hour. You're fine now.* What if we could pay someone to figure out what's wrong with Cass or Denny? What if I had someone to talk to who would really be listening? I look at the silhouette of Tim's profile, eyes open and glinting in the moonlight. I feel an anxious wave rising deep in my chest, but instead of letting it flatten me I decide, for once, to jump in.

"You know what I think about?" I say. "The fact that every single day for the last eleven years, he's woken up in the morning with a choice. And that every single day for eleven years, he's chosen to not be my dad. That seems even worse than how he left my mom with two little kids and a drug habit he gave her." I blink back tears and keep going. "I mean, he could have picked up the phone anytime. Or written a letter, or even shown up out of nowhere just to say . . . I don't know, *something.* He could have sent money so he'd know we'd be eating, and that Cass would have her medicine. But he never did. Not once."

"What about now?" Tim asks. "He's trying now. He could have just died without telling anyone."

"Are you kidding? I *wish* that's what he did!" I say, the tears finally spilling over my lower lashes, running messily down the sides of my face into my ears. "He doesn't love us. This isn't an epiphany about all the mistakes he's made. This is the Hail Mary of a sick man afraid of going to hell." I wipe my eyes with the heels of my hands. "I hope Leah understands that."

"I don't know," he says.

"Seeing him won't do anything for us, except make the mental image we have of him even more depressing."

"Then why did you decide to go?"

"Whatever Buck has for us, we need the money," I say flatly. "I'm just hoping it's actually worth something. This is *my* Hail Mary. I've got no other options. I just hope whatever it is, it's enough to keep us afloat for a while."

Tim swallows hard. "What about your mom? Doesn't she have a job?"

"She used to. She was a housekeeper at the Embassy Suites out near the airport. But then a few months ago, some earrings went missing. They weren't even expensive, not diamonds or anything. She told me they were little gold starfish owned by some tacky woman who didn't tip." I remember this detail specifically because my mom *hates* starfish—every time she sees one in the ocean she screams—and I remember being so relieved, because I wanted so badly to believe she wasn't stealing again. But in the end it didn't matter.

"That sucks," Tim says.

"Yeah, well. It is what it is." That's something Mom says when she can't fix a problem. That, or she tells me that if we all threw our worries in the air and saw everyone else's, I'd want to grab mine back. But I don't think so. I'm pretty confident I could find better ones.

We lie in silence for a few minutes. The talking in the tent is slowly dying down, making me think of all those nights Cass and I spent lying in our beds giggling and telling stories while we waited to fall asleep, how our voices would soften and the intervals between words would stretch and stretch until finally I would say, "Cass, are you still there?" and hear only breathing.

"My mom used to be a nurse," Tim says. "She worked really long hours, and sometimes I wouldn't see her for a day or two, and when she was off she was always sleeping or just kind of out of it. Dad said it was just exhaustion. But then the summer I was eight they caught her stealing prescription meds, really high-dose painkillers."

"Oh." I don't know what else to say. I know from experience all the *I'm sorry*s in the world aren't going to change anything.

"She went to rehab for a while, and things were okay, but then she started feeling sick all the time, going to a ton of doctors who couldn't diagnose anything. Then she got beat up in a mugging."

"Jesus," I say.

"That's not the worst part," Tim says, closing his eyes. "It didn't actually happen. There was a camera in the lot where she said she was, and Dad tracked down the tape, and it just showed her getting into the car and driving away. But she had all these bruises . . ." I watch his Adam's apple bob as he tenses his jaw. "Anyway, by the time he caught on, it was too late—she already had the meds she wanted."

"Did she get arrested?"

"No, you can't get arrested for kicking the shit out of

yourself, apparently, as long as you don't file a false police report. But she got divorced."

"Where is she now?"

"She lives in Annapolis. My dad has full custody, but I see her every couple of weeks. She makes a lot of excuses, though. She always has some reason she has to cancel. And I worry all the time. I don't know if she's taking care of herself or what she's capable of. I guess I just don't . . ."

"Trust her?" I finish.

"No." He closes his eyes. "Not at all."

"I know what that's like," I say, and without even thinking about it I grab on to his hand and squeeze three times. He squeezes back three times. And then we just let them stay, as Cass's voice rises up over the crickets, thin and uncertain and sweet, singing Denny his lullaby.

ELEVEN

Friday
Bristow, OK ➔ Oklahoma City, OK ➔ Amarillo, TX

The next morning brings sunshine, chirping birds, and Leah and Tim knee-deep in water, holding Denny by the wrists and ankles as they swing him out over the lake. I change clothes in the backseat and watch as my brother communes with nature, his soaking SpongeBob SquarePants briefs swinging a few inches below his actual butt.

"One . . . two . . . THREE!" they chant, and Denny lets out a Tarzan yell before he splashes down.

The tent flap is open, and I spot Cass sitting just inside, a cracker held between her teeth, giving herself a shot. I wait till she puts her shirt back down and then drop into the sand next to her.

"What's your problem?" I joke. "Too early to cannonball?"

"Haha," she says. "And it's not early. You just slept forever." I was uncharacteristically the last one up and probably would have slept even later if Denny hadn't clambered into the car dripping wet and asked me if I wanted to join him for a "lake bath."

"Yeah, I don't know what happened." I stretch my arms over my head and yawn. "I must have just crashed."

"Mmm hmmm." Cass gives me a look.

"What?"

"Nothing." She zips up her backpack and crawls out of the tent.

"*What?*" I prod.

"*Nothinnnng.*" She skulks off toward Goldie, and I take out my frustration over her constant moodiness on the tent, ripping it out of the ground like the Hulk.

"Hey, can I help?" Tim comes jogging over, his khakis rolled up over his knees, damp hair sticking up in what I hope is an unintentional mohawk.

"Yeah, can you fold this monster?" I brush my hair out of my eyes self-consciously, realizing I must look like one of Lil Wayne's mug shots by now. First order of the day will definitely be stopping somewhere to clean up.

"It's a beautiful morning, huh?" He smiles up at me as he wrestles the poles into submission.

"Yeah, not bad." I feel a little awkward talking to Tim after last night. It's not like anything really happened, but I'm not sure how I'm supposed to act. Are we friends now that we know each other's secrets? Is it incredibly pathetic that holding his hand gave me more butterflies than kissing Ernest Hudson?

"I think it's going to be a beautiful day," he says, wrapping up the now-cylindrical tent in a Velcro strap. "In fact, I've got a wonderful feeling that everything's going my way." Tim shoots me a big, goofy grin. "Get it?" he laughs. "*Oklahoma!* The musical!"

"Nerd," Leah says with a smile, walking up behind him, her arm draped around a still-damp Denny. I guess a night in the tent was all they needed to get past the Chocolate Frosting Incident.

"Is he like this all the time?" I laugh, and Leah nods.

"He serenaded me in the cafeteria on my birthday last year. It was *soooo* embarrassing."

"It was not!" Tim says, feigning offense. "I was totally on-key!"

"That's not what I meant," she groans, following him to the car. "It was the dancing. The *dancing*! Why did you have to choreograph it?"

"I thought you loved *Glee*!" Tim says playfully. He lifts up the trunk door and starts moving stuff around to fit the tent poles in. Alongside our bags of clothes and food, there are piles of old magazines wrapped in twine and plastic shopping bags filled with stuff Mom stores in the car for unknown reasons. I've never looked in them because I'm too afraid I'll find something illegal, so when Tim goes to open one, I freeze.

"What *is* this stuff?" he says, reaching in. Then he sees something, stops, and says, "Oh my God."

"Just leave it!" I lunge over to grab the bag, but Tim's faster than me and is already pulling out a silver cylinder attached to a long, clear tube. I snatch it from his hands and toss it onto the grass. "That's none of your business!" I shout, and he and Leah look at me like I'm crazy.

"Michelle," he says. "It's a siphon pump."

"What?"

"A siphon pump," he says, breaking into a smile, grabbing my shoulders. "For gasoline. And I saw an empty can in there, too."

"Oh!" I start laughing, I'm so relieved.

"What's so funny?" Denny asks.

"We're gonna make it," I say, lifting him up and kissing him on the cheek. "We're actually gonna make it to California."

"We weren't before?" Leah asks, stricken, and Tim and I exchange a guilty look. "Whatever, you guys are so weird," she says, climbing into the backseat.

To work the siphon pump to our advantage, we have to stage a breakdown on the side of the road. Goldie's jacked-up exterior is for once a plus; the only potential snag is that we're a bunch of kids without a chaperone, and it's a good half hour past when even the crunchiest hippie schools would start. This, I tell myself, is why four cars pass me without so much as slowing down, even though I'm doing my best down-on-my-luck half smile and Miss America wave (Devereaux rule #5: Work what you've got. As Mom likes to remind me, "You won't be this cute forever.")

"Maybe you should have Denny get out with you," Cass calls through the open window.

"Nah," I yell as a freight truck screams past, making me

jump back even farther on the shoulder. "If anyone's going to die trying to steal gas, it should be me. Besides"—I lean out tentatively, squinting at the flat, wheat-colored horizon shimmering like a desert oasis—"I'm sure somebody will stop."

But five minutes and as many cars later, no one has. My cheeks hurt, and I can feel my hairline starting to sweat. Aren't Midwesterners supposed to be really nice and trusting? Did I just pick the wrong spot, some stretch of state highway only traversed by dicks and the legally blind? I know there's a third possibility, but I really don't want to believe it's that. So when Tim offers to take over, I say no, both out of stubborn pride and because I don't want to see a car stop for him that wouldn't have stopped for me.

"Let me stand with you, at least," he says and steps out into the blinding sun before I can stop him. Before we left the campsite, he changed into one of Denny's clean(ish) oversize T-shirts, a silkscreen of Obama's face with BARACK THE VOTE! in big red block letters. With the khakis and the loafers, it makes him look like an overeager canvasser who doesn't realize his guy already won.

"I'm really okay," I say, shielding my eyes from the glare.

"I need some air," he says. "And besides, I want to learn from the master. In case I ever need to do this someday."

"Yeah, I can really picture you with a Tommy Hilfiger hobo bindle."

"You know," Tim says, bending slightly to whisper in my ear, "I'm not as clean-cut as you think I am."

"Is that right?" I put my hands on my hips and look at him expectantly.

"I'll have you know that after junior semiformal I drank

three rum and Cokes and ended up sleeping in a stranger's hammock."

I grin in spite of myself. "Hey!" I yell to a passing pickup truck, pointing at Tim. "Public enemy number one right here!" The driver, an elderly man wearing a baseball cap, frowns in confusion.

"Is that your sales pitch?" Tim laughs. "No wonder you can't get anyone to stop."

"Shut up."

"Maybe you should show a little leg, like in *It Happened One Night*."

"What happened one night?"

"It's just this movie," he says, smiling. "It's old. This reporter and this socialite end up traveling together and—"

"He's a raging misogynist?"

"What? No! He's Clark Gable."

"But he makes her pimp herself out to stop a car?"

"He doesn't *make* her. It's her idea."

"Yeah." I shake my head, looking back out at the empty highway. "That's not my style."

"I know! I was kidding. It was stupid. I'm sorry."

I cross my arms and level my eyes at him. The sweat's slowly crawling down the back of my neck now. "Why don't *you* show some skin?"

Tim raises his eyebrows. *"What?"*

"Show off that a cappella body. And get some color so you look less like end-of-life MJ."

"MJ?" he asks.

"Michael Jackson," I clarify. "Please tell me you've heard of him."

Tim puts his hand in his pockets and looks down at the ground, and I'm about to really lay into him when he executes a perfect moonwalk, his face suddenly all kinds of smug. In response, I launch into the "Thriller" dance, which Cass and I taught ourselves the summer MJ died, when Denny was a newborn and all Mom wanted to do was sit on the couch and watch tribute concerts on TV.

Neither of us notice the white SUV pulling up alongside Goldie until it stops a few feet away and a short-haired, middle-aged woman with wraparound sunglasses and aggressive highlights peers out from her window.

"Car trouble, or y'all having a dance-off?" she asks with a friendly smile.

"Oh!" I wipe the damp hair off my face and try to smile through my humiliation. "A little of both."

"We were driving our brother and sisters to school when we ran out of gas," Tim jumps in, his dimple in full effect. "My mom told me it was low, but I thought we could make it. We've been stalled here for over an hour now, and we're really late." He could have more conviction in the delivery, but I have to hand it to him: His body language is great. He's leaning a little against her car, like he's so exhausted he can barely stand, even though he's wisely keeping a nonthreatening distance at the same time. I try to look pained, like the thought of missing school is unspeakably awful, when the truth is that I haven't thought twice about it since I made that U-turn Wednesday morning.

"Oh, honey, nobody's stopped?" the woman asks. Her voice has a slight drawl to it, which for some reason makes me think of pie. It's probably all those cooking shows. "Did you call your mom?"

"Uh . . ." Tim looks at me, and I feel a pang of shame at not having talked to my real mom yet. "We left her a few messages," I improvise, "but she had a big meeting this morning, so she probably hasn't checked. Anyway, I called school, and they know and we're all fine but . . ." I give Tim a look, and he picks up right where I left off, like we've been practicing this grift for years.

"If you could let us siphon some of your gas, we have our own pump, and we'd be happy to pay you for it," he says. "We only need a gallon or two to get us there, and then we can figure it out, call a tow or something."

I look hopefully into our reflection in her sunglasses, holding my breath.

"Well, no," the woman says. "I will *not* take your money." I feel Tim exhale at the same time I do. "And I will not give you a gallon and then just leave y'all to fend for yourselves. I just filled up, so you take what you need."

"Are you sure we can't give you a few dollars?" I ask.

"Please," she says. "If you were my kids I'd want someone to do this for them, so consider it a gift." She raises an eyebrow. "And listen to your mother next time!"

"Yes, ma'am," Tim says and jogs over to Goldie to get the pump. He's the only one who knows how to work it, so I fall back and watch as he makes charming chitchat with the woman while he fills up our two-and-a-half-gallon container. When it's full, I see her gesticulate out the window, and he comes back over with a shocked smile on his face.

"She says she won't leave until I fill up at least two more times," he says, pouring the gas into Goldie's tank. I grin into my fists in the shadow of the rear bumper.

Our success puts me in such a good mood that on the way to Oklahoma City I try to make surviving for the next few days into a fun game, more like *Extreme Cheapskates* than *Lord of the Flies*. "Each of us has to come up with our own way to score free food or goods," I say, shouting a little over Goldie's now constant clanging. "The only ground rules are no stealing—if it has value, it has to be given to you willingly—and no straight-up begging for money." I have nothing against panhandlers—hey, you do what you gotta do—but I want to save that as a last resort.

To my surprise, Leah volunteers to go first, citing the mall as her target. "I can do way better than leftovers," she says confidently.

Malls are a goldmine for scavengers, a glittering oasis full of free samples, public restrooms that actually get cleaned on the regular, and dressing rooms where you can change clothes in private. Picking through Cass's and my luggage (which is really just a garbage bag stuffed haphazardly with wrinkled clothes), Leah finds a gray T-shirt she deems "not horrible" and a pair of dark jeans that ride loosely on her hips. (She seems very excited about the brand, which is apparently high-end, and I don't want to burst her bubble by telling her I got them for $20 at Marshalls' on-fire sale.) We put it all in Cass's backpack along with dry underwear and a clean shirt for Denny and walk through the automatic doors into the blast of Cinnabon-scented air conditioning and streams of midday shoppers.

We head straight for the bathrooms, and while Tim helps Denny de-lake himself in the men's room, Cass, Leah, and I take over a bank of sinks in the ladies' and start scrubbing our faces, arms, and any other exposed skin we can reach. I show

Leah how to put a blob of dispenser soap on a paper towel and rub it under her arms for "deodorant" (Devereaux rule #7: Be prepared to improvise), and she helps me restore some bounce to my curls with an application of soapy water and a few minutes under the hand dryer.

"If there's a Sephora, we can even do our makeup!" Leah says enthusiastically, and Cass retreats into a stall, either to administer a shot or just to hide. Much to Leah's disappointment, there is no Sephora, but there is a Bath & Body Works, and she's able to find a pot of clear lip gloss with a TRY ME! sticker that she insists on applying to both my lips *and* eyelids. "Trust me, you look really pretty," she says, and when I turn to Tim to crack a joke, I catch him looking at me in a way that makes my stomach flip.

Leah leads us to the food court—your typical brightly lit, abundantly littered square of fragrant chaos—and starts to tentatively case the joint, pretending to look for a table. I see her pass by perfectly good half-full sleeves of fries and lonely, untouched broccoli spears left on greasy Chinese-food trays, and it's all I can do not to jump in and show her the ropes. Finally, she homes in on a half-eaten burger. She stands over it, looking around nervously, combing her hair with her fingers, before finally snatching the tray. Even though it's not what I would have chosen (I try to pick things that haven't touched anyone's mouth if possible—stuff you eat with a fork), I'm weirdly proud of her. But then, instead of coming back over to us, Leah makes a beeline for the Burger King register and starts talking animatedly to the cashier. Almost instantly, she's holding a tray with a brand-new, uneaten burger and a side of large fries.

"Ta-da!" she says, smiling broadly even though her hands are visibly shaking.

"What did you *say*?" I ask, plucking a golden, still-grease-hot fry from the top of the pile. The taste of warm, fatty food after thirty-six hours of dry crackers is positively transcendent.

"I said I found a hair in it," she says with an innocent shrug.

"So you lied," Tim says.

"That's not a rule!" Leah protests. "Right, Michelle?" She hands the burger to Denny, who takes a bite much larger than he can chew.

"It's not a rule," I say, cramming another fry in my mouth and swallowing it nearly whole. "If it means the difference between starving and eating, it's allowed. Plus, it's Burger King, not a mom-and-pop shop. They can swing a freebie."

"If you say so, coach," Tim says with a little smile.

Leah's con is quickly forgotten as we pass the tray around, demolishing the meal in what seems like seconds. Only Cass doesn't eat much, claiming she feels sick. But somehow the rest of us are all even hungrier after getting some real food in our stomachs, so Leah repeats her trick at Wok 'n' Roll with a plate of General Tso's chicken.

"You have officially earned your scout badge," I say, and she does a little curtsy.

It's after school hours by the time we tear ourselves away from the buffet, and as we pass a Chuck E. Cheese's on our way to the exit, Denny spots a bunch of balloons inside.

"My turn, please?" he begs. "Max has an idea."

"We'll never see him again," I joke as he sprints into the noisy restaurant.

"On the bright side, maybe Max will fall in the ball pit," Tim says, and we high-five.

But the meatball comes through, dashing out ten minutes later with a cupcake clenched in one hand and a slice of pepperoni pizza in the other.

"Hey," I say gently, kneeling down to meet his eyes, giving him a reassuring squeeze. "Did you take that stuff off someone's table?"

"Nope," he grins. "There was a birthday party, so I just sat down and someone gave me food."

I give him a big, wet kiss on the forehead. "Don't let anyone tell you you're not a genius," I say, and he takes a victorious lick of blue frosting. He hands the pizza to Cass.

"I know it's your favorite," he says.

"Thanks, buddy." She takes a small bite from the end but grimaces a little as she swallows. I hope she doesn't have a stomach bug or something. If Goldie gets vomited in, we'll have to spend my last $61 at the car wash. That, or set her on fire and walk away in slow motion like cool action-movie heroes. Right now I could go either way.

"So what's *your* game?" I ask Tim as we get back on the highway heading toward the little top hat of Texas.

"I'm still fine-tuning," he says, rubbing his chin with one hand. "But I had to go last because I didn't want to make you guys look bad."

"Trash talk, okay, I see how it is," I laugh. "Bring it. Next city we stop in, it'll be you and me, head-to-head, winner take all."

"What do I win?" Tim asks. "A car that actually runs?"

"Go ahead, keep talking," I say, batting my glossy lids. "You're digging your own grave."

We score another full tank of gas between Oklahoma City and Amarillo, split between three Good Samaritans who stop in quick succession, no dancing required. After watching Tim do it the first time, I learn to do the siphoning myself. It gives me a cheap thrill to add to my list of self-sufficiency skills, and I want to show Cass and Leah that you don't need a man to do the dirty work for you. There are a lot of ways I don't want to turn out like my mom, but I have to give her credit for teaching me how to survive on my own. Just as many nights as she locked herself in her bedroom with a bottle of wine, she was down under the sink perched on her bare toes, banging away at a leaky pipe with some dog-eared how-to book open on the floor next to her. She figured it out because she had to, because she didn't have anyone else who would help voluntarily, and because she couldn't afford to pay anyone. And that's how she taught me to live.

Which gives me the idea. Wiping my hands off on my gasoline-splattered jeans, I know how I'm going to completely school Tim.

We drive into northern Texas on a long, cracked stretch of Route 66 dotted with pawn shops and legitimate Mexican joints that make Taco Bell look like the Disney cartoon it is, their bright storefronts faded to lazy pastels by decades of unflinching sunshine.

"Jesus saves, ask Him!" Tim says as we pass an RV park, and it takes me a minute to realize he's reading off a bumper sticker and not just suddenly professing his Christian mission.

We reach downtown Amarillo just as the sun starts to set, and while it's mostly as low and sparse and beige as a Texas tumbleweed, it's still a spring Friday night, so there are people milling around outside of a few busy-looking bars and restaurants. It's too late to execute my master plan, which requires both natural light and local library Internet access, but I know Goldie's death rattle will still be there tomorrow—and Tim doesn't seem to be exactly off to a running start—so I try to enjoy the warm evening breeze and turn my mind to dinner. I park in front of a big old-school theater marquee adorning an otherwise nondescript office building. It must have been gutted to make dozens of tiny, soulless cubicles, but I guess it's nice they left the sign up. It's a beautiful scar.

"Want to scout for food?" I ask as I turn off Goldie's engine, giving her rusty old bones a rest. "There's probably not much here, but if we can find a coffee shop, they should at least give us a few cups of hot water to make noodles."

"I think I need to check my messages," Tim says, pulling out his phone. "That okay?" I nod. He hasn't tried to turn it on once without asking since I laid down the law yesterday.

"I'll stay with him," Leah says.

"What about you?" I ask Cass and Denny. "Any important calls?"

"Haha," Cass says.

"Can we call Mom?" Denny asks.

"No, buddy, calls only go one way where Mom is." I haven't turned my own phone on in over twenty-four hours, too afraid of what might be waiting for me.

"Can we find a bathroom then? One where I can stand up?" The great thing about being six is that talking to your absent mother and finding a urinal to practice on are basically equally exciting.

"Sure thing," I say, and we trudge off into the dusk, just three disheveled minors out for an adventure pee in the Texas Panhandle.

Of course the first open place we see is a Taco Bell. I mean, of course it is. Even Cass starts laughing at the irony, and she hasn't cracked a smile since Indiana. It's on the other side of a big highway intersection, though, so we have to wait for about ten minutes for the light to change and then dash across like frightened deer because, since no one ever walks across highways, the walk light only flashes for about five seconds. I usher Denny into the men's room with the best instructions I can guess at and then give Cass a few bucks to get a bean burrito and a soda, because she looks so pale she could pass for a Kardashian. "You *need* to eat," I tell her, shoving the bills in her clammy hand. I'm hoping we can get some downtime in California, maybe even get a room at a motel with a pool if Buck's parting gift comes through, and spend a day lying around in the sun before we have to figure out how to rejoin civilization.

While Cass is waiting in line, I finally bite the bullet and turn on my phone. And sure enough, the voicemail icon instantly lights up.

"Hi, Michy . . . . it's been a few days, baby, and I'm ready to come home as soon as you can get that money together. I'm doing good now—well, better, anyway—and I'm ready to change a lot of things. I hope you believe me. Even if you can't post the bail yet, could you come and see me? It's getting lonely in here, and I miss my babies. Take care of them, okay? I know you will. You always have. You're all they got

right now, though, till I come home." There's a long pause, which I let myself hope is some kind of period of existential reflection until I hear her blow her nose. I forgot about the runny nose. When Mom stops using, she leaks for days. *"Sorry. Anyway, I put you on the visitor list, so come anytime."* By way of goodbye, she shouts, *"I'm done now. Damn, relax!"* presumably at someone waiting to use the phone.

Standing in a Taco Bell, listening to my mom's excuses . . . 1,500 miles and I can't seem to get anywhere I haven't been before. I chew nervously on the insides of my cheeks as I delete the message and stuff my phone back in my pocket. She does sound better, at least—not that it means anything. She's always better, until she's not. In some ways it's worse when she's good, because then I'm just waiting for something to happen, wondering if this will be the day, or the next one, or the next one. I always find a reason to go in the house before Cass and Denny, just in case, so I can be the one to find her if she ODs. I've never found any tips for that scenario on the cover of a teen magazine.

Luckily, I can't dwell on it for too long, because Denny barrels out of the bathroom with a big wet splotch on the front of his pants.

"It's from washing my hands!" he says, scowling, as I attempt to suppress my laughter. A big bald guy comes out of the men's room and gives us a long, piercing look, but luckily Denny has his back turned. I wonder if he knows yet that he's in for a lifetime of looks like that—and that the looks won't be the worst of it. I glare at the bald man and pull Denny toward me.

"Whoa, D, you fall in or something?" Cass appears with her burrito, which bends limply over her fist in its foil sleeve.

"He washed his hands *very* thoroughly," I say, planting a firm kiss on my brother's forehead.

You're all they got right now.

"Um, congrats?" Cass holds the burrito out to Denny, but I push it back.

"That's for you," I say. "Eat."

Cass grimaces. "I feel like puking."

"Just eat the wrap then."

Cass groans in protest but leans against the wall and reluctantly begins to peel open the foil. Across the room, Baldy is sitting with a younger, bleached-blonde woman with sunburned shoulders. She's talking to him, but he's not looking at her. He's still staring at us with narrowed eyes, like the very sight of us offends him to his core. He's got an *American Gothic* face, kind of pruney and all kinds of mean. Instead of Family Circus, we must have stumbled into the Racist Rodeo hour. Lucky us.

"Hurry up," I say to Cass, who is tearing off minuscule strips of the soft, damp tortilla and placing them on her tongue like Communion wafers.

"I'm done," she says, looking peaked and pitiful under the fluorescent lights. I should give her some serious shit about her blood sugar, but we have to get back to the car and I'm not in the mood to force-feed a feral teenager, so I let Denny dispose of the evidence as I usher them both out the door, feeling the bald man's eyes on my back the whole time.

When we make it back to the block where we parked, there's a little crowd gathered, and my first chilling thought is that maybe Tim's dad was just baiting him to call so he could trace our location, and that he already sent the cops straight to us.

But as I get closer I hear clapping, and then I can see Tim standing under the theater marquee with a rolled-up paper bag at his feet, doing some sort of white boy shimmy as he sings an a cappella rendition of "San Antonio Rose." His voice is smooth and sweet, like a dorkier Bruno Mars.

"Oh no," Cass says, instant humiliation draining even more color from her face. She hangs back while Denny and I move in closer. Just as he's finishing, I see Tim see me, and he smiles wide and wiggles his eyebrows, like, *top this.* That sneaky bastard. This was supposed to be a battle of wits, not *American Idol.*

After the last note, the onlookers clap and holler, and a few of them step forward to drop coins and dollar bills into the bag. Leah is leaning on Goldie's hood, arms crossed tightly on her chest, looking reluctantly proud but sitting far away enough to safely deny any association with him.

"Thank you so much," Tim says. "This next one goes out to a girl I know." Someone whistles, and he laughs. "No, it's not like that. She once told me to buy a taco or step aside. But"—he pauses and winks, to the crowd's delight—"I think I'm growing on her." And then he launches into a song I haven't heard in so long, it takes my breath away—"Michelle," by the Beatles.

Buck used to sing that to me all the time when I was little. He doesn't get too many points for creativity—it's the only popular song with so much of my name in it—but I didn't know it was a real song back then; I thought he made it up for just me, and it always made me feel special and safe. I find myself blinking back tears.

I want to meet Tim's eyes, but I can't. It's too dangerous, what I'm feeling right now, this combustible concoction of new euphoria and old, aching rage. On the one hand, this is the first time a guy has ever sung to me—in public, no less—and it makes me feel dizzy and hot, like my plasma has been replaced with champagne bubbles. But then, the song also reminds me of the man who took away my trust, who's at least half the reason I've spent the past decade avoiding getting close to anyone. Your parents are supposed to teach you how to love, so what the hell are you supposed to do if they leave you hanging? How are you supposed to know what to feel or even how to express it? I stare at the pavement sparkling under my shoes in the glow of the streetlamps and try to let whatever this is—this song, this boy, this moment—wash over me, and when he's done I clap so hard my palms sting.

"Thanks," I say when he comes back to the car clutching the bag filled with bills.

"Not bad, right?" He smiles nervously and searches my face for a reaction.

"Not bad." I try to smile, but I'm afraid it looks too fake, like I don't mean it.

"So what did you get?" he asks.

"Nothing." I hold my hands out to prove it. "It's all you. You win."

"How much did you make?" Leah asks, grabbing at the bag. "Is it enough for sushi?"

"Yeah, got your fishing pole?" He laughs, holding it over her head. His arm brushes my waist, and I jump back like he's on fire.

"We should probably get back on the road," I say. "I want to make it into New Mexico before we camp." Tim nods but doesn't say anything. Now he's the one staring at the ground.

You're great, I think. *I'm sorry. I'm just no good at this*. But my telepathy only works on Cass . . . and maybe not even on her anymore.

"Hey," I say, grabbing his hand. I notice that each nail has a perfect half-moon beneath it, not waxing or waning—just constant. Tim looks up, and our eyes meet. My heart beats in my ears like a snare drum.

But the words, whatever they are, die in my throat as I see the bald man emerge from the crowd and make a beeline for Leah. He's broad-shouldered and over six feet tall but must be pushing sixty-five and moves like he doesn't have all of his original parts. *I could outrun him*, I think wildly.

"Hey!" Now I'm yelling it. I drop Tim's hand, push past him, and instinctively step in front of Leah and Cass, who are pawing through the crumpled ones and piles of quarters like winos. "Get in the car, let's go," I say. But physics fail me this time; he's in motion and we're standing still, and he closes the distance before the last word is out of my mouth.

"Excuse me." His voice is raspy and thin like a rusted-over flute.

"What?" I ask, a little too sharply. He frowns in my direction but doesn't seem to see me; he's looking back and forth between Tim and Leah, finally settling on Tim.

"Can I speak to you for a moment, son?" he asks.

Tim looks confused but offers up a tentative half-smile. "I guess so. What about?"

"Maybe he wants to give you a record deal," Leah quips.

"No, nothing like that, I'm afraid." Baldy smiles, but his eyes are steely. I feel Denny's hand close around my wrist. "I was just wondering . . . is your car an old beige station wagon?"

Tim looks at me and furrows his brow. "Yeah," he says. "Why?" I can see Goldie about fifty feet down the block, slumped against the curb. Apart from her general appearance nothing seems amiss.

"I thought so," Baldy says.

"Is there a problem?" I ask.

"You tell me." He sounds angry now. The glare is back with a vengeance.

"Hey, man," Tim says. "There's no need to talk to her like that, she didn't do anything to you."

Baldy ignores him and turns to Leah. "Where are your parents?" he asks.

"Um, none of your business?" she shoots back.

"I think it's time for us to leave," I say as calmly as I can manage. For once I'm going to follow Buck's sole contribution to the Devereaux Rule Book: When it starts to get bad, *walk away.*

"Where you headed?" He won't let it go.

"*Home,*" I say.

"Do you live nearby? I couldn't help but notice your car had out-of-state—"

"Dad!" The blonde he was sitting with at Taco Bell appears behind him, looking pissed. She's got a thin, angular, aggressively tanned face, but there's a softness to her eyes that seems to defy her genetics. "Jesus, Daddy, I told you to leave them alone."

"Stay out of it, Natalie," Baldy says. "I know it's them." A chill runs up my spine, but I try to channel Cass and keep my face bored and blank.

"I'm sorry," Natalie says. "Please forgive him; he's just a music teacher who wishes he was a private detective."

"I don't understand," I say.

"We just—well, we heard something on the radio earlier," she says. "An AMBER alert about some missing kids. Two white ones and three, um—" She looks at me apologetically. "African American."

Radio. AMBER alert. For a second I wonder if I'm dreaming, or in some weird exhausted fugue state where I'm hearing things that aren't there. But then I see Tim's face, slack with disbelief. He heard it, too. This is happening.

"Not missing," Baldy interrupts. "*Kidnapped.* And the car exactly matches the description. Exactly! It's even got Maryland plates!"

My heart threatens to burst out of my chest, *Alien*-style. They know about Goldie. And about the three of us. Not even Tim's dad knows we're involved. The only place anyone could trace us to is—

"You're wrong," Tim says softly.

—the hotel. The parking lot. *Shit.* Of *course* they had cameras. So much for identifying my obstacles.

"I'm not wrong, you said so yourself!" Baldy sputters. "A beige station wagon, you said!"

"With *New Mexico* plates," Tim says calmly. "We just came over from Santa Fe for the day."

"Spring break!" Leah chirps with a big smile.

"I don't want to go to Mexico!" Denny whines, but luckily his voice is muffled by my back.

"See, Daddy?" Natalie says, tugging on his arm. "I told you, it's not them. They're probably looking for three big black guys, anyway, not a couple of girls and a little kid." This master stroke of racial profiling seems to finally pacify Baldy.

"Sorry to bother you," he mumbles into his neck.

"Sorry to bother *you*," I say icily.

As we walk as inconspicuously as possible back to the car, Tim tries to take my hand again, but I shrug him off. A few minutes ago I was almost falling for him, but now I can't even look at him. He was supposed to keep this from happening. He promised it wouldn't. And he has no idea how much I stand to lose now that it has.

"Well, fuck," I say once we're back on the highway. I say it a few more times for good measure. For once I don't care what Denny hears. He'll probably hear a lot worse in his new foster home, anyway, which is where he'll be going once the cops catch up with us. I'm so numb from shock and fear that I can barely feel the steering wheel under my fingers. I have to get off the road soon, or I might get us all killed.

"I thought you were taking care of your parents," I say to Tim, the acid in my mouth sharpening my tongue.

"I didn't think they'd go through with it," he says.

"So you *knew*?" I feel betrayed in a way I wasn't prepared for.

He looks at me helplessly. "I tried to stall last night, like you said, but the story just doesn't hold. They saw right through it."

"What exactly did you say?" I ask.

"I told them we were going to keep going." He takes a deep breath. "And Dad told me that he was going to report us missing."

"Thanks for telling me."

"I was trying to find the right time," he mumbles.

"Bullshit," I snap. "You had plenty of time."

"Well, would it really have helped?" he asks irritably, fiddling with the radio dial. A burst of deafening static fills the car.

"Yes," I shout over the noise. "It! Would! Have! Helped!"

Tim lowers the volume. "What I don't understand," he says, "is why some random dude in Amarillo heard about us on his local radio station. I mean, how could anyone know we were anywhere near there? If we got spotted by a cop . . ."

"Then we'd already be in custody," I finish.

"This might be a stupid question, but there's no way Goldie has, like, a tracking device, right?"

"She can't even charge a cell phone, so no. And yes, that *is* a stupid question."

"Oh no," Tim says, turning around. "Leah. Did you turn on your phone?"

"Just for a second," she says. "When Denny went in Chuck E. Cheese, I got bored. I didn't post anything, I swear!"

"You don't have to post anything! Karen installed software that can remotely track your location!" Tim runs his palms over his face. "Shit, I can't believe I didn't think of that."

I did! I want to scream, but I know the damage has already been done. "Throw it out the window," I tell Leah. "*Now.*" Her eyes get wide, and I repeat myself, more forcefully.

"But it's not even on!" she cries, her voice shrill and wobbly. I'm about to unleash a tirade of curses when the radio static gives way to a crisp female voice emerging from Goldie's ancient speakers:

". . . say both teens have blond hair and are approximately five feet eleven and five feet nine inches tall, respectively. They may be wearing school uniforms. If you see anyone matching this description traveling

without adults, please call your local police precinct. After this brief break, stay tuned for an uninterrupted hour of golden oldies on this Flashback Friday—"

As an ad for a car dealership begins, I take the next exit and park on the shoulder of a sleepy rural road. After I kill the engine, the only sound is the incessant *click, click, click* of the ancient hazard lights, sending out a useless SOS into the darkness.

"Well, the good news," I say hollowly, "is that they only care about finding you."

"How would they know about *you*, though?" Tim finally asks. "How do they know that you're—what you look like? Or the car?"

"The hotel," I say. "Security footage."

"Dammit." Tim rubs his eyes. "We should have listened to you."

"Too late now," I say.

"So what do we do?" Leah asks.

"We wait for them to find us."

"Are we in a chase?" Denny asks, not sure yet whether to be excited or alarmed.

"Who says they'll find us?" Cass asks.

"If that guy knew the make of the car, the cops probably have the plates already," I say, struggling to keep my voice steady.

"But if they're going by Leah's phone GPS, they think we're in Oklahoma."

"We've only gone a hundred fifty miles. And they must know we're headed west. Every squad from here to LA probably got the memo." Bile rises in my throat as I weigh our very few remaining options. If we ditch the car, we're stranded. If we ditch Tim and Leah, they are—although probably not for long. For all I know Daddy Harper is already on his way.

"What's gonna happen?" Denny asks shrilly. I turn back to look at him, and as soon as I lock in on those big, scared brown eyes, I know I can't give up yet. I didn't make it this far to throw it all away now. If the cops want to take me in, they'll have to drag me kicking and screaming. Like mother, like daughter.

"I'll tell you what's going to happen, meatball. We're all going to keep our phones turned off—*no exceptions.*" I say, glaring at Leah. "We're going to get off the highway and take side roads. And we're not going anywhere outside the car as a group. Everyone got it?" I look around at them one by one. Only Tim avoids my eyes. "You two especially need to stay out of sight," I say.

"Like Max?" Denny asks.

"Yup," I say. "You're invisible from now on. No more malls. No public places. If you have to go anywhere, you can't be seen together."

"This is so humiliating," Leah moans.

"Well, the silver lining is, at least your parents give a shit," I say.

"Hey," Tim says, perking up slightly, "can't your mom call the cops? If they know who you are and that you're related to Leah—"

"She can't do that," I say, avoiding *his* eyes this time. Tim's not the only one who's withheld important information. My face burns with shame.

"Why not?"

"She's in jail."

There's a beat of not-quite-silence—*click, click, click*—as Tim and Leah ingest this revelation.

"So she doesn't know," he says, his voice low and even.

I shake my head.

"Are you guys running away?" Leah asks.

"No," I say firmly, mostly for Denny's benefit. "We just . . . didn't have anywhere to go. And when you came and told me about Buck . . ."

"I shouldn't have done that," he says.

"Too late now," I say softly.

"So what happens to you if they catch up with us?" he asks.

My head pounds. If the cops find us, then I violate the most important rule I grew up with, even worse than begging. The rule to end all Devereaux rules, and the one Mom has the most trouble following: *Don't get caught.* "I don't know," I say shakily. "Nothing good."

Tim looks straight at me, his eyes flashing with something that's not anger, exactly, but just as frightening.

"Then we have to make sure they don't," he says.

TWELVE

Friday Night/Saturday Morning
Amarillo, TX → Tucumcari, NM

We drive west on back roads until we're out of Texas, and then I spend an hour on the New Mexico byways looking for a place to camp that's not populous enough to blow our cover but not remote enough to remind me too much of *The Texas Chainsaw Massacre*. Finally I find a spot near Tucumcari Lake that shows signs of human life in the form of bonfire ruins but has no other campers. Leah doesn't fight me when I tell her I'm sleeping in the tent. No one really speaks, actually; we just shut down, one by one. And I can't sleep, but I could see that coming. In a way it's more comforting to be awake, lying between my siblings, hearing them breathe.

"Are you asleep?" I whisper into Cass's back once I'm sure Denny is out cold.

She doesn't answer, but I can feel her muscles tense through her shirt, the sharp triangles of her shoulder blades drawing together.

"I'm sorry about all this," I say. "I should have listened to you." I don't mean that, exactly. As much as it would make our lives slightly easier from a legal standpoint, I can't pretend that having Tim, and to a lesser extent, Leah, with us hasn't helped. Up to now, at least. But it doesn't matter; Cass doesn't take the bait.

"I probably overreacted in the car," I say—another lie. "I'm sure the cops have better things to do than look for a couple of kids on a road trip. As long as we don't tip any cows, we should be okay."

"Will you stop?" she finally hisses. "I'm trying to sleep."

"Hey," I say, resisting a sudden urge to grab on to her and hold tight, making spoons like we did when we were little, feeling the shift of her thin bones under my bigger ones as I curled around her like a human safety net. "I just need you to know that I'm here. And that I won't let anything happen to us."

"You can't promise that," she says, still with her back to me. And she's right; I can't.

"Okay then. I'm still here. I won't leave." I reach out to lay a hand on her arm, but she shakes it off.

"Getting taken away is the same thing as leaving."

A lump forms in my throat, and I try hard to keep the pattern of my breath from giving away the fact that I'm fighting back tears. After I compose myself, I try a different approach.

"When we get home, I'll help you transfer schools," I whisper. "Maybe we can get you into one of those fancy ones with financial aid. You could even go to Hogwarts." Cass lies stiff as a corpse. If she hadn't just spoken, I'd check her breathing. "In a weird way, this could all be a blessing. I think things will start to get better," I say.

In one swift and jarring motion, she flips over to face me, her head just six inches from mine but its contents still completely out of reach.

"No," Cass says. "They won't." Then she turns away again.

I lie awake for hours sending silent prayers out into the universe. *Just get us to California*, I think. If we can make it that far, I'll know there's hope for us, that things *can* get better, and I'll prove it to Cass, too. Now that Tim and Leah are national news, though, getting the rest of the way means throwing out our old rules for a new set. We can't just take whatever we can find to survive, by whatever means necessary. We have to move like ghosts, drawing as little attention to ourselves as possible. It means no more stopping strangers on the side of the road to siphon gas. It means we're down two bodies when it comes to scavenging for food. It means avoiding any and all rest stops, toll roads, and speed traps. It means we can't trust anyone but each other. *Just get us to California*, I beg the bowed ceiling of the cheap polyester tent. *I don't care about the journey, just get us to the destination.*

In the morning—or what passes for morning, when the sun is just starting to pink up the sky—I crawl out of the tent and look across the lake at Tucumcari Mountain, which is swathed in mist like a Q-tip. A sign at the entrance to the campground last night said that *Tucumcari* comes from a Comanche word, *tukamkaru*, which means "to lie in wait for someone or something to approach." It's a little creepy how much it applies to us at this point.

But I want to regain some control, take action instead of lying in wait, which I think I can do if I can just fix the goddamn car. Somehow this beige behemoth—which existed long before I did and was broken long before we were, and which has carried my family on every journey we've ever taken, however brief or ordinary, however fraught with tension or filled with wild, fleeting joy—seems like the key to turning things around. I know it makes no logical sense, but I wake up convinced that if I can fix Goldie, I can fix everything.

The only problem is I don't really know anything about cars except for where to put gas and how to do a jump start. Since Buck left I think Mom took her to a mechanic maybe once, when the muffler fell out (and only then because the neighbors complained after a few days). Otherwise when something goes wrong she just kisses her hand, smacks it on the dash, and holds it up to the sky, the way people do when they run a light just as it's turning from yellow to red. She stopped going to church a long time ago and barely talks religion, but I know Mom thinks God has kept Goldie running all these years, which gives a whole new meaning to the phrase "Jesus, take the wheel."

I was going to hit up a library and find some DIY repair books or web pages, but since that's no longer an option, I'll have to wing it. Luckily I do remember some of the things Tim said it might be—wheel bearing, shock mount, heat riser, exhaust pipe—and if there was a siphon pump I bet there's also a tool or two banging around in Goldie's trunk with the rest of Mom's junk.

But when I get to the car and peer through the streaky back window, I notice two things immediately. One, Tim is splayed on his back in the driver's seat, lips slightly parted, his left arm wedged between the seat and the door, his right hand disappearing into the cup holder. He's still wearing the Barack shirt (at least Mom's haphazard thrift shopping was good for something, and he'll no longer be recognizable by his school clothes) and a pair of comic book boxers. The second thing I notice—and the thing I should have seen first, really—is that Leah is gone. I walk around to the front of the car and scan the lake, holding my breath, until finally I see her about a hundred feet away, her long hair blending in with the tall yellow grass. Reluctantly, I put my mechanic ambitions on hold and walk over to where she's sitting.

"Hey," I say, crouching down next to her.

"Hey."

"You been up long?"

"I couldn't sleep."

"Yeah, me either."

"I've never slept well," she says, pulling up blades of grass from the ground and letting them sift through her fingers. "My mom says when I was a baby people kept telling her I would start sleeping through the night, but I never did." She rips out another handful of grass and examines it before letting it go. "I still don't."

"Me either," I say.

"Must run in the family," she sighs.

"Listen," I say. "I'm sorry this has all gotten so crazy. I should have known something like this would happen. I probably should have just left you alone."

"It's okay," she says. "I'm glad you found me."

"You are?" It's hard to hide my surprise. So far everything about this girl's life has been downgraded since she left Maryland.

Leah nods. The sunrise lends her face a golden cast, turning her eyes into twin pieces of sea glass. "I'm sorry I was so bitchy at first," she says. "I was just . . . it just felt so unfair."

"What did?"

"That that was how we had to meet, you know?" Her chin trembles a little bit. "I knew you guys existed when I was about five. I overheard them fighting, and my mom said something about me not even knowing my sisters. But when I asked her later, she told me to ask my dad, and when I asked him"—Leah stares down at the grass between her crossed legs—"he said you lived far away and that I could never meet you." She breathes in deep in that way people do when they're trying not to cry.

I stare out at the mountain, a big, squat pile of rock rising out of the valley like a sloppy sandcastle. I bet I could break it with my rage right now, just bust through like a bullet and send it crumbling into pebbles. *Thanks, Buck*, I think. *Thanks for everything, you piece-of-shit excuse for a human being. Thanks for giving me your eyes so I can see so clearly the ruins you left for us. Thanks for robbing us of our childhoods. Thanks for robbing us of our sister. Thanks for setting Mom on a collision course and then leaving us to pick up the pieces.*

"By the time I found out he was lying," Leah continues, "I was too scared to look for you. Because I thought you didn't want to find *me*." She swallows hard, blinking back tears. "Or else you would have."

"We did want you," I say, grabbing her hand. "We always wondered about you. We just didn't know your name. We used to make up stories, and we would just call you Sister."

"Really?" A shadow of a smile. "What were they?"

"Usually we'd get reunited and then go kick some bad guys' asses," I say.

"So, this trip, basically?" she says, and we both laugh. Leah's a lot sharper than I first gave her credit for. "I made my mom make up stories about you guys, too," she says, shaking her head. "That must have been so weird for her."

"What were we like?" I ask.

"Um . . . usually princesses," she says with a smirk. "You would come in this big fancy coach and tell me I was your sister and I could come live in the palace with you. Like Cinderella, basically. I watched a lot of Disney."

"Believe me," I laugh, "you don't want to live in our palace. We'd rather move into yours."

"I'm sorry about your mom," she says. "I don't know what I'd do if my mom was in jail."

"You'd survive," I say.

"Maybe," she says, looking unconvinced.

"Besides, you have Tim," I say.

"He's pretty great," she says. "I mean, he can be annoying, but I'm just glad I'm not an only child anymore." I know she's talking about Tim, but she looks at me when she says it.

"Yeah."

"He likes you, you know."

I'm caught off guard by the change in subject. "What? No." I reach down and rip up my own handful of grass, feeling the blush rise in my cheeks.

"He does," she says. "He's got no poker face. And that song last night, I mean, come on." She rolls her eyes. "He is so obvious about everything. It's embarrassing."

"Well, he made some money, at least. Which reminds me"—I glance back at Goldie, slumping as unimpressively as ever in the early morning light—"I still have to show him up."

"What are you planning?" she asks.

"I'll tell you if you help me," I say with a grin.

We open the trunk as quietly as possible and grab indiscriminately at bags, pulling them out onto the grass. In addition to a few pairs of seemingly clean underpants, a roll of paper towels, a circa-1992 Aerosmith cassette tape, and a crumpled pack of cigarettes, we find a socket wrench, a small pair of pliers, a weird diamond-shaped hunk of metal that neither of us can identify, and—most amazingly—a beat-up copy of *Auto Repair for Dummies*, which at first makes us high-five but then brings a wave of guilt as I picture my mother doing the same thing I'm doing right now—paging through it while her children slept, searching desperately for some key word she understood, hoping she could pull it off. Maybe Mom's the only reason Goldie's made it this far, no matter how bad she looks. Maybe she's been doing a lot more good I can't see.

"I think checking the wheel bearings means we have to take the wheels *off*," Leah says, pointing to a diagram of a confounding tower of tiny plates and screws.

"Okay, let's check the heat riser and exhaust pipe first." I prop open the hood, and we stare for a while at the jumble of dull tubes and cylinders connected by crisscrossed wires. I can identify the engine and the battery and that's about it, but luckily the book really does seem to be written for stupid people, so finding the little metal plate in the diagram isn't too hard. While Leah reads aloud from the manual, I poke around and try to wiggle it with my fingers, but it's so rusty that it seems glued in place permanently; it doesn't budge. So much for that.

Checking the actual exhaust pipe requires more work, since

it's under the car. We can't jack it, but I can fit my head and shoulders underneath without feeling like I'm inviting death, and after some experimentation we discover that if Leah holds her compact mirror at the right angle, she can catch enough light so that I can see. I trace the loose pipe with my fingers, dirt clumps falling into my eyes and hair, until I come to a bigger piece of metal covering part of the pipe. It gives immediately when I touch it, and when I shake it I can hear rocks or something rattling around inside.

"I found it!" I cry triumphantly. I would raise my arms *Rocky*-style if I wasn't worried about accidentally amputating a finger. I shimmy back out to wipe my face and get some tools to find Tim standing next to Leah, looking down at us sleepy and confused.

"What are you *doing*?" he asks.

"Fixing the car," Leah says excitedly. "It was Michelle's idea."

"You couldn't wait an hour?" he asks. "I could have helped."

"She asked *me*," Leah says.

"I wanted to do it myself," I say.

"Well, I could have jacked the car, at least."

I put my hands on my hips. "We don't have a jack."

"What do you call that, then?" he asks, pointing at the diamond-shaped thing on the ground.

"Oh," Leah says. "Oops."

"Whatever," I say. "I don't need it. I figured it out. There's a rock or something in the heat shield. I just have to take it off and put it back on."

"Well, you could have hurt yourself. Or Leah." I can't tell if he's actually concerned or just mad that I didn't let him swoop in and save us.

"But I didn't," I say, raising an eyebrow.

"That's not the point!"

"Yeah, the point is I *fixed* it." I grin and do a little touchdown dance to drive the point home. I'm just rubbing it in now.

Tim shakes his head. "Fine, but I'm driving today. I no longer trust your judgment."

"Says the boy wearing Captain America boxers."

His face reddens. "Now you're just being mean."

"I'm sorry," I say. "But you can't drive. You're supposed to be lying low, remember?"

"Am I supposed to lie on the floor again?" he asks.

"No. Just sit in the back." In my peripheral vision I see Cass and Denny unzipping the tent flap. "Cass, you want shotgun today?" I call, a weak attempt at making up for last night.

"Whatever," she croaks.

I grab the wrench and get back to work, my confidence fading fast. I might be able to fix the car, but there are much more important things that are broken. And I'm terrified they might be beyond repair.

THIRTEEN

Saturday Afternoon, Part 1
Tucumcari, NM →
Grand Canyon National Park, AZ

We spend the rest of the morning driving through New Mexico's sandstone mesas and ponderosa pines listening to nothing but the blissful hum of tires on asphalt. I brag about my rattle-repair skills only once every five miles or so. Breakfast is cold, thin instant oatmeal made with water from a fountain near the campsite, but I try to stay grateful—despite the awful development of last night, our luck hasn't run out just yet. We've been listening to the radio all morning for any updates, but Tim and Leah haven't been mentioned once so far, and we have enough gas to get us a ways before we have to figure out how to score more. Plus, the rising temperature that makes my hair start to frizz and stick to the back of my neck reminds me how close we're getting to California, to the reality of Buck and what he might give us. I mean, he ended up in Los Angeles; maybe he actually made something of himself. Maybe he's a sleazy Hollywood guy who makes deals over martinis and calls everyone babe. Maybe he invented an app or something and is living large in Silicon Valley. Maybe he's rolling in it, and thanks to his deep regret and even deeper pockets, we will be, too.

"Hey," I ask Leah as we pass through Albuquerque, "do you know what Buck's doing out in California? Did he tell you anything?"

"Nope," she says. "Last I heard he was in Utah with Grandma Polly."

Grandma Polly? "Did you know her?" I ask, trying to sound casual.

"No. She just sent me birthday cards." Leah sounds bored. She has no idea that she's exposing my grandmother as a racist bitch who only deigned to recognize the birth of her all-white grandchild.

"Why was he in Utah?" I ask.

"Who cares?" Cass says angrily. I think she can sense the newfound camaraderie between Leah and me.

"Because my mom kicked him out," Leah says. "He was cheating on her with a legal secretary."

What goes around comes around, I think, but to Leah I just say, "I'm sorry."

"Whatever. He was always out at weird times and acting shady. I knew something was wrong before Mom did."

"Even when you were that little?"

"Well, I wasn't *that* little," she says. "I was seven."

I look over at Tim, waiting for him to correct her, but he's just looking out the window, yawning. "You couldn't have been seven," I say. "That would mean—" The math takes shape in my head, each number like a punch in the throat. Buck left us when I was six, Cass was two, and Leah was already three. If he didn't leave Leah until she was *seven*, that would mean he stayed in Baltimore for *four years.* I would have been ten, Cassie six, Denny a cluster of cells dividing in Mom's belly. Four years he could have spent still knowing us. Four years that could have changed everything.

"That would mean he's an asshole," Leah says, looking over guiltily at Cass, who's busy biting her lip and avoiding eye contact.

"You said it," I say and then switch the radio over to some loud rock station. If I can't change the past, at least I can drown it out.

We cross into Arizona around one P.M. to find ourselves entering the city of Window Rock as well as the border of Navajo Nation, an unintentional detour that Tim insists is a game changer.

"The reservations have their own police force," he says. "I don't think they would know about us."

"You don't think, or you know?" I ask, my fear of getting caught battling to the death with my fear of losing control of my bladder.

"I *know*," he says. "At least I think I do."

"Okay," I say. "We can stop quickly, but we have to take turns going in, and no talking to anyone. Hell, no *looking* at anyone." Within a few minutes I spot a Navajo shopping center and park in a barely visible spot between two vans. I go in first, alone, keeping my eyes down until I'm locked safely in a bathroom stall. But on my way out I can't help but notice a big, glittering food court full of scraps for the taking. I don't want to mess with the Navajo spirits—some seriously bad juju—but the kids need to eat, we have seven hundred miles to go, and we're down to a single sleeve of crackers. So I do what I have to do, pretending to look for a seat while I slip pizza crusts into the sleeves of my hoodie like I'm doing a party trick. I'm so nervous walking back to the car that when a nearby baby shrieks, I nearly faint.

"So where are we going today, Magellan?" Tim asks as we chew the stale dough, waiting for the kids to finish up in the bathrooms. I sent Leah in wearing one of Cass's hoodies and some sunglasses, but I'm still on edge.

"As far as we can get before nightfall," I say, tapping the steering wheel with my knuckles.

"'Cause I had an idea for a day trip."

"Would you mind keeping your head down?" I ask, glancing back at him in the rearview mirror.

"Do you want to hear it?"

"Not really."

"Don't you want to see something cool?"

"No." I pop the last bite into my mouth and frown at him. "Please at least slouch a little. You fail at stealth."

"Okay, fine, I'll give you a hint," he says, ignoring me. "It's big—some might even say *grand*—and canyon-y."

"No," I say firmly. "We are *not* going there."

"Why not? It's on the way. Kind of."

"Do you understand the concept of not having people see

you?" I ask, spinning around. "It's Saturday, and that's the most popular tourist attraction in the entire southwestern United States. Maybe the entire country."

"That's the thing, though," Tim says. "Maybe you're thinking about it wrong." I glare at him. "Hear me out," he presses. "Maybe sticking to podunk towns and empty roads makes us *more* visible, you know? In a huge crowd that's busy sightseeing, we could really disappear for once."

"Even if that's true," I say, peering out the front window for any sign of the kids, "it's a waste of time. If we drive straight through, we can make it before midnight."

"We won't be able to see him until tomorrow morning anyway," Tim says. "So what difference does it make if we get there at eleven P.M. or eight A.M.?"

"It makes a difference to me." I don't know how to explain that I just want to get there as fast as I possibly can and that until we hit the LA city limits, I won't be able to breathe. I have this growing sense of unease that whatever's approaching—the cops, the devil, the future—is faster than we are.

"Well, I just wish you could see it," he says. "Dad took me on a trip after the divorce. A lot of what we did was pretty corny—the world's biggest ball of wax and stuff—but the Grand Canyon . . . man, it blew my mind."

"We went to Washington, DC, once when I was little," I say. There are pictures in an album, including one of Mom and Buck bisected by the Washington Monument in some heavy-handed foreshadowing. "But we never really leave the city. I've never seen much natural beauty."

"Somehow I doubt that," Tim says, and I reflexively press down on the gas pedal. Luckily the car is off.

I don't want Tim to think I'm being cold, but I have no idea what to say. Boys have told me I'm pretty before, mostly murmuring stuff as I pass them in the hallway, some of it nasty, most of it harmless. My least favorite catcall, and the one I get the most, is "Come on, beautiful, give me that smile." I always think about spinning around and telling them I don't smile on command, that I don't have all that much to smile about, and that they can mind their own damn business. I'm used to tuning out those comments, just walking away—but they've never been from someone I actually liked before. They've never been from someone who deserved an answer.

But before I can come up with something, the girls and Denny emerge from the front entrance of the mall. All three are inexplicably holding hands, and for the second time in ten seconds, I'm rendered speechless.

When Cass gets in the car, it's clear she's been crying. "I'm really sorry," she says.

"Sorry for what?" I ask.

"Everything," she says.

"Did something happen in there? What took so long?" Cass won't meet my eyes, so I look to Denny. "Are you okay?"

"She's sad about stuff," Denny says.

"She wouldn't tell us what," Leah adds.

"Hey," I say, touching Cass's cheek as she sits down in the passenger seat. "I love you. You know that, right?"

She nods, but her eyes are watery, threatening to spill over. I'm not sure what broke this dam in my sister—given the past few days, there are plenty of contenders—but if there was ever a time to give her a break, it's now. Tim's right—it doesn't matter if we get to LA tonight or in the morning, and camping's probably safer out here anyway. We haven't so much as seen a police cruiser in the past eighteen hours, and we all need a rest from the tension that Buck's previous dickery and imminent non-absence is bringing up. As long as we're careful, a stupid sightseeing detour might be exactly what we need.

I learn a few key facts about the Grand Canyon as we pull up to the South Rim entrance in the late afternoon. One, it's popular on Saturdays; the line to get in is a quarter mile long. Two, it's not free; it costs $25, over a *third* of our funds, which Tim neglected to mention but swears he'll make up for with as many al fresco concerts as it takes. Three, he wasn't kidding; it's breathtaking. Even before we get all the way to the visitor's center I can see the scope of it stretched out in front of us, an unbelievable panorama of sunset-colored rock rising out of the Colorado River.

We finally find parking and leave Goldie to bake in the searing Arizona sun. Cass, who's been fidgeting for most of the four-hour trip from Window Rock, seems out of it, but at least the angry edge that's been clouding her eyes all week is gone. Any trace of Leah's former attitude has also evaporated, and walking up to the sprawling nexus of the park, it almost feels like we're just a normal family taking in a tourist attraction on a road trip. Especially since all the kids want to do is eat junk food and go to the gift shop.

"You can go in the gift shop, but don't try to steal anything," I say to Denny, drawing side-eyes from age-appropriate moms who don't have to coach their children not to break laws. Cass sits down on a bench looking sweaty and shaky, and I dig a five-dollar bill out of my pocket. "Can you get her something?" I ask Leah, who's also looking limp under her heavy disguise. "She needs to eat; don't take no for an answer." I look for Tim, but he must have taken Denny someplace, because they're nowhere to be found. Cass slips on her sunglasses and turns away, and I take that as my cue to get lost, if only for a few minutes.

I go in the opposite direction of the masses of cargo-shorted, sunburned tourists and follow a sign for a greenway that leads to the Kaibab Trailhead. It's just a little road lined with rocks and brush, but after a few hundred feet the canyon opens up on one side, vast and awe-inspiring and almost instantly profound, like nature smacking you in the face and saying, "Get your head out of your ass and just *look* at this glory," and so I listen. I climb my ragged, city-kid butt up on a rock (far enough from the edge so I don't have to worry about coughing and tumbling to my death), fold my knees Indian-style, and just *look*. It's been so long since I just stopped to breathe, I've almost forgotten how.

The canyon makes me think of Buck, the absence of it. The lack of something coming to define it, like the lack of him has come to shape me in so many ways. It reminds me of Mom, too, the depth of it that could swallow you whole if you don't watch your step. Mom hasn't fallen yet, but she's hanging by her fingers, scratching at the stones, waiting for someone to reach in and pull her up while all I want is for her to stop doing drunken cartwheels along the edge.

But it's not depressing somehow. It's the first place I've seen where the absence of matter is what makes it mean something, what makes it special. And the canyon's huge rock formations aren't mountains, even though they look like mountains. They're just parts of the earth that haven't fallen into the fissure. They're survivors.

"Hey, is this rock taken?" Tim asks. I shake my head—not taking my eyes from the vista even though the sun is so strong I'm seeing spots—and feel him sit down next to me. "It's amazing, isn't it?" he murmurs.

"Beats the hell out of Baltimore," I say.

"Don't rub it in, I'm stuck there for four more years," he says.

"But you get to go to college."

"'Get to!'" He laughs bitterly. "More like 'have to.'"

"It's a privilege," I say, finally turning to him, narrowing my eyes. "Not everybody has it."

"You're right. I'm sorry."

"It's okay." I rest my chin on my hands and look back out at the canyon. I try to imagine all my anger and resentment, all my jealousy at the things I can't, don't, and will never have tumbling in. What would life look like without those ugly filters? There might be colors I don't even know exist yet, things I can't even see.

"You know, you're amazing," Tim says after a while. "We never would have made it this far without you."

I let myself smile, just a little. "Yeah, but without me you'd be sleeping in a bed with fresh sheets and taking real showers and not forced to sing for your supper."

"It's worth it," Tim says. "If Leah gets to see Buck just for a few minutes, it'll be worth it."

I frown down at my scuffed boots. "Have you considered the possibility that he'll disappoint her?"

"What do you mean?"

"He could refuse to see us, for one."

"But he called and *asked* for you to come."

"He could have been drunk."

"In a hospice?"

I shrug. "He's done worse. Or he could say something wrong, or mean, or make her feel guilty—"

"What would she have to be guilty about?" Tim asks. "She was just a kid when he left."

"We were *all* just kids," I remind him. "He abandoned *three* of his kids."

"I know."

"So what does that tell you?"

"Point taken."

"I don't know," I sigh. "Maybe I'm just afraid he'll be okay, nice, even. And that I won't completely hate him anymore. And then he'll be dead."

Tim's quiet for a minute and then says, "That would be *such* a dick move," and our laughter sends a flock of birds scattering into the sky.

"So where on the spectrum of dick moves does accosting someone in a Taco Bell fall?" I ask.

"Oh, somewhere in the middle, I think, just below kidnapping strangers and then making them recycle underwear for four days."

I try to elbow him playfully, but instead I lose my balance and just sort of end up leaning on him. And it's nice, so I stay there. I can feel his warmth through the thin cotton of the T-shirt, like I'm getting sunshine from all sides.

"Hey," he says into the top of my head. "While I have you,

um, on me, I wanted to say I hope I didn't make you uncomfortable last night. You know, with the song."

"Shut up," I say. "It was sweet. And I told you, you won. You get bragging rights for the rest of the trip."

"Yeah, well," Tim says softly. "I was kind of hoping it might win me . . . something else."

"Like a giant teddy bear?" I say.

I tilt my face up toward his, and all of a sudden there are his lips, soft and warm and full and pressing into mine with an urgency that nearly topples me over. I freeze for a second. I wanted this in a vague, soft-focus, fan-fiction way, but here? Now? I don't need anything else to worry about, much less my first set of boy problems. Physics problems, yes. Boy problems, no.

But then his hands cup my chin, his fingers tracing circles on my neck that send tingling waves down my entire body, and my brain stops talking. I open my mouth and let his tongue meet mine, and it's nothing like that first time in the schoolyard, not awkward and rough and frightening but gentle and tentative and intimate, like we're improvising a dance with no music. It's hard to find the space to breathe, but it feels too good to stop. When I pull away, we're both dazed. We should probably move back from the cliff.

"Sorry," he says. "I had to do that."

"Don't be sorry," I say, running my tongue against the back of my teeth.

"So . . . you're not going to hit me?" He grins, and I shake my head, leaning in.

"No," I breathe as our lips brush again.

But that's when I hear it: the scream, high and loud, its two syllables breaking into the still mountain air like a firecracker.

"MICHELLE!"

Tim and I jump to our feet to see Leah racing up the path, her face at least four shades whiter than normal, her eyes full of fear. What really chills my bones is that the look she has makes me think it's not the cops but something worse. She doesn't just look scared, she looks haunted.

"Michelle!" she cries, groping for my arm, her hands shaking. "It's Cass. You have to come. I don't know what's wrong, but she's on the ground, twitching. She can't talk, her eyes are weird—" The words tumble out so fast it's hard to process what they mean at first, but my body reacts before my brain has time to catch up. I break into a run, pushing Tim and Leah aside, racing past tourists with their Nalgene bottles and raised cameras, the canyon fading into blackness along with everything else in my peripheral vision.

My feet pound the ground, but I can barely feel them. I taste coppery blood in my throat. I can't even think, except for three words that keep breaking through the chaos in my head: *Nothing else matters.* The money doesn't matter. This trip doesn't matter. That kiss doesn't matter. Nothing else matters but getting to Cass. Nothing will ever matter again if I lose my sister.

FOURTEEN

Saturday Afternoon, Part 2
Grand Canyon, AZ → Flagstaff, AZ

Here's what I remember before the tidal wave hits: Running across what seems like miles of concrete, not understanding how I possibly could have gotten so far away. A cluster of people, three or four bodies thick, standing in the sunlight, silent, like a prayer circle. Just watching. Pushing through them, tearing at their clothes, their purse straps, not caring if it hurts. Their angry glances turning to pity, features melting into the periphery. *Nothing else matters.* And then Cass, on the ground, flopping, her eyes rolled back in her head. Bathed in sweat, so bad that at first I look to the sky for the rain I can't feel. A man in madras shorts crouched over her, his finger in her mouth. Her teeth are bared; she doesn't look like herself. I think: *Come on, beautiful, give me that smile.*

I fall to my knees. *Cass, are you there?* I grab her hand, clenching so hard the knuckles crack.

Michelle. MICHELLE! Denny wrestling away from the elderly woman who's been comforting him—*not me, of course not me, I wasn't there, I was with Tim*—and throwing himself on me, his voice shrill and scared.

What's happening? Why is she moving like that? Is she okay?

I'm a doctor, the man in madras says. *She's having a seizure. Does she have any preexisting . . .* And then the siren drowns him out. I fumble for her backpack, splayed half-open at her feet, with hands that feel like lead pellets in rubber gloves. The front zipper won't open. It's stuck on something. I pull and pull until it rips apart. A truck parts the crowd. Two men in black jackets jump out as my fingers close on the bracelet.

The man in madras talking to the paramedics as they hold her down and check her vitals. *Could tell something was wrong . . . hard fall . . . don't think she's breathing.*

She's diabetic, I say—scream, really—holding the bracelet out like it's some kind of magic wand and not just a crappy scrap of titanium. Like it can do anything at this point.

I need an Accu-Chek and D50 NOW! The guys in black are all over her, and the only thing I can do is hold on to the toe of her sneaker, and not even that once they lift her onto the stretcher.

We need to intubate, one says. Within seconds, they're fastening a plastic collar around Cass's neck, and one of the paramedics holds her head steady while the other feeds a clear plastic tube into her throat. I cover Denny's eyes.

A burst of static from a walkie-talkie. *I've got an unresponsive teenage female who needs immediate transport to Flagstaff! We're intubating in the field. Have an airlift meet us at the clinic.*

Denny's eyes, looking up at me, terrified. This can't be happening.

Where is she going? I'm her sister. A voice behind me: Leah. I didn't even see her.

Flagstaff Medical Center, the other paramedic shouts, lifting Cass onto a stretcher. She's moving less, just twitching now. *I need you to move back, ma'am.*

Someone's arms lift me up, dragging me back. Tim? A stranger? Does it even matter? *Nothing else matters.* Then doors slamming. The taillights of the ambulance. The earsplitting scream of the siren.

Denny, clinging to my waist. *Is she gonna be okay?*

Waiting for a sign. Waiting for the three squeezes I can't give.

I don't know.

(Take care of them, okay?)

I don't know.

(I know you will. You always have.)

I DON'T KNOW.

(You're all they got right now.)

And then I'm gone.

This time, though, it doesn't pass after a few seconds. I feel dizzy and numb. Somehow I make it to the car and sit down in the passenger seat, still clutching my sister's backpack.

"Can you buckle yourself in?" Tim asks gently, and I nod only so that he leaves me alone. But the truth is I don't want the buckle. If we hit something, I want to fly through the windshield, and I want to feel it. I want to get what I deserve.

I know the symptoms of hypoglycemia like I know my times tables. Pale skin. Sweat. Hunger. Confusion. Agitation.

Hadn't she looked pale to me for days now? Hadn't I seen her vibrate like a live wire in the backseat all afternoon? Saw her wipe sweat from her eyes even with the windows rolled down, doing sixty on the highway? Watched her wander over to the visitor's center like she didn't know where she was? The seizure might have been sudden, but the warning signs were all there, and I noticed them. I just didn't *see* them.

"It'll take us about an hour," Tim says, pulling onto the highway entrance ramp. "I'll go as fast as I can."

"What's wrong with her?" Denny asks, his voice uncharacteristically quiet.

"You saw it, Lee," Tim says. "What happened?"

"I didn't, actually." Leah's face is still paper white. "I was inside with Denny. Then I heard . . . screaming."

I close my eyes. I should have been there, and not just today. I should have been there all week. Cass has barely spoken in days, and I chalked it up to moodiness. I *saw* her get bullied, and I let it go after one half-assed attempt at a talk. I thought running away would just fix her problems (well, *my* problems, anyway), like on one of those makeover shows when some formerly frumpy lady walks out from behind a curtain wearing fitted jeans and a blazer and her whole family cries. They don't show you what happens after that, though, because it probably just goes back to how it was. People don't change from the outside in.

"She seemed okay earlier," Tim says, glancing at me. "Right? I mean, she seemed normal."

"Well." I stare at the floor mat, a faded maroon the color of dried blood. "Normal for Cass isn't really normal."

"But, I mean, this must have been sudden. Some kind of accident."

"She gets mad when she doesn't eat enough," Denny says.

That's true. If Cass doesn't time her shots to her meals right, she can dip below the blood sugar threshold. But that doesn't happen often. She's been diabetic since she's been alive, so she knows how to handle it—I *know* she knows. So I never pay that much attention to what she eats.

But this week has been different. I've been with her twenty-four hours a day, so I know what she's had: not much. Cass, who needs to eat well to live, survived on crumbs and scraps while I hoarded my money for gas, spent it on a totally unnecessary tent, and paid for parking at a tourist trap so I could explore second base in the open air.

"I should have made her eat," I say to the floor.

"No," Tim says and puts his hand on my arm, but I shrug him off. I don't know what to say to him. I can barely even *look* at him. It's not his fault I wasn't with Cass, and if he hadn't followed me I probably would have stayed just sitting there, doing nothing, trying to get inspired by nature. (God, was that really just hours ago that I had the fleeting luxury of not feeling like the world was collapsing around me for a second?) But he *did* follow me, and now I can't think of the velvet feel of his lips without my stomach churning with guilt, because nothing will ever change the fact that while we were kissing, she was seizing on the concrete, afraid and alone. I'll never forgive myself if something happens to her, but I'll never be able to forgive him either. And I think he knows it.

"Is there anything else that could make her . . . do that?" Leah asks.

"Too much insulin," I say, zipping and unzipping the front of Cass's backpack, watching the teeth click into place and then fall apart, over and over.

The only time it happened was when she was five. That was before she could give herself shots, and it was up to Mom to do them. She had just two shots a day back then. The morning shot was much more potent than the nighttime one, and it must have been easy to mix them up. That's what I've told myself ever since: *It must have been easy to mix them up.* Even sober. Because of course she was sober, right? She didn't get high and then inject her own daughter with a potentially lethal dose of insulin, right after pajamas but before she'd brushed her teeth with her light-up Hello Kitty toothbrush. The reality is that I'll never know, and I never want to know. We spent that night in the ER, all three of us wide awake, Cass nauseous and ghost-pale and tethered to an IV that made her cry, nurses coming in to adjust her dosage every hour until they were confident she could stabilize on her own. After that, I took over the shots, and Cass started doing them herself when she was nine. She has never slipped up in four years. Ever.

I look down at my sister's backpack and notice something odd. Except for the MedicAlert bracelet and a few snack-food wrappers, the front pocket's empty. The ever-present Ziploc baggie filled with needles and insulin is gone. I tear open the main zipper, hoping she just moved it, but all that's in there are dirty clothes.

In a flash, I see it laid out before me like a horrible road map I didn't bother to read: the silence, the tears, the delay in the Window Rock bathroom, her face when she came out. *I'm sorry.* For what? *Everything.* The insulin, gone. *All of it.* Gone.

Agony cuts through the fog with the precision of a scalpel, and I literally gasp as the truth dawns on me. There's no way this was an accident. Cass is trying to die.

FIFTEEN

Saturday Night
Flagstaff Medical Center, Flagstaff, AZ

The ICU waiting area is a little three-walled enclave with one couch, twelve chairs, and two loveseats arranged back-to-back so that we don't have to see anyone else's grief up close. Not that I could think about anyone else right now. There's a flat-screen TV playing sitcom reruns on TBS and a spread of magazines, and I wonder who could sit here and watch *Seinfeld* or read about Selena Gomez's new eyebrow shape without wanting to break shit and start wailing. The nurse at the desk looks like she's seen it all; she looks like that Munch painting, *The Scream*, only with bangs.

We've been here an hour. Cass has been here an hour and forty-five minutes. Her doctor, Dr. Chowdhury, who wears green scrubs and has a handsome, angular face with a prominent forehead vein, told me I can't see her until she stabilizes. She seized for twenty minutes, they're guessing, from the time she fell to the time she responded to the dextrose solution they gave her in the ambulance. They don't know how long her brain was without oxygen—probably not long, they think, but combined with the overactivity from the seizure ("like an electrical storm") and the mild concussion, it could cause lasting side effects. She's still intubated and has been given barbiturates to keep her nervous system suppressed, so she's still unconscious—not coma-unconscious, but heavily drugged. Her body will live, but her brain is anyone's guess.

"We've been able to pick up activity in many of the major areas of concern," Dr. Chowdhury said when we got there. "I'll keep you updated."

Many of them. Meaning not all of them. I think for the thousandth time of Cass on the verge of tears and me turning up the radio. Cass sitting down on that bench and putting on her sunglasses, turning her face away. How I'd thought she was just freezing me out like usual . . . how relieved I was that I could get away from her for a few minutes. Not knowing that they were the last few minutes she was planning on living.

A flood of tears sends me down the hall to a cavernous, antiseptic bathroom, which is lined floor to ceiling with gray tile, to double as a shower. I crouch on the toilet in the corner and weep into my knees, turning the sink water on full blast to drown out my primal, hiccupping sobs. In the car, I managed to hold it together for Denny, but now that I'm actually here at the hospital, the numbness is gone and my nerves are raw and bloody. How many mistakes have led up to this moment? How many were my fault? Mom's? Buck's? I know it's useless now, but I desperately backtrack, looking for the point of no return that I missed. If I hadn't pushed Cass aside so much lately—if I hadn't invited Leah and Tim—if Aunt Sam hadn't been such a cold bitch to us—if Mom hadn't gotten arrested—if she hadn't relapsed in the first place—if she had been happy—if any of us had been happy—if Buck hadn't left—if, if, if.

I finally pull myself back together and scrub my face under the ice-cold water, knowing that my red-rimmed eyes and swollen features will give me away in a heartbeat anyway. But at least maybe it'll get me some sympathy with the nurses. They treated Cass because it was a life-or-death emergency, but when I filled out her intake forms they told me parental consent is required for moving her to the pediatric psych ward, which is protocol for suicide attempts once she recovers. *If* she recovers.

I plop back down on a chair across from Leah and Denny, who are coloring with the pen he stole from Child Protective Services. Amazingly, the MVP of this disaster is turning out to be Leah, who has been calmly distracting Denny for hours now, discreetly showing him YouTube clips on her phone, walking him back and forth to the water fountain, and even making a DIY bowling alley with upside-down Dixie cups and a crumpled page of *Prevention* magazine. All this time I assumed Tim was the strong one, but now I'm not so sure. Because right now he's freaked out and pacing, making things even more tense, while she's quietly and unassumingly locking shit down. I've always assumed that's what I do in my family—hold it together, balance out the crazy. But maybe I'm not the strong one. I certainly don't feel strong right now. I feel like I'm unraveling.

"Hey," Tim says, grabbing my hand and pulling me into the corner, next to a potted palm. "Are you okay? You look . . ." He pauses to consider his options before making a save with "upset."

"I *am* upset. My sister tried to kill herself." I look past his face to a pastel painting of a sunset hanging on the opposite wall. Or maybe it's a sunrise. That would be less of a metaphor for imminent death, at least.

"I'm sorry, that was a stupid thing to say." He takes my other hand, but I still can't look at him. We're standing a foot apart now, making an inverted drawbridge. "Is there anything I can do?"

Leave, I think. I tried to get him and Leah to stay in the car—I don't know how far the Harpers' witch hunt has spread, and I don't want to find out while Cass is being kept alive by machines—but they wouldn't.

"I don't think so," I say. I catch Leah looking at us in my peripheral vision and snatch my hands back.

"Oh." He clears his throat, takes a step back. "Well, I was thinking maybe I should call my dad."

"Don't do that," I say. "It'll just complicate things."

"We have to tell *someone*," he says. "And your mom is, uh, hard to reach, so . . ."

"Parents aren't just interchangeable," I snap. "Your dad doesn't know us. He wouldn't care. Plus, what could he even do?"

"He would care," Tim says, sounding hurt. "And he could get us a hotel room, buy us some real food. He could make sure they take care of her here—people listen to him."

"Of course they do, he's a white man."

"That's not what I meant."

"You don't have to mean something for it to be true."

"Fine, well, I just think . . . we can't do this on our own anymore," he says.

I look him straight in the eyes. "Maybe you can't."

"What?"

"*I* could do it," I say, anger suddenly filling the emptiness in my chest. "We were doing fine before you."

"I don't—" Tim frowns, wounded and confused. "You're the one who brought us."

"I didn't know what I was doing," I say. "I didn't know it would make everything worse." That's my fault, I know it is. I should have seen the second Cass ran out of the car at the Family Dollar that taking Leah was a bad idea. We should have left her where she was, on Facebook, smiling and abusing exclamation points in her white picket life. But it's Tim's fault I got curious. He was the one who barged in on us, who made me care in the first place. He was the one who knocked me off my feet when I should have been standing guard. "If I hadn't had to babysit you and her all week," I seethe, gesturing to Leah, who's now full-on eavesdropping, "I could have paid attention to my *real* sister."

"Wow, okay," he says, his cornflower eyes turning steely. "Because it seemed like you were pretty happy with the distraction." He's talking about the kiss. I can't *believe* he's bringing that up now.

"That didn't mean *anything*," I whisper.

"Got it," he says, his jaw hardening. "Then I'll get out of your way."

"Great," I say. "I could use some peace."

"Good luck with that," he says. "Leah, let's go take a walk."

"Why did you make them leave?" Denny asks, scowling, once they disappear around the corner.

"Don't worry, they'll be back later. They've got nowhere to go." I sink down into one of the loveseats, the thick imitation leather squeaking under my weight, and close my eyes. I want to tell him the truth, that it's for our own good and that I'm just preparing him for the inevitable, but I don't think he'd understand.

He'll have to learn for himself, like I did: Whether you push them or not, everyone leaves, eventually.

SIXTEEN

Early Sunday Morning, Part 1
Flagstaff, AZ

I can't sleep—big surprise. But the thing about hospitals is that the lights never go out, and while the cast of doctors might rotate, they never stop moving, even when the big round clock above the nurse's station reads three fifteen A.M., like it does now. The bitter irony is that after four days, we've finally found a free, twenty-four-hour shelter. Denny is stretched out on one of the loveseats with Mom's purple sweatpants covering his face. Leah's on the other one, wrapped in one of the Walmart blankets. Tim is slumped in a chair across the room, head bobbing against his chest. He's frowning while he sleeps, making me feel guilty even while he's unconscious. *That didn't mean anything.* Of course it did. Of course he does.

But I can't think about that right now. Until I see Cass's eyes open, I won't be able to think about anything else.

The latest news from Dr. Chowdhury is that she's breathing on her own (good) but still on seizure watch (bad). They've been slowly easing up on the barbiturates and expect her to wake up fully in the morning, which everyone acts like is great, jump-on-Oprah's-couch news. But a part of me is dreading the moment when she realizes she's still alive. Will she be relieved, or will it feel like one more failure? All I know is that I have to be there.

I feel a vibration against my leg and dig my phone out of my pocket. But it's off, and when I turn it on there's nothing new, no texts or voicemail. Who would be texting me anyway? Yvonne's given up since I ignored her last text on Thursday—Thought any more about that asst mgr gig?—Mom can only make calls from eight A.M. to ten P.M., and I don't think anyone else even has my number, except for Cass. But then something vibrates again, and I realize it's coming from Cass's bag. It's *her* phone, not mine. I didn't even think she'd turned it on since we left Maryland. I open the backpack and dig through her laundry until I find it, a slim black rectangle housed in an unmatched sock. I smile down at my sister's DIY phone case and then, feeling more than a little bit guilty, take it out and look.

The voicemail is from a restricted number, which instantly raises my blood pressure. On the same day my sister decides to end her own life, she gets a shady, anonymous call in the middle of the night? I try to access the message but get prompted for a password, and after various combinations of the numbers of Cass's birthday fail, I give up and scroll through her texts instead.

Other than one-word missives to Mom and me, her only

texts are to Erica. There's an endless string of short, boring back-and-forth, mostly "Where u?" "My house today?" "There soon," that kind of thing. But then the pattern breaks abruptly. On April 2nd—three and a half weeks ago—Cass writes:

Hey

?

U around?

Need 2 talk

On April 3rd:

I'm sorry

Don't ignore me

Fine

On April 10th:

Who did u tell??????

Fucking bitch

April 13th:

I hate you

April 14th:

No I don't

You hate me tho

Right

??

Thought so

And then Wednesday, the day we left:

Leaving 4 a few days

Can u talk now?

Please???

Thursday:

Might not be back

Last chance

And then Friday, finally, a response from Erica, two words long:

Good riddence

While I'm somewhat gratified that the bitch can't spell, my heart breaks. I don't know exactly what happened, but clearly Cass said or did something that made Erica turn on her. And while Erica barely spoke, and Cass rarely talked about her, I know what their friendship meant. That was her safety net. Lord knows we don't have one—we Devereaux stumble across high wires like the down-market Flying Wallendas (of course, we're falling, not flying, but the wind's moving fast enough we can't tell the difference). I try to imagine what my sister must have felt getting that text on Friday, on the heels of seeing Mom dragged off, finding out about Buck, and Leah, all of her life's rejection getting thrown back in her face at once. And not having anyone she could talk to about it. Not even me.

I turn off the phone and shove it back in her bag. It's three twenty-five now, and the hall is quiet, except for the distant beeps of monitors. The nurse at the desk—not the Munch painting, a new one who looks like Mrs. Mastino's good-witch twin—is on the phone, turned away from me. I can see the double doors that Dr. Chowdhury comes in and out of just fifty feet down the corridor. There's a button on the wall he pushes to make them open. As far as I can tell, he doesn't have to swipe an ID.

I stand and start walking to the water fountain; Nurse Mastino doesn't flinch. So I don't waste any time. I walk quickly and keep my head down, punching the red button and slipping through the doors to the ICU just as she hangs up.

I first see her through a thick wall of glass, like she's a diorama in a museum, lined up with a bunch of other, equally static and depressing scenes. And it's easier to think of her as a wax figure, lying there motionless, hooked up to so many machines. Her normally coffee-colored complexion has an ashen pallor, and her closed eyelids are dark, like she's wearing shadow for the first time. There's a thin tube emerging from her nose, and the tape used to secure it gives her the look of a boxer after a bad KO. Not my sister but a stand-in, an actress—one of our childhood fantasy scenes come to life. The deathly ill "orphan" princess waiting for a kiss from her long-lost father to bring her back. (That was a real one; sometimes they got weird.)

There's a nurse attending to one of the patients at the end of the hall, so I tiptoe around the glass partition and sit in the empty chair next to Cass's bed. The room feels like the set of a play: Everything's on wheels; nothing seems permanent. Someone else must have been in here yesterday, with different equipment, different injuries. Either they moved on to another floor, or . . . my shoulders sag as the tears start up again. My sister isn't going to die this time, but if she tried once, what's stopping her from doing it again? No. I can't think like that. I have to keep it together.

"Hi," I whisper, needing to talk but not sure what to say. Cass's heart rate monitor climbs and falls, a range of tiny mountains. The electrodes taped to her forehead and scalp feed data into a computer. The IV bag drips steadily and silently. "It's me," I say. I lay my left hand on her right, the one not attached to a needle. I splay my fingers out and cover hers. Mine are half an inch longer and a shade lighter but otherwise nearly identical, thin and tapered, with nails chewed down to ragged nubs, spots of dried blood at the cuticles—nails that defy manicures but wouldn't cut your fist if you had to throw a punch.

We've been fighting for so long, though. We've done it because we've had to, but if where we are is any indication, it's time to stop. I thought we'd hit rock bottom back at Aunt Sam's, but I was wrong. I thought leaving town would buy us time, but instead it's just made things crumble faster. Nothing I can do—no amount of work, or vigilance, or prayer, or clever roadside tricks—can fix what's been broken inside my sister. Inside me. It's time to give up, go home, and face our demons. At the very least, our mother.

"I'm sorry," I say, weaving my fingers in hers. "I'm sorry I kept putting you off. I'm sorry I wasn't there for you when you needed me." I wipe my nose with the sleeve of my free arm. Cass's face remains motionless, serene. Even with the cracked lips and gray tint to her skin, she's stupidly beautiful. I lean over and kiss her on the forehead.

"Excuse me!" A sharp voice behind me: the nurse. "You can't be in here until nine A.M. And don't touch her wires!" I turn to see good old Munch glaring at me from the door, her eyes little slits in her long, tired face. "Do you need me to show you back to the waiting area?"

I shake my head. Reluctantly, I let go of my sister's cool, limp hand.

"See you tomorrow," I say to Cass. Her monitor beeps noncommittally.

Back in the waiting room, the sweatpants have fallen off of Denny and onto the floor. I replace them and kiss his cheek, burying my nose in the soft, warm skin that doesn't smell half-bad, actually, for the time he's gone without a proper cleaning.

"Mmmmmph," Denny sleep-groans, rolling over, his elbow smacking me in the chin. "You're squishing Max."

Fantastic. The return of Max. I hope Denny doesn't talk about him around the doctors too much, or we'll be looking at two psych evaluations. Three, if I can manage to wake up paralyzed. I wonder if they offer family packs.

I slink back to my preferred crying bathroom and gargle with plain water, wiping the surface of my teeth with a paper towel, washing my face with abrasive, Pepto-Bismol-colored soap. It's only as I'm making a move to leave that I see the OUT OF ORDER sign dangling from the shower rack. I briefly weigh my options—the waiting room with my little brother, his imaginary adult cowboy, the estranged sister I recently insulted to her face, and the good-hearted crush I brutally rejected; the backseat of a smelly old car parked in a dark hospital garage; the sidewalk—before hanging the sign on the doorknob, locking it from the inside, shutting off the lights, and lying down on the hard tile. I settle in with my arms behind my head, stretching my aching legs out across the floor, the bleach-scented air stinging my nostrils, when I feel my phone start to buzz against my hip.

The light of the screen reflects off the glossy walls, casting the whole room in an eerie blue glow. A restricted caller. At four in the morning. That can't be good news. I'm about to let it go to voicemail when curiosity gets the better of me. Could it be the same person who was trying to reach Cass? I click the talk button, biting hard on my tongue.

"Hello?"

"An inmate at the Baltimore City Detention Center is attempting to contact you," a cheerful robotic voice says. "Please press one to accept the charges."

Mom. But how could she be getting phone privileges in the middle of the night? Don't they have wardens who lock down that kind of thing? I hold my breath and look up at the industrial showerhead bolted into the ceiling. If I'm sleeping at eye level with a toilet, I don't have much left to lose. And every instinct I've had so far has led us further and further astray, so maybe it's time to stop running.

I press one and wait for the telltale click of connection.

"Hi, Mom," I say into the darkness.

SEVENTEEN

Early Sunday Morning, Part 2
Flagstaff, AZ

"What in the *hell* is going on?"

I'm back in the hallway now, making a beeline for the exit to the stairs. Mom has been asking some variation on this question since I picked up, and her voice is steady and strong, not a trace of the junk-sick shakes of a few days ago. Cass and Denny call it her pastor voice, because it goes up and down like a preacher delivering a fiery sermon. She only uses it when she's angry, so I know there's going to be yelling. That's why I had to get out of the bathroom, to someplace with less reverb and fewer witnesses. I might have some yelling of my own to do.

"What do you mean?" I ask, lowering my voice as I push through the heavy metal door. The stairwell is empty and gray, yellow moonlight filtering in through a gated window. Buck's rhyme whips through my head: *Look real quick, it will soon be gone.*

"You tell me," Mom says, indignation seeping through the receiver. "I got dragged out of bed because some *hospital* in *Arizona* called the warden about my daughter." My stomach drops. I remember the intake nurse asking for Mom's contact info, but I was so upset I didn't even think to lie. I didn't have a number, though. I never thought they'd call. "Is it true? Is she in the hospital?" Mom asks, less mad and more scared this time.

I swallow hard. "Yes."

"Oh my God." The receiver drops, and a sharp, metallic clang rings in my ear. Fumbling, then whimpers. "Oh my God, is she okay? What happened?"

"She was hypoglycemic," I say. "She had a seizure."

"Are you skipping meals?" The hyperventilating gives way to irritation again. Mom's temperature rises faster than mercury. "Tell me you're not letting my baby skip meals!"

"No!" I cry, more defensive than I have to be, probably because I know I'm guilty. "No. She . . . gave herself too much insulin." I don't want to have to say what that means out loud, but I don't have to—Mom knows as well as I do that Cass would never slip up by accident. There's a long pause, and when she speaks again, her voice is husky and raw with anger and pain.

"How could you let this happen?"

It's a question I've been asking myself for the past nine hours, raking myself across the coals over and over until it burns, but for some reason now that Mom is asking it I'm filled with rage. How could *I* let this happen? None of it ever would have happened if she hadn't let us all down. I'm not supposed to be in charge, I'm not supposed to have to make these kinds of decisions.

"Excuse me?" I say stonily.

"She's your little sister," Mom says, her voice breaking. "You're supposed to take care of her."

"No, *you're* supposed to take care of her," I spit. "They're *your* kids. I'm your kid. You're supposed to be here for us."

"You're almost eighteen years old, don't act like a child," she says, and I bristle.

"You're almost thirty-four," I shoot back. "Act like a mother."

"You're lucky we're on the phone so I can't smack you. I didn't raise you to talk to me that way."

You hardly raised me at all, I think. Out loud I say, "Right."

"And another thing," she snaps. "We haven't even talked about the fact that you're in Arizona. Why the hell are you way out there? What about school?"

"It's Saturday," I say.

"Don't be a smartass, you know what I mean."

"What does it matter?" I lean my forehead on the bars of the window just as the moon emerges from behind a cluster of clouds. It's waning now. Like everything else.

"It doesn't matter. It doesn't matter if I graduate, I'm not going anywhere. Oh, they're kicking Denny out of his school, too, by the way."

"What?"

"And Cass," I say, a lump forming in my throat. "Cass is getting called all kinds of ugly names. She hates it. She cried when I tried to take her to school last week."

"This is all news to me," Mom says.

"Well, it shouldn't be."

"No." She softens a little. "I guess it shouldn't. But what about your aunt? Didn't you go with her like I told you?"

"Yeah, that didn't work out so well."

Mom sighs heavily. "Michelle, I know she can be hard to take, but she's family."

"She doesn't act like it," I say. "She basically extorted me and threatened to ship us off to CPS!" Mom mumbles some choice curses under her breath. "And guess what?" I cry, gathering steam. "We've been gone since *Wednesday*, and she hasn't even called me once to see what happened. She doesn't care. When are you gonna learn she doesn't care about us?"

A pause. "Why didn't you come to me then?"

"What could you do? From in there? Seriously, Mom." I kick the wall, and paint chips off, scattering on the floor.

"You could've got me out," she says. "We could have gone home, picked up where we left off."

"With you still using?" I ask bitterly. "No thanks."

"That's over," she says. "I'm off it now, Michy. For good this time."

Yeah, right. It's on the tip of my tongue, but I clench my teeth to keep it from slipping out. I might not believe it, but she does. It's all she's got. And I can't take that away, no matter how much I want to hurt her right now.

"Hello?" She sounds annoyed.

"I'm still here."

"So when are you coming back?"

"I don't know."

"When does Cass get out?"

"Depends on when they release her," I say. "They need your consent to give her psychological treatment. For, you know . . ." We mutually and silently acknowledge the ellipsis.

"Our insurance cover that?" she asks.

"I don't know. They haven't kicked us out yet." I attempt a laugh.

"That's not funny. Those heartless sons of bitches will take me to the mat just to avoid paying for a prescription, let alone therapy."

"It's okay, Mom," I say.

"Oh, what, you got the money?" Now she's laughing, the quick *rat-a-tat-tat* giggle that makes her sound like Sweet Sixteen Maddie Means instead of inmate 2247 or whatever her number is this time.

"No," I say, "but maybe I will soon."

"Taco Bell start paying in gold bars?" she laughs, and I'm so pissed off by the mockery that I consider not even telling her. But she's going to find out eventually, so it might as well be now.

I take a deep breath. "The reason we're out here," I say, "is Buck. He's sick, I guess—says he's dying—and he's leaving us some heirloom. That's why we left. We're going to see him, to collect it."

I brace myself for screams and tears, but instead Mom gets quiet. "Well," she finally says. "Something was bound to get him sooner or later."

"It could be good for us, though," I say. "If he saved something. You could finally get what he owes you."

"Oh, honey," she says. "He can't repay me what he owes me. There's no way to get life back."

"But something, at least. We could pawn it, have some cash to get by for a while."

"He's never going to deliver," she says, her voice cooling. "Whatever he says he has for you, don't believe it for a second. It's probably an heirloom tomato. He'll probably end up shaking *you* down for cash. He's a liar, Michelle. Always has been, always will be."

Resentment flares in my belly. "This coming from the person who let him live a neighborhood away for four years and never even told us."

She clicks her tongue. "I was just doing what I thought was best for you girls."

"By not letting us see our father?"

"Please," she cries. "You think he tried to see you and I stopped him? Barred the door? I was trying *not* to let you see who your father really was. And *is.* A coward who runs away the second things get tough, who's too selfish and prideful to look back just in case it makes him feel something for one second of his miserable life."

"Well," I say, "he wants to see us now."

"Of course he does! He's got nobody else. He knew you'd feel bad, that's why he called you. He plays people, that's what he does."

"Why can't you accept that maybe he actually feels sorry?" I yell, my voice echoing off the increasingly claustrophobic-feeling walls. "You know, that's a thing people do sometimes when they screw up their children's lives, apologize?"

She's quiet for a minute. "That's what you want, huh, an apology?"

"Yeah."

"Well, I'm sorry," she says. "I've been sorry every day of my life since I had you. Not because I didn't want you but because I wanted *more* for you. I wanted more than I knew you would get from us." She sniffs loudly. "Believe me, I did my best, but I've been sorry every day. For you and your sister, and Denny. Because no matter how hard I try, I'm never going to be good enough."

Tears spring to my eyes. "But you *were* doing good. What happened?"

"I wish I could tell you, but I can't," she sighs. "Sometimes one bad decision just starts a chain reaction."

I nod, letting the tears spill down my cheeks. The truth is I've never understood how my mother can live the way she does, scrambling and desperate, trying but failing to steady herself again and again. It's maddening to watch someone you love mess up so much, and it's hard to keep loving them. The resentment just grows and grows until it covers up the love like ivy on a wall. But now, after this week, I can see how things can get out of control so fast, even with good intentions. I believe for the first time that my mother really might be trying, in her own way.

"We're gonna get you out, you know," I say. "As soon as we get the money from Buck, we'll come back and get you out, maybe even get you into a good rehab."

"That's sweet, baby," she says. "But don't worry. I called Violetta yesterday, and she has the money to spring me this time. She's a dental assistant now, can you believe it? Clean for five years." I wipe my eyes, trying to picture the rail-thin, gap-toothed woman I remember in any kind of medical environment.

"Violetta is allowed to put sharp tools in people's mouths?" I ask incredulously.

"People change, Michelle," she says.

"Okay then," I counter, "what about that rehab?"

"We can talk about it."

"That's not good enough."

"Baby—"

"I'm not your baby anymore," I say. "And your word's no good this time."

"Okay then," she says wearily. "You're the boss."

I want to tell her that's not the point, that I don't want to be the boss anymore, not of her, not of anyone but myself. I just want my own life, where I can choose where I go and what I do and who I see. I want a life where I don't spend all my time worrying when the sky is going to fall again. She can be in that life, and so can Cass and Denny—maybe even Leah and Tim—but they can't be all of it anymore. She has to let me go.

But instead of saying all that, I decide to let her go. I hang up. And then I sit in the stairwell and cry.

When I get back to the waiting room, Denny and Leah are still sleeping, but Tim is gone.

"If you're looking for your boyfriend, he's looking for you, too," the Mastino lookalike at the desk says with a knowing smile.

"Oh, he's not—" I start to say but then let it go. Explaining would only make things weird.

"He got in the elevator a few minutes ago," she says. "I'd check the lobby."

"Thanks." I stand there, the phone still warm in my hand, sinuses screaming from all of the flooding they've suffered through today. I want to go back and hide in the bathroom till morning, not talk to anyone until I stop feeling so emotional. But maybe that's my problem. Maybe I inherited a little more from Buck than just his eye color and love of action movies. If I run from everything I'm scared of, I'm no better than him. And if I keep pushing Tim away just because the feelings I get when I'm around him make me uncomfortable, I'll never know what it's like to really let someone in—a someone I'm not related to, anyway. Before I can change my mind, I spin around and head back to the stairs, taking them two at a time.

I find him sitting on a bench outside the automatic front doors, under a streetlamp. I thought the Southwest was supposed to be all dry heat and cacti, but it's freezing out, and he's in a flimsy Hanes undershirt. As I get close I can see goose bumps running up and down his arms, which are so tense that muscles I never noticed were there are thrown into relief. Not that I care about that kind of thing.

"Come inside," I say from behind him. "You'll get sick."

He doesn't turn around, but his shoulders visibly relax. "I thought you left," he says.

"Where would I go?" Clutching my arms for warmth, I sit down next to him, and we share a few seconds of awkward silence. For the first time all week, he's starting to show the wear and tear of life off the grid—his hair's sticking up like permanent bedhead, and there are dark circles under his eyes.

"I don't know," he says. "I just got worried. It's a strange city, the middle of the night . . ."

"Thanks," I say. "I'll be okay."

He gives me a look. "Really?"

I let my chin drop to my chest, the weight of everything centering at the top of my spinal cord, curling me in like a snail. "No."

"Well, I have *some* good news," he says. "My dad talked to the cops, and the search is officially off."

"So you called him."

"Yeah." He looks at me with an expression of heartbreaking guilt. "I know you asked me not to, but I didn't know what else to do."

"Did you tell him where we are?" I ask.

"No, not exactly," Tim says. "But I did tell him we were with you and that Cass was in the hospital. I asked him to call off the AMBER alert so that we could focus on getting her better without looking over our shoulders for sirens."

"And?"

"He said yes, on two conditions."

"Which are?"

"That he can wire me some money for food and that he and Karen can come meet us in LA," Tim says. "To take us home on a plane."

I let out a long, shaky breath. Mr. Harper doesn't sound like such a bad guy after all. Just a worried-sick father. A foreign species I have never observed up close. "That sounds fair," I say. "You guys have roughed it long enough."

"No, *all* of us," he says. "That means you, too. And Cass. And Denny."

"But why would they—they don't even know me. If they did, they would know I'm nobody's charity case. They probably hate me anyway."

"They don't hate you," Tim says. "And it's not charity; you're Leah's family. Plus, they know how much you mean to me." He reddens. "I mean, I told them about you."

I pull my legs up to my chest and hug them, pressing my face into the soft denim at the knees, rubbed so thin from months of squatting for condiment packets below the counter at work that they feel ready to split at any second.

"Tim—" I start.

"No, I should say it," he says softly. "The thing is, I care about you. A lot, actually. More than I probably should after just a few days. When this all started, I just wanted Leah to feel better. I had no idea how big it was."

"What?"

"Everything," he says. "The three of you coming together, going to see him. I can actually *see* Leah changing. And I'm changing. I mean, you're changing me." He blushes again. "Not that it's about me, I know I wasn't even invited."

"I need to stop saying that," I say.

"It's true, though." His eyes are full of determination. "Denny and I could stay here in Arizona, for all it matters. If I'm good for anything, it's just to help you and Leah and Cass make it the rest of the way. And I know it wasn't fair for me to try to start something between us when you have so much going on. I won't do it again, and it's okay if you never want to see me again after this, but I just need you to know that—"

"It didn't mean nothing," I say quickly.

"What?"

"On the rock. At the canyon. It didn't mean nothing."

"Oh." He looks completely shocked. "That's . . . not what I was expecting."

"Yeah, well, welcome to the club."

"Come here." He pulls me in for a hug and holds me there until I can hear his heart beating through his T-shirt, a comforting bass line cutting through the stillness.

I press my forehead against his chest. "I just don't know how to do this," I say. "I've never—no one's ever . . ."

"Kissed you?" He tilts my chin up and kisses the tip of my nose.

"Once, but it lasted, like, four seconds."

"Well, believe me, that guy doesn't know what he's missing." He holds my face in his hands as he presses his lips to mine, soft and slightly parted, like he's drinking me in breath by breath, and a feverish buzz starts down in my toes, somersaulting up through my body so fast that I have to break away before I start laughing or weeping, I'm not sure which.

"I'm sorry." I look up to see Tim grinning. This level of vulnerability is new for me. I don't know how people do it; it feels like being bare-ass naked in the freezing snow. It's definitely going to take some getting used to.

"No, *I'm* sorry," he says. "I told you, I can't help it." I smile and rest my head on his shoulder, looking out at the Subway sandwich sign illuminating the parking lot of the shopping center across the street and wondering if it's like this for everyone: miracle moments hiding in plain sight, like fireflies flashing in the dark.

"I've never flown before," I say.

"Once you take off, it's like nothing," he says, squeezing my hand.

"Just hurtling through space."

"But the faster you move, the less you feel it."

"We'd have to leave Goldie."

Tim pulls back slightly and gives me a small, pitying smile. "Do you think she'd even make it back?"

"Maybe. She's gotten us this far. I can't just leave her."

"It's up to you," he says. "But I noticed this morning, she's about to turn over."

"Turn over?"

"Yeah, the odometer. It's almost at a hundred thousand. Just a few dozen miles, and it'll turn over to zeros."

"Oh, right. It's actually the second time that's happened."

"I figured, on a car that old. Do you remember it?"

I shake my head against his ribcage. "It was before I was born." I try to picture Goldie's odometer clicking over to one again. Starting from scratch doesn't sound bad, but there's something a little bit sad about it, too. All those miles, gone, like they never happened in the first place. All that distance traveled and then erased from memory.

"Let's go in," he says, rubbing my arms. "You feel like you're made of ice."

"I don't know," I say as we walk back to the front doors and step on the mat together, sending the automatic panels groaning open. "I think I'm starting to thaw."

EIGHTEEN

Monday Morning to Tuesday Afternoon
Flagstaff, AZ → Kingman, AZ

Cass comes to at seven fifteen the next morning. Thanks to a heads up from Munch, who has apparently forgiven me my trespasses, I've been sitting by her bed since 7:07, waiting. Bracing myself, really. I know I can't predict how she'll react, but I want mine to be the first face she sees. That much I can control, at least.

Her still-closed lids flutter for a while before they finally start to lift. I'm holding her hand again, and as those big, dark eyes come into view, I squeeze, just once. No code, no cop-out, just *I'm here.* She blinks a few times, and I realize I'm holding my breath, hoping she'll say, "What *happened*?" or "Where am I?"—anything that would make it just an accident. But she doesn't, because it wasn't. She looks at me, and then beyond at Dr. Chowdhury and Munch, with a kind of grim acceptance. She glances down at my hand on hers but doesn't move.

"Hey," I say, struggling not to let my smile turn into the ugly-cry grimace it wants to become. "I missed you." Dr. Chowdury has warned me not to bring up the suicide attempt because they're transferring her to pediatric psych at eleven, and he doesn't want Cass to feel ambushed. But now that she's awake, it's actually the last thing I want to talk about. "Are you hungry?" I ask. I'm glad the feeding tube is gone; I hope she never knows it was there.

Cass shakes her head and winces.

"You sustained a minor concussion, Cassidy, so you're likely to have some pain for a few days," Dr. Chowdhury says, crouching down on the opposite side of the bed. "I'll have the nurse bring you some ibuprofen with your breakfast, how does that sound?"

"I'm not hungry," Cass whispers. Her voice is soft, hoarse, and a little slurred.

"You still have to eat," he says gently. "We've been keeping your blood sugar stable with a glucose, lipid, and amino acid solution, but now that you're conscious I think it will be much more pleasant for you to take food orally."

Cass looks at me, her eyebrows slanted down slightly, the way they've done her entire life every time she needs me to reassure her that something is okay.

I nod. "You should eat. The food here's not bad. Denny likes it."

Her cracked lips part in a shadow of a smile that makes my heart leap. "He'll eat anything," she says.

I stay with Cass through her meal of jiggly eggs, an English muffin with strawberry jelly, a bruised banana, and a grade-school-style carton of milk. She doesn't say much, which tempts me to make a joke about how her brain seems undamaged, but I want to keep things light, so instead I just sit there and tell her stupid, mundane details about the past sixteen hours, from describing the nurses' identifying moles and tattoos to the contents of the vending machines. Before she gets carted off for a follow-up MRI, Denny comes in nervously and hands her a get-well card that Leah helped him make, featuring rainbows and shooting stars and a pack of carnivorous dinosaurs.

"I'm framing this one," she says, giving him a weak but affectionate squeeze. I leave her room clinging to that sentence like a life raft. You frame something you're going to keep. Framing means longevity. Framing means she wants to live. I know it's a stretch, and that I'm pinning a hell of a lot of hope on something you can get for $2.50 from a discount craft store, but I don't care. I'll take what I can get.

Tim's dad comes through with a money transfer through Western Union around lunchtime, and we pick it up at a grocery store in the strip mall across the street. Tim won't tell me how much it is—I think he feels guilty—but he says it's enough so that we don't have to siphon any more gas and can eat at restaurants and do our laundry. I feel pretty conflicted until he drives us to a cabin at a nearby campsite that he's put two nights of rent on and that comes with a fridge, microwave, cable TV, and, most importantly, a shower, a bare-bones outdoor stall with a wooden latch door that looks like the bathroom at Versailles, under the circumstances. I dig out some of the stolen bottles of hotel shampoo from my bag, and while the kids attack some take-out burgers on their bunk beds, I stand under that shower for fifteen minutes, gazing up at the sky. I've always thought those instructions on shampoo—*wash, rinse, repeat*—were dumb, because seriously, who needs to repeat? Now I know. I repeat and repeat and repeat until the bottles are empty, and then I turn off the water and scrub myself with a ratty towel until I have what feels like an entirely new layer of skin. I fall into bed still wrapped in the towel and sleep like a brick until four thirty, when Tim wakes me up to let me know we have to get back to the hospital before visiting hours end.

Cabin, hospital, cabin. Wash, rinse, repeat. We do this for forty-eight hours while the doctors watch Cass to monitor her blood sugar and make sure she's not a danger to herself anymore. I stay with her most of the time and let Tim take Leah and Denny out to do normal kid things that ideally don't involve police or paramedics. The doctors tell me she's cooperating but not talking much, which sounds like typical Cass, only I don't know if typical is okay anymore. The doctors don't think so. They're thinking of putting her on an antidepressant but are waiting for Mom to approve the prescription from behind bars. Mostly when I visit we just sit and watch TV and avoid addressing the Grand Canyon–sized elephant in the room.

"How's it going?" I'll ask, and then she'll say, "Okay." She calls her therapist Dr. Zhivago, even though his name is Dr. Zinsser. Snark seems like a good sign, but I know it'll be cold comfort when she's doing her own shots again. She's asked me for her phone a few times, but I keep pretending I can't find it. I don't want anyone to be able to get to her. I'm even thinking she shouldn't come with us to see Buck. Maybe Tim's newfound cash can buy her and Denny some hot dogs and a ride on the carousel at the Santa Monica Pier. Ironically, she might be safer dangling over a boardwalk than in a room with her biological father—from a psychological standpoint, anyway.

Both nights, Tim and I share a bed. It's not premeditated, but there's only a queen and a set of bunk beds. Denny is *all about* the bunk beds, and Leah does not want to share a mattress with anyone, if she can avoid it. We both act like it's no big deal, even though we know it is. We've hardly touched since our frigid bench détente—turns out the combo of a hospital setting and a cabin room with two younger siblings isn't exactly a recipe for torrid romance—and so we ease under the covers like we're playing a game of old-school Operation, trying not to touch any of the wrong parts. But the first morning we wake up hardcore spooning, and on the second morning he wakes me with a sleepy kiss.

"Oh my God, *gross*," Leah groans from her bed, pulling the blanket over her face.

Just like in the movies.

Cass is discharged Tuesday afternoon, thanks to a fax from the Baltimore City Detention Center signed in my mom's jagged scrawl that looks like two *M*s having a fistfight. I bring Cass a freshly laundered hoodie, socks, underwear, and jeans, but she takes hours to emerge, and when she does I see that one of the nurses has braided her hair into thick cornrows. They look good, even if they turn my stomach a little thanks to Erica, and Cass seems to be in an okay mood. She actually high-fives Dr. Zinsser, and when they snip off her hospital bracelet, she gives it to Denny as a present. He loses it in the elevator down to the parking lot, but still, it's the thought that counts.

Dr. Chowdhury leaves me with an awkward demi-hug and a Xerox listing the warning signs for suicidal ideation. "She already knows this," he tells me, "but for the foreseeable future Cassidy should not have access to her insulin. She can continue to give herself the shots, but someone else needs to measure them out and make sure they don't exceed the prescribed dosage. And she needs to be supervised for every injection until you trust her again."

"Got it," I say, but my insides feel like they're eroding. I've been Cass's sister my whole life, so it's a job I've always felt sort of prequalified for. I never thought I could fail at it. Now I'm vibrating at this weird, high frequency, hyperaware of everything I do and say, not to mention everything *she* does and says. Plus, she doesn't know about Tim and me yet, and I feel like that might not go over well. The prospect of going back out on the road again like everything is normal, and like this was just a pit stop, fills me with dread.

But we've made it this far—barely—and so we have to keep going, even though I don't think any of us wants to. There's a vibe of grim determination as we trudge over to Goldie's boxy silhouette in the hospital parking lot. We might be cleaner and better fed, but we've lost any illusions that this is some kind of adventure. It's a mission now, one that almost had a casualty. The cops may not be after us anymore, but I've never felt less safe.

I insist on driving so that I can have something to focus on besides the subtly shifting planes of my sister's face. I'm shamefully relieved when she chooses to sit in the backseat even after I offer her shotgun.

"Nothing's changed," Cass says, which nearly stops my heart until she adds, "Tim's legs are still longer."

For about an hour, no one really says anything. But then Denny comes through with a classic "Are we there yet?" and since they can use their iPhones again without worrying their locations are being tracked, Tim and Leah tag-team mapping a route that will get us to Buck's hospice—the Golden Palms—in six hours and nine minutes, or about eight P.M. Which is, of course, after visiting hours. We'll have to wait until tomorrow morning.

"That'll make it exactly a week since we left," I say. "Almost to the hour."

"It would have been faster to walk," Denny says. I can't tell if he's making a joke.

"Where are we staying tonight?" Leah asks. "Can it have an indoor shower, please?"

"Picky, picky," Tim says, surreptitiously squeezing my leg.

"And no IVs," Cass says. It's her first attempt at levity, and the rest of us don't know how to react. I freeze up, and Leah makes a weird grimace-smile, and Tim chuckles a really fake-sounding chuckle that someone could bottle and use on the laugh track for a bad TV show. Goldie shudders in agreement.

"Done and done," Tim says. "We all could use some decent sleep."

I take the opening. "I was thinking," I say, trying to sound nonchalant, "maybe you and Denny should sleep in tomorrow or do something fun while we deal with Buck."

"Why Denny and me?" Cass asks. "Why not Denny and Tim? They're the ones who aren't related to him." Her voice is calm, but I can tell she's acting, just like me, trying to keep things light while much darker feelings roil just below the surface.

"I know, I just thought . . ." I take a breath and take a leap, deciding to be honest. "You've just been through a lot already this week. I would totally understand if you didn't want to see him on top of it."

In the rearview mirror, I can see Cass purse her lips. "It sounds like you don't want me to go," she says.

"That's not what I said."

She flares her nostrils. "Right."

"Hey," Tim says. "We should play license-plate bingo."

"What's the one with the purple cactus?" Denny asks.

"Arizona," Leah says.

"Arizona!" Denny cries, craning his neck to look out the window. "Arizona . . . Arizona . . . This is boring."

"You can go," I say to Cass. "I want you to go."

"Good," she says. "I'm gonna go. But not because *you* want me to."

"Okay," I say.

"I see a California!" says Tim.

"*Stop*," Leah groans.

"Stop trying to control everything," says Cass.

"I don't try to control everything!" I say.

"Yes you do!" she shouts.

And then there's a kind of metallic wheeze and then another shudder and then nothing. Goldie goes silent, and when I step on the gas, the pedal goes all the way down to the floor with a dull thud.

"No," I say. I watch the needle on the odometer float down to zero as we coast, slowly losing speed. I jam the gearshift back and forth in its base. "No, no, no, no, *no*!"

A tractor-trailer leans on its horn as it screams past on the right; I'm in the middle lane.

"Get over," Tim says, looking out his window. "Get over now." I steer the corpse of the car into the right lane and then onto the shoulder as it slows to a crawl.

"Well, this sucks," Leah says.

"That's the theme of the trip," Cass mumbles.

"Can we just go home?" Denny whines.

I look over at the odometer. It's at 99,998. But then, like the slow rise of a cruel, discreet middle finger meant only for me, it clicks over to 99,999. And stops.

That's when I start to scream.

NINETEEN

Tuesday Afternoon
Kingman, AZ

It tears out of me like it's been waiting in the wings for years, perfectly formed, this long, loud, ragged yell that goes and goes until my vocal chords give out and the muscles in my neck start to shake. I slam my palms against the steering wheel, the thin, hard band digging into my skin, making it sting. Good. I want it to hurt. I hit it again, closefisted this time, and a flare of sharp pain shoots through my knuckles.

"Michelle," Tim says, and I feel his fingers encircle my right wrist, holding it back. But he can't reach the left. I slam it into the steering wheel a few more times, hitting the horn, producing a series of staccato honks. "Michelle, *stop.* You'll just break something."

"What's left to break?" I yell, jerking my hand out of his grasp. I feel a weird, dead calm settling in as the adrenaline drains from my limbs. I'm used to panic. I'm used to the swells of anxiety that turn my breath quick and shallow, that turn my pulse into a surround sound marching band, that dry my throat and dilate my pupils. I've lived with it as long as I can remember—fight or flight, every second of every day. This is different. I just feel . . . done.

"You need to relax," Cass says, looking at me like I'm insane.

"That's easy for you to say." I drop my throbbing hands into my lap. "You don't even know how easy you have it. You don't have to take care of anything or anyone but yourself." The next sentence comes out before I can stop it, a series of bullets at pointblank range: "And you can't even do that." I turn to face her, my voice rising to a shout. "How could you do that to yourself? I'm doing this, *all* of this, for *you*."

Cass's mouth screws up, and she looks away, out the window. There's nothing but mesas and dying brown grass as far as the eye can see. We're in the middle of nowhere, a metaphorical destiny we've finally managed to make literal.

"Stop it," Leah says, putting an arm around a terrified-looking Denny. "It's not about you."

"Oh, what, did she tell you?" I ask angrily. "In the bathroom, when she was stabbing herself with all those needles, did you guys have a bonding moment?" Leah looks like she just got slapped, and Cass starts to cry.

"*Michelle*," Tim snaps, and I feel a wave of guilt, but I'm too worked up to let it go.

"She was *there*," I say, slamming the steering wheel again. "She was right there."

"Don't blame Leah," he says. "That's totally out of line, and you know it."

"I can't take this," I say to no one in particular.

"Why don't you ask her what happened instead of *yelling* at her?" Leah says, leaning forward in her seat, her cheeks getting red.

"Stop fighting!" Denny cries. "Max wants you to stop fighting!"

"Max can shut the hell up," I snap. "And it's none of your business," I say to Leah.

"It is my business!" She shouts. "She's my sister, too!"

Another semi wails by just inches away, making me flinch. In the back, both Denny and Cass are sniffling. I remember when Mom and Buck would fight right here, in these same seats, trading bitter accusations and hurling threats back and forth, screaming at each other to shut up and at me to stop crying. The arguments always died down as quickly as they escalated, but that was almost scarier; it made the whole world seem frighteningly off-kilter, something that could shift under your feet and topple you at any second.

Now I'm passing on that feeling, sowing the seeds my parents gave me, and my anger is immediately replaced by a crushing shame.

"I'm sorry," I say, first to Cass and then to Leah, to Tim, to Denny. "I'm so sorry." I check to make sure I'm not about to get sideswiped by a Mack truck, and then I get out of the car and start to walk along the shoulder. *I give up*, I tell the universe, kicking the guardrail for emphasis. *I'm taking the hint.* Hopefully there's enough cell reception on this stretch of highway for Tim to call his dad and get him to change plans and pick us up here—if any of the Harpers are even willing to associate with me anymore.

"Hey!" I look over my shoulder to see Cass slamming her door shut and starting after me. "Where are you going?"

"Get on the other side of the rail!" I yell as a line of cars shoot past.

"*You* get on the other side."

She has a point. I jump over the low metal fence and into a circle of grass. We're at a bend in the road now, which creates a shallow little meadow for a few yards before the ground swells into a hill. We meet in the center.

"Where are you going?" Cass asks.

"I don't know," I say. Wind from a passing truck whips my curls across my face, and I bat them out of the way.

"Well, wait."

"For what?" I cross my arms. "A cartoon anvil to drop out of the sky?"

Cass shoves her hands in the pockets of her hoodie. "For me."

"You think I would leave you? Now?" I cry. "I would *never* leave you behind. You're all I've got, Cass. That's why when you—" I have to close my eyes for a few seconds and will the tears away. When I open them again, Cass is wet-eyed, too. "I've never been that scared," I say.

"Me neither." She always looks small in her oversize clothes, but right now I can see back a decade, to the little girl clinging to her mother's legs, squeezing her brown eyes tight, trying not to be seen. "And I'm sorry," she says. "I did think about you. And Denny. It just . . . wasn't enough." I know she doesn't mean that to sting, and I try not to show that it does. I sit down in the grass and lean back on my elbows. If I tilt my chin up I can't see the road, and with the sun beating down on my face it almost feels like I'm back in our yard. When it gets really brutal in the summer, we all set up back there on towels, even Mom sometimes. The crabapple is somehow still alive, so we have to clear away the rotten fruit first, but all we really need is some lemonade and a radio to make a day of it.

"Can you tell me why?" I ask. Cass drops down next to me, and a little black zippered case I didn't notice she was holding falls to the ground between her knees. It's the new insulin kit from the hospital. I made Tim hide it in the glove compartment. She catches me looking at it and blanches.

"I was bringing it so you could . . ." She picks up the case and lobs it at me like a live grenade. "I wasn't going to . . ."

"Do you want to, though?" I ask. "Still?"

"I mean, not right this minute," Cass says. "I feel a little better."

"Good." I turn the case over in my hands. She'll still have to do shots for the rest of her life. I wonder if she'll think about it every single time. I know I will.

"It wasn't one specific thing," she says after a minute. "It was a lot of stuff."

"Mom," I say.

"That didn't help."

"No, I was going to say I talked to her. A few days ago."

Cass frowns and chews on her lower lip. "Was she mad?"

"No," I say. "She was just scared and sad. Kind of all over the place, like normal." When Cass won't meet my eyes, I put my hand on her knee and shake it gently. "She's mad at *me*, and Buck. But not you. Nobody's mad at you."

She gets quiet for a minute and drops her elbows to her knees, then her chin to her elbows, folding in like one of those Jacob's ladder toys. We have one at home that Mom got from church as a kid. Apparently they were allowed to play with them at Sunday school because of the biblical reference, but there's not much you can do with a staircase to heaven that doesn't actually go anywhere.

"It's one thing to not have Buck. Or even Mom sometimes. But if we got split up . . ." She shakes her head, picking at the grass.

"That's not going to happen," I say. "If Mom slips up again, I'll file for custody myself."

Cass looks up at me, surprised and a little bit suspicious. "But then you'd be stuck with us. Like, for life."

I'll admit, I haven't thought the legal guardian thing through yet—and I hope I never have to. But after this week, staying in Baltimore for a few more years doesn't sound so bad anymore. Seeing some of the rest of the country has been cool, but no place has felt quite like home. Just call me Dorothy Gale, I guess.

"I'm already stuck with you for life," I say to Cass. "You'll never get rid of me."

"What about school, though?"

"I can take night classes or put it off for a year or two." If I take that assistant manager gig—if Yvonne will still give it to me—I could probably pay my way through the University of Maryland without too much aid. They have a great law school, actually. I could up and do a one-eighty on the family business. Who knows? "And I'm serious about getting you into a new school, too," I say. "If you want."

"Maybe," Cass says. "It's not going so great."

"I know." I take a breath, trying to tread carefully. "While you were in the hospital . . . I read some of your texts."

"Oh." She doesn't look angry, exactly. More hurt.

"I'm really sorry, I was just so worried."

Cass blinks nervously. "It's okay."

"So . . . you and Erica aren't talking anymore?" I ask gently.

"Nope."

"That sucks."

"Yeah."

"Do you want to talk about it?"

"There's not much to talk about," Cass says with a far-off look. "I liked her, and she didn't like me. Not in the same way, anyway." She lets out a shaky breath. "I'm glad you know," she says. "It's kind of a relief."

"I love you no matter what," I say. "And someday I know you'll meet someone who loves you like I do, for exactly who you are. Don't settle for anything less."

Cass nods, but there's a vacant, sort of despairing look on her face. I recognize it—it's the same feeling I get whenever I think about falling in love. Because what if he wants to get married someday? Love is one thing, but marriage is something else completely, something murkier and infinitely more frightening. Marriage, to us, means Madison and Buck. It means an electrical storm that burns everything in its path.

"I'm scared to see him," Cass says, as if reading my mind. "I don't remember him at all. Not a smell, not a mental picture, nothing."

"It's probably for the best," I say.

"Not for me." Her brows knit together, pain flashing in her eyes. "I'm jealous you knew him. I don't want to be, but I am. It's always been like he's *your* dad, not mine."

"He's just as much yours . . ." I say, trailing off, the modifier *unfortunately* dangling on my lips. I'm not sure where Cass is going with this, and I don't want to say the wrong thing. She's opening up more now than she has in years.

"But I got used to it with you," she says. "And it was just our ages, it wasn't like he *chose* you." Her eyes well up, and she covers them with her fists. And then I realize what she means.

"Leah," I say.

"He was already cheating," Cass says, choking out the words, gasping for breath in between. "He could have just kept doing that. She was already born. It wasn't until *me* that he left."

"No," I say, putting a hand on her back. I'm tentative at first, bracing for her to shrug me off, but the resistance never comes. I fold her into my arms like when we were young and she would hop into my lap for stories. "It wasn't you," I murmur into her cheek.

"Then what?"

"He's just a piece of shit, Cass. I wish there was a reason that would make it make sense, but there isn't. *He's* the reason. He makes bad decisions and hurts people. That's why we don't have a dad. Not because of you. And not because of Leah."

Slowly, my sister's sobs get quieter, punctuated by loud sniffing and nose wiping.

"The worst part," Cass finally says, "is I kind of like her."

"Yeah," I say. "Me too." The whine of an airplane fills the sky overhead. If the Harpers come through on their promise, we'll be on one in a matter of days. Our first time flying. I haven't even had a chance to wonder if it scares me. Life on the ground has been scary enough.

We sit side by side looking out at the cars for a while, and then Cass lifts up the bottom of her sweatshirt. "It's time," she says. "Will you do it?"

I unzip the black case and take out the bottle of cloudy medicine, rolling it between my palms. "It's been forever," I say. I tear open an alcohol wipe and clean my fingers, then use it to swab Cass's side—what would be a love handle if she had any fat on her.

"I liked when you did it," she says. "You'd do the funny voices and everything."

I take the cap off a needle and pull back the plunger to fill it with air to the right dosage line. It's true, I used to make the needles talk, pretending they just wanted to give Cass a kiss, unaware of their own sharpness. It made her laugh, at least until the actual puncture.

"So, is it true about you and Tim?" she asks as I insert the needle into the bottle and turn it upside down. I give her a look. "Denny told me," she says. "He said you were hugging a lot."

"I don't know if there is a me and Tim," I sigh, filling up the syringe. "It's weird. He's my half sister's brother."

"*Step*brother."

"Still, it's not exactly a story I'd want to tell my grandkids."

She doesn't even wince at the injection. "I think he's nice," she says, with the needle still in. "He sat with me awhile the other day. He taught me how to harmonize."

As I pull it out she starts to sing, "*Michelle, ma belle . . .*"

"Shut up," I laugh.

"Nah, but seriously, he's crushing hard."

"Whatever."

I'm putting everything back in the kit as Leah rounds the bend in the highway, my two-sizes-too-big jeans hanging low on her hips.

"Hey," she calls, stepping gingerly over the guardrail. "Tim just wanted me to tell you that he found a bus we can take the rest of the way—oh, sorry!" Her face gets weird, and I realize I'm still holding the needle.

"It's over, don't worry," I say. "We're just doing some sisterly bonding."

"Well, just come back to the car when you're done then," Leah says with an embarrassed wave.

"You can stay," Cass mutters.

Leah freezes in place for a few seconds like she's not sure whether to call the bluff, if it even is one. But then she swallows a smile and sits down across from us, self-consciously tucking her hair behind her ears.

"So, the bus leaves tonight," she says. "The station's just a mile from here, according to Google Maps, so we can hitch or even walk. We would get to LA first thing in the morning . . . if you want to keep going."

If we want to keep going. It's weird to hear it like that. So far it hasn't felt like a choice.

"I know you're only here because of me," Leah continues. "I mean, because I got that call from Dad." Cass and I exchange a look—*Dad*. It's such a foreign word to associate with him. A father is biological; a dad is something else entirely. "And even though part of me wants to see him before he's gone, I won't do it if it'll hurt you," Leah says. "*Either* of you." I look over at Cass, asking her for permission this time.

"He told you we moved away, right?" she asks Leah, who nods, wincing slightly at the memory. "Then I know it's petty, but I kind of *want* him to see us together. To know he couldn't keep us apart."

"Yeah," Leah says, fixing us with a look so fierce I'd swear she had some Means blood in her, too. "That he couldn't break us."

"Okay then," I say. "I guess we better go catch that bus."

I look into both of my sisters' eyes and realize we're all thinking the exact same thing right now:

We could take him.

Back at the car, Denny is busy scratching the letters R.I.P. onto Goldie's hood with the four-color pen.

"I hope it's cool," Tim says sheepishly. "He was pretty adamant."

"Sure." I run my finger along one of her more impressive dents. "She deserves an epitaph."

"You know, we don't have to leave her," Tim says. "We could call a tow. Maybe it's fixable." Even he doesn't sound convinced, but it's sweet that he's trying.

"That'd cost a lot of money, plus, what are we gonna do, swing back through on the way home?" I shake my head. "She's gone." Tim looks more upset than I would expect.

"I'm sorry I was mean to her," Leah says, staring over Denny's shoulder like she's at an open-casket wake.

"It's okay, she'll just haunt your dreams," Cass jokes. "You'll be about to make out with Justin Bieber, and then you'll realize you're in the backseat sitting on a bag of Funyuns."

"She did us proud, though," I say. "We couldn't have made it without her."

We pack as much as we can fit into our backpacks, and the stuff we can't take I arrange into a little shrine in the trunk: Mom's cassette tapes, the siphon pump and sock wrench, some rags made out of ripped-up T-shirts, two crushed packets of ramen noodles.

"Why don't I find a junkyard that can come and get her?" Tim asks.

"I just don't want to wait for them to come," I say. "I don't want to see her get dragged off."

"Max can wait," Denny says.

"If we leave, though, that means Max gets left behind. For good." I try to sound sad instead of hopeful, but it's hard when Cass and Leah are struggling not to laugh.

"I know, *duh*." Denny rolls his eyes.

"So . . . you're okay with that?"

"Yeah," Denny says. "Tim says when I get scared, I can talk to real people. Plus, I have a picture of him at home I can look at if I miss him."

"A picture?" Cass asks skeptically.

"Mom has it in her room," Denny says, "on the dresser." Mom's clothes are usually strewn around like a tornado hit, pooled on the floor, hanging on chair arms and doorknobs, piled on the bed. I don't know if I can even remember what the dresser looks like under all of the crap she's got stacked on it. But I know the photo Denny's talking about. In it, a man is sitting on a stoop, smoking a cigarette and giving the camera a mischievous grin, exposing his dimples. His dark hair is shaggy and hangs in his eyes. He's wearing a white undershirt, jeans, and Converse sneakers. In the picture he looks like he could be any bad-boy flirt at any high school, the kind you can't stop thinking about even though you know he'd hurt you if you ever let him in. He could be anyone, but he's not. He's my father. All this time Denny's been making imaginary friends with Buck. No wonder I never liked him.

"I think you're right," I say, laying a hand on his shoulder. "I think it's time to let Max go."

We take one last look and then file onto the shoulder, walking away from the car, one by one, in silence.

TWENTY

Tuesday Night/Wednesday Morning
Kingman, AZ → Los Angeles, CA

The bus ride goes by in a blur. It's pitch black outside by the time we leave, and the sun comes up just as we're entering the Los Angeles city limits, the downtown skyscrapers encased in a haze of majestic-looking smog. I sleep in fitful spurts, each time dreaming I'm walking into the hospice center for the first time. In one dream, Buck is sitting at the front desk, beaming, looking healthy but dressed in a paper gown. *I just wanted to see you*, he says. *Don't be mad at me, baby.* In another, he's suddenly wizened and elderly, unconscious in a bed with Dr. Chowdhury standing over him. *We've been able to pick up activity in most of the major areas of concern*, the doctor says and then turns on a shower that begins to flood the room. In the last one, Bucks's gone missing. *He was just here*, a nurse says. *Would you like to wait?* And in the dream, even though I know he isn't coming back, I sit down on a plastic folding chair and put my hands over my eyes. I wake up from all of them relieved at first and then filled with empty dread.

Tim sits with Denny, who almost immediately passes out on him, but a few times he reaches over and grabs my hand from across the aisle. Once we both fall asleep that way, and a woman has to wake us up so she can get back to the bathroom. Cass and Leah sit behind me, but I hardly hear them exchange a single word, and when I look back I see them dozing, the ear buds from a shared set of headphones making a Y between their heads. The thought occurs to me somewhere in the midst of the Mojave Desert that maybe it's not the destination *or* the journey that matters in the end, but rather who's there to help you haul your baggage around. The five of us have gone from distrustful strangers to something approaching a family in less than a week. Tim and I have gone from fast-food nemeses to something approaching a couple.

There's a fear, too, of course, that goes beyond whatever we'll find when we really do get to the hospice. Tim's dad and Leah's mom are flying into LAX in the afternoon. We're supposed to meet them at the airport for a seven P.M. flight back to Baltimore. I'm worried about what they'll think of us—or what they think of us already. I don't know how they expect me to act with Tim. How much has he told them? And what's going to happen when we get back home? Will we really try to be together? Will I step beyond that white picket fence for family dinners? Will he climb our cracked front stoop for study sessions? Or will he gradually recede back into the ether, like one of my tidal waves—only one I don't want to ever end?

These questions are still knocking around in my burned-out brain as we step off the bus into a perfect, dry 72-degree breeze that makes me briefly consider never going home at all.

"Look, a palm tree!" Denny says excitedly. We're standing in a back alley surrounded by squat little clusters of buildings the same color as Goldie's anemic paint job, but he's right—the palm trees overhead lend the bus-stop landscape an exotic, even glamorous feel.

"Finally," Leah grins, stretching her arms over her head. "I love California weather!" She throws her arms around Tim's shoulders. "Can we move here?"

"You've been here?" I ask.

"Just for Disneyland," she says, and I make a slashing motion across my neck. If Denny hears we're anywhere close to the Happiest Place on Earth, we will hear about nothing else for the rest of the day.

"So I guess we just . . . go now?" Cass asks, slinging her backpack onto one shoulder. Except for Denny, who's busy tossing a stick at a stop sign, we all look at each other, waiting for someone to find a reason to stall. But there is none. We made it. This is what we came for. My stomach lurches in the same way it did the time my seventh-grade class took a field trip to a Six Flags knockoff called Adventure Park and I got on the roller coaster only to change my mind at the last second—that *nevermind!* nervous system double-back that's probably a Darwinian adaptation designed to save us from our own dumb decisions.

"You ready?" Tim asks and reaches out for my hand, weaving his fingers through mine. I squeeze, hard.

"No comment."

"You'll feel better in the cab," he says.

But I don't feel better in the cab. In addition to my churning insides, there's a bad feeling I just can't shake. It's not panic or fear, exactly, it's just the sensation that something is wrong, something I can't pinpoint. I tell myself that maybe it's riding in a car that's not Goldie, a compact Prius taxi with smooth, clean seats and no food smells. Or being so far from home now that Mom is out of jail, on her own with no one to keep her in check. I take deep breaths and try to calm my nerves. I want to be clear-headed when I see Buck. I need to be able to tell him what I have to say, exactly the way I've been practicing all these years.

When we pull up to the Golden Palms just after eight, the feeling in my gut is justified: Something is very wrong. In fact, I'm so convinced the driver has the wrong address I make him circle the block twice. In my mind, and in the dreams, it was a sprawling, free-standing complex that was set back from the road like Tim and Leah's school and surrounded by meaningfully manicured trees to look like swans or something. There might even have been a fountain or a koi pond. Palm trees, definitely. It would have an air of serenity and almost unbearable gravitas. What I did not picture was a crappy plastic sign in one of eight slots on a two-story medical plaza sandwiched between a liquor store and a car wash. It's a strip mall. My father is dying in a strip mall. And as much ill as I've wished on Buck over the years, I would never wish for that.

"This is more depressing than I pictured," Leah says, taking in the colorless stucco, the neon sign for the nail salon (with only the *N* unlit, turning into the cruelly accurate ail salon), the family dental practice, and the two homeless men slumped against opposite sides of one of the concrete columns separating the parking lot from the stores.

"Damn," Cass whispers.

"Can we get doughnuts first?" Denny asks.

"After," I say. And I intend to keep that promise. After whatever awaits us, I am going to face-plant into a plateful of simple carbohydrates like it's my job.

I lead the way across the parking lot, into the shady, faintly urine-scented stairwell, and up to the second level, my adrenaline pumping so hard I feel a little woozy. This is not a dream. I'm about to walk in and face the reality of Buck. He won't be a scapegoat specter I can design in my head to my desired specifications; he'll be right there, in front of me, an absolute truth of bones and flesh who will say things and do things I can't control. Twenty feet now. Fifteen. Ten. There are double doors covered with screens from the inside, glowing an opaque yellow, golden on one door, palms on the other. *Palliative care . . . from people who care!* in smaller script below. Taped above the doorknob is a hand-lettered sign that reads *Please ring bell.* Without looking back at the others, I put my finger on the button and push.

A few seconds later, there's a sharp buzzing sound, and I pull the door open, misjudging its weight so I end up stumbling back into Cass. Inside, it looks like a normal doctor's office waiting room, with chairs and wall-mounted racks of magazines and a conspicuous restroom right next to the main desk where people get sent to pee in cups. The only things that make it weird are the strong odor of dying flowers and the prominently displayed funeral brochures. I walk up to the desk with Tim and my siblings trailing behind me. The woman sitting behind it looks a lot like Aunt Sam. She looks up at us with a tight smile, and I get that bad feeling again.

"Quite a crew for first thing in the morning," she says. "Are you on the list?"

"The list?" My heart drops.

"Yes, each patient has a list of visitors. You have to have been requested. We can't be too careful, especially in this neighborhood. Hence the buzzer." She gestures to a small monitor on her desk, a black-and-white video feed of the balcony we came in from.

"We're here to see our father, so . . . I think we should be on it," I say.

"And your father is?" She blinks up at me.

"Buck Devereaux." I'm expecting her to flip through papers, so I'm taken aback when she stays frozen in place, her mouth falling open slightly, confusion in her eyes. "Or Allen," I say quickly. "It could be under Allen, that's his first name."

"No, sweetheart," she says, and the sudden change in tone of her voice and manner tells me immediately what's really wrong, what I knew was wrong since I stepped off the bus. The blood rushes to my head so fast I can hardly hear the words as she says them out loud. "I know who your father is, honey. It's just—I'm sorry to be the one to tell you this, but Buck Devereaux passed away last night."

The first feeling is shock, plain and simple, like getting body-checked from a blind spot. Buck is already dead. We're too late. This realization knocks the wind out of me. But once its meaning sinks in, there's a wave of relief that dovetails with a swell of anger and then something else, a kind of bitter, throbbing sadness—is that grief? It all happens in the span of a few seconds, as the nurse looks up at me with naked pity. *What kind of daughter doesn't know her father is dead*, she must be thinking. I want to explain, but I can't form the words. So I just say, "Oh." I look back at the others. Cass is stone-faced, but Leah's face is threatening to crumple, the muscles around her mouth trembling as she tries to control them. Tim, who just looks worried, puts his arms around both of the girls. Denny takes my hand and looks up at me.

"Dad is dead?" he asks. "But I really wanted to meet him."

Me too, kid, I think.

"We didn't have any next of kin," the nurse says apologetically, "or we would have called. The only person who's been to see him is his girlfriend. She's coming in to pick up his personal effects."

Personal effects. That's a good name for what we are. The effects of his miserable existence. I suddenly have a strong urge to see his body. I always look away when they show dead people on the crime shows Cass loves, but I'm afraid if I don't see Buck I'll always wonder if this wasn't just one last way to avoid us.

"Is he—" I try to keep my voice steady. "Is he still here?"

"No, the funeral home came and got him," she says apologetically. "I can give you the number."

I nod, and she pulls a business card from a drawer. All Faith's Funeral Home. Next to the address there's a cheesy picture of an orchid lit by a celestial beam. I'm sliding it into my back pocket when the doorbell rings, a loud, almost cartoonish *ding-dong!* I can see a woman standing outside on the monitor screen, with messy black hair and big sunglasses.

"That's Carly, his girlfriend," the nurse says, pressing the buzzer, and we all turn to brace ourselves as the last guest to our sad little party arrives.

Carly is small and skinny, swimming in cutoff shorts and a tank top with a big pair of red lips silk-screened on the front. She's wearing flip-flops, and her toenails have chipped green polish. From her body I'd guess she was in her twenties, but when she pushes up her sunglasses, her face is sun-damaged and kind of puckered, probably more like forty-five. She's got watery blue eyes and eyebrows drawn in with pencil. If she's not a junkie now, then she's definitely had a past—you can tell just by looking at her.

"So you made it," she says, giving us the once-over, looking totally unfazed by our color spectrum and various stages of dishevelment. Her voice has a pack-a-day smoker's rasp. "You missed him, but he wasn't awake much for the past week anyway. Probably just as well." She walks past us to the front desk and leans her elbows on the counter. "You got a box for me, Gina?"

I didn't even know Carly existed two minutes ago, so maybe it's unfair to have any expectations, but I'm instantly thrown by how casual she is, as if she picks up the effects of newly deceased boyfriends in front of their bands of estranged children every other week or something.

"We made it," I say. "Barely." But Carly either doesn't hear or chooses not to respond. Cass makes a *WTF?* face at me, while Leah shoots daggers into Carly's back.

The nurse—Gina, I guess—bends down, reemerging with a shoebox a minute later, marked on one side with *Devereaux* in black Sharpie. It's not even a large shoebox, either. It looks like the kind sandals might come in.

"Thanks," Carly says and then turns back to us. "You guys want any of it?"

"What's in it?" Denny asks.

"Probably just a bunch of crap, little man." She puts her hand on Denny's head, and I jerk him back, but she doesn't seem to notice. "He promised me a ring, but he didn't get to that. Bought himself a used car, though. Typical." She sounds more pissed off than sad.

"What did he die of?" Leah asks. She's more composed now, but her nostrils are still flaring.

"Well, he had hep C," Carly says. "But so do I. The difference is, he kept drinking. I told him he had to quit, but he couldn't. So his liver went. And once the liver goes . . ." She shakes her head and looks down at the shoebox. She takes off the lid, revealing a beat-up brown wallet, some car keys, a pair of aviator sunglasses, and a half-full pack of cigarettes. She puts the cigarettes and the car keys in her purse and then looks through the wallet for bills, finding none.

"Can I see that?" I ask. Carly shrugs and hands it to me, and I pull out Buck's driver's license from behind a scratched plastic window. The photo's not too sharp, but he looks pretty much the same as I remember him. Longish hair, handsome face, maybe a little thinner in the cheeks. There's an address listed for Venice Boulevard. "Does he have an apartment?" I ask.

"Please, that man had no credit," Carly says. "That's an old girlfriend's place where he used to get mail. Since we hooked up, he's been staying with me." Drinking, bouncing from place to place, making promises he couldn't keep—it seems like

Buck didn't change much. The thought is both depressing and oddly comforting.

"I'm Michelle," I say, realizing I haven't introduced myself. Not that she seems to have been wondering.

"Nice to meet you, honey," she says, extending a bony hand. "You look like him. All three of you girls." She smiles at Tim. "You, not so much, but you're a cutie like Buck. Just don't be a jerk like him, okay?"

"I won't," Tim says and puts a hand on the small of my back.

"Buck called," I say, glancing at Leah. "He said he had something for us. Did he leave a will or anything?"

"There's nothing but a lot of debt that I know of," Carly sighs. "Luckily his mother's taking care of that. She's living large out in Utah someplace. Stopped giving him any money a while back, though." She frowns into the box. "Unless you count paying for the funeral."

"What about the car?" I ask.

"He left that to me," she says a little sharply, closing the shoebox with a possessive thump. "It was one of the last things he said." She laughs bitterly. "It figures he'd spend his last living minutes yakking about a stupid car."

I turn back to Leah and Tim. "He didn't say anything about what it was?" I ask. Leah bites her lip and shakes her head, and Tim frowns apologetically. "It was an heirloom," I say to Carly. "Something from his family, maybe?" Hearing that "Grandma" Polly got rich gives me a sliver of hope. Maybe there was a piece of jewelry she gave him specifically for us. Maybe he didn't tell Carly because he knew she'd try to cheat us.

"*Oh*," she says, smacking her thigh. "Of course. I remember now. There's another car somewhere, one he got from his dad. That one's yours. Hope it's worth something."

A hysterical giggle rips out of my throat. Goldie. The "heirloom" he left for us was Goldie. I don't know what's worse, that she's as dead as Buck is or that he had the nerve to leave us a piece of property that he already left behind eleven years ago and that we already owned by default.

"You okay?" Carly asks, and I nod mutely. I look back and see Cass and Leah whispering furiously. "Well," she says, standing up, clutching her worthless box. "I have to get to work. The funeral's Friday, if you're sticking around. All of his Venice Beach buddies are coming. It's gonna be a good time, just like Buck would have wanted." Her eyes are watery and unfocused, and for a second I'm afraid she'll burst into tears. But instead she just blinks a few times, gives us a limp wave, and bangs the door open with one bony hip. It slams shut behind her with a brittle clap.

"*Wow*," Cass says.

"Who was that lady?" Denny asks.

"No one," Leah says, clenching her jaw. Her eyes flash. "So that's it?" she asks, looking back and forth between Cass and me. "That's all we came for?" She sits down hard on a chair and bursts into tears.

"Hey." I crouch down and rest my hands on her knees. It's kind of a relief to be able to snap into comforting mode instead of dealing with my own feelings, which still are shifting kaleidoscopically from guilt to disappointment to anger and back again. "I know it's not what we wanted, but if we had never come, we'd always wonder." I look up at Cass; this is meant for her, too. "And now we know."

"It just seems so unfair," Leah cries.

"That's because it is." It's all unfair: what Buck did to us, what happened to Mom, the fact that we traveled this far, sacrificing so much, only for Buck to peace out for good while we sat on a Greyhound bus just hours away, leaving us with nothing but a broken-down car full of bad memories. There's nothing that's ever going to make that fair. I try to think of something to say to soften the blow, but instead I find a lump forming in my throat. "Excuse me," I whisper and make a break for the bathroom. I know I need to stop crying in them—it's so pathetic and clichéd. But in order to break down I need a closed door, and that's the only one I see.

It's the size of a small closet, painted a buttery yellow, with one of those fans that turns on when you flip the light switch so it feels like you're emptying your bladder under a low-flying helicopter. But I'm grateful for the white noise. It pulls double duty, drowning out both my tears and the voices outside.

I don't know what to think about any of it. I think I'm still in shock that Buck's gone, not just gone like I'm used to, but *gone* gone. I thought it would feel more freeing. Isn't that what I told Cass back in the tent however many nights ago? That it would be a blessing? It doesn't feel like a blessing; I don't think any death can be a true blessing, even if the person was horrible. And now that he's gone, I won't ever know firsthand if he was so horrible.

So much of my hatred is rooted in what Buck *wasn't*, not what he was. He was selfish and unreliable, a bad husband and a bad father and a bad boyfriend till his dying day, if I take Carly's word for it. But I'll never know any of his redeeming qualities, beyond being able to make a five-year-old girl laugh until her sides hurt, when he was in a good mood. I'm kidding myself if I try to pretend like I wasn't hoping I'd get here to find him changed, and maybe we could have connected, and I could have walked away knowing something—*anything*—about my father besides the fact that he left us.

I tear off a long sheet of toilet paper and blow my nose. It's weird, but I feel a lot sadder about not getting to see Buck than I do about not getting any money from him. The truth is, I stopped really caring about the supposed heirloom when Cass got sick. I guess that's when I realized we had more important things to worry about than money. And maybe, deep down, I knew the whole time that it would end up being nothing, just the last in an endless string of disappointments.

I peel myself off the toilet and move to wash my hands, which is when I see it.

There, on the sink, wedged between the hot-water faucet and a container of antibacterial wipes, is a small cylindrical soap dispenser. And inside the clear plastic, amid a viscous, cloudy sea dotted with air bubbles, floats a miniature Christmas tree. The secret icon I've coveted all these years of some perfect, unattainable life is here, in what has got to be in the running for one of the saddest places on earth. The fact that it's four months past New Year's is almost beside the point.

I slowly depress the nozzle and let the soap pool in my open palm. Maybe no one's life is what it looks like from the outside. Maybe Mom's right, and if we all threw our problems in the air and saw everyone else's, I'd grasp for mine (well, mine or Ivanka Trump's). Whatever this sad bottle of soap means—if it is a sign from the universe and not just a sign that there was a recent local discount on out-of-season cleaning products—I need to stop wishing for an easier life, because no one's going to hand it to me. I just have to suck it up and work with what I've got.

When I come back out, what I've got—all four of them—are waiting patiently, sitting in a row.

"Did you fall in?" Denny asks with a smirk.

"No," I say. "But I think I just successfully removed my head from my ass." I sit down across from Cass and rest my elbows on my knees. "I'm sorry this has been so hard," I say. "And I'm sorry for making all of you come so far for nothing."

"It wasn't nothing," Cass says. She takes Leah's hand.

"Nope, not nothing," Leah says, taking Denny's.

"I got a cool pen," Denny says, holding it up. We all bust out laughing, and Denny joins in.

As we file out the door, I double back to the desk to thank Gina. "Sorry about all the histrionics," I say. "It's been a long week."

"Believe me, I've seen worse." She cocks her head and studies my face. "You do look like him," she says. "But if you don't mind my asking, where are the other two?"

"Cass and Leah?" I ask, confused. "They're right over there."

"No, Madison and Karen," she says. "He had the names all in a strip down his left side. Used to tell me, 'These are all my girls.'"

"Oh, right," I say, like I knew all along I was in his skin, that we all were, side by side, a tribe of survivors. I back away from the desk and give her a shrug. "They couldn't make it."

I push through the door to find Tim leaning against the railing, the searing California sun turning him into a human hologram. Denny's voice echoes in the stairwell—he's singing "Michelle" now, too. Soon we can form a band.

"Are you okay?" Tim asks. "That was intense, to say the least."

"I think so," I say. Although I have no way of knowing, really; right now my feelings are bobbing over my head like untethered balloons. It's all so surreal.

"Is there anything I can do?"

"Just . . . keep being a good person," I say, taking his hand and threading my fingers through his. "Open doors for old ladies. Lower your carbon footprint. Always tell the truth. That kind of thing."

Tim nods solemnly. "Okay," he says. "Then I should probably tell you, I'm falling in love with you."

I close my eyes, not sure what to think. I'm still aching from the shock of losing Buck—or the idea of him, anyway—before I even had him, and now there's a sudden swell of euphoria crashing up against the pain, hitting all the keys in my heart at the same time, like a cat running across a piano. I start to get anxious, bracing for the tidal wave, but then I open my eyes and look at Tim and realize that I don't have to just wait for it to hit me this time. I have another option I've never considered. I can dive in.

"Me too," I say. Tim grins, and we both lean forward, two atoms succumbing slowly to an electromagnetic force.

"Are you gonna kiss again?" Denny's yell is punctuated by barely concealed giggling, and Tim and I leap back, hanging our heads to conceal our self-conscious smiles.

"I don't know," he says, letting his fingertips brush mine as we make our way to the stairs. "I think we can find someplace more romantic, don't you?"

"Definitely," I say.

TWENTY-ONE

Wednesday Night
Los Angeles, CA → Baltimore, MD → ?

"Please direct your attention to the front of the cabin for a safety demonstration."

There's shuffling throughout the plane as a flight attendant with thick foundation and a bad case of bitchy resting face steps out into the aisle and begins miming buckling a seatbelt.

"Do they do this every time?" I whisper to Tim, who's sitting to my left, in the middle seat between Denny and me.

"Yup, there's even a video." He points to the tiny screen on the back of the seat in front of me, where actors are inflating life vests and jumping onto emergency slides with the calm, blank faces of people who've recently been given heavy doses of sedatives.

"If this plane goes down, I will kill you," I say, only half joking. I was all right until we got into the twisting, narrow jetway that led us from the terminal to the plane. Then I started feeling like Alice falling down the rabbit hole, my old, familiar panic winding around my ribcage and pulling tight. But Tim's been explaining everything—every ding and snap and a terrifying whooshing sound like we're about to be sucked through a wind tunnel to our untimely deaths (which apparently is just the flush of a chemical toilet). It also doesn't hurt that Denny thinks the inside of an airplane is the coolest thing he's ever seen and has been painstakingly illustrating a replica of our Boeing 737 ever since one of the flight crew brought him up to meet the pilot.

"Relax, everything's going to be fine," Tim says. He means the plane. As for everything else, that's a big ellipsis with no end in sight. But I feel ready to take it one day at a time. We land in Baltimore at ten P.M., which means first it's back home for a reunion with Mom and then back to school tomorrow to beg for makeup tests and extra-credit projects so I can finish out the semester without my grades tanking. After that it's time to run for the border to ask Yvonne for my job back. I'll need all the income I can get, since we're now without a reliable mode of transportation—although Mr. Harper did mention he has an old Volvo from the mid-'80s rusting in his spare garage and that if Tim and I can get it running, I can have it. I told him it's a deal, except I want to do it with Leah as my co-mechanic. Just the old two-long-lost-sister-princesses-fixing-a-car story, you know how it goes.

The Harpers seem great so far. They bought us dinner at the airport and listened to (an abridged version of) our story and managed to be warm and open even when they were clearly pissed. They weren't mad at any one of us individually, just understandably freaked out by the whole thing. Tim's not allowed to drive without an escort until he graduates, and Tim and Leah are both grounded until their parents can devise what they called "a more original punishment." But Tim and Leah didn't even seem upset. When they all got reunited in front of the JetBlue ticket desk, everyone cried a little bit, even Cass. Tim says he didn't, but I know what I saw.

Up front, the flight attendant demonstrates how to use a seat cushion as a flotation device, and Cass taps me from across the aisle.

"There's a whole empty row behind us," she says. "I say we stockpile them to make a raft." I nod, and we discreetly fist-bump. That's Devereaux thinking right there. That's why we pull through.

As the plane taxis away from the airport, all I can see is a lot of concrete and some far-off trees listing in the wind, as small as dandelion heads from here.

"Not much of a view," Tim says, seeing me stare. "But every airport looks the same, anyway." Strip malls, airports, hotels—all trying to make me feel like I could be anywhere. Walking down the hallways at school, trying not to stand out, like I could be anyone. It worked for a while, but I don't want that anymore. I want a place to belong. I finally want to land.

"Excuse me, sweetie," an older, kinder-faced flight attendant says, stopping in front of our row and grinning forcibly at Denny. "I'm gonna have to ask you to lock your tray table for me."

"But I have to finish my assignment," Denny protests, and I do a double take. My brother has never once passed up an excuse to avoid homework. One of us usually has to sit with him and physically force him to focus.

"Well, aren't we the model student?" she says. "Don't worry, you can pick up right where you left off once we're in the air." Denny begrudgingly slides his paper and pen into his lap as Tim helps him get the tray table folded.

"What are you doing?" I ask once she moves on to her next victim.

Denny holds up his airplane drawing and flips it over. On the back, he's sketched out a copy of the family tree from the handout he showed me at the police station. Me, Cass, and Denny are the roots that anchor the tree, with our parents dangling perilously over our heads. I wonder if whoever designed the worksheet knows that it's supposed to be the other way around.

"Why didn't you just use the one your teacher gave you?" I ask.

"There weren't enough branches," Denny says matter-of-factly. "I had to fix it." He points to a new line emerging from Buck's branch, shooting over to Karen and then to Jeff, with lines for Tim and Leah curling down like improbable grape vines grafted onto a maple.

"That's perfect, meatball," I say.

"Mrs. M will probably give me a check-minus, though," he frowns. "She doesn't like it when we don't follow directions."

"You know what?" I say, reaching across Tim's lap to tussle Denny's hair. "Who cares what she thinks?"

"Yeah," he grins. As I sit back upright, Tim catches my hand and holds on tight.

"Listen," he says to both of us. "Any minute now, we're

going to start to move really, really fast, and the plane will start to rattle, but that's just because the pilot has to pick up as much speed as he can to give us momentum for takeoff. It's normal."

"Mmm hmmm." I press my spine hard against my seatback and take a deep breath. I know he's just trying to help, but I wish Tim hadn't told me that. I had almost forgotten about the whole leaving-the-ground thing. And while I'm familiar with the physics of flight, lift and thrust and drag and all that, it's one thing to study it on a page in a textbook and another to actually be sitting in a four-hundred-ton machine about to wage a war with gravity. When there's such a strong force pulling you down, it's hard to imagine there could be an even greater one lifting you up. But it happens to millions of people every single day, so why not now? Why not me?

"Flight attendants, please be seated for takeoff."

I look over at Cass, but she's engrossed in conversation with her new best friend, Leah. It's just as well. I don't want to make her nervous. I sit still and try to ignore the adrenaline flooding my veins, telling every bone in my body to get up and bolt.

"Are you okay?" Tim massages my hand with his thumb.

"Define 'okay.'"

"Alive?"

"For now." I concentrate on taking slow lungsful of air, in through my nose and out through my mouth. I've heard that keeps your heart rate in check, but judging from my skyrocketing pulse, it's not working yet.

"Remember, once we get in the air, it'll feel like we're not moving," he says.

As the plane picks up speed, the overheard bins start to sway. "Uh-huh," I say skeptically.

"This is the worst part. It'll be over in a minute. You'll see."

"This. Is. *Awesome*," Denny says, pressing his face against the window.

Suddenly we really accelerate, and I feel like I'm sucked back against my seat, helpless and lightheaded.

"I can't do this," I whisper, squeezing my eyes shut. "I can't, I can't, I can't."

"I thought you could do anything," Tim says.

"I lied!" I say, almost laughing I'm so terrified. Everything's shaking violently now—the seats, the trays, the wings, my faith. We must be going a hundred and fifty miles an hour, hurtling through space toward an uncertain landing. I feel like I'm going to faint.

"Hey, I almost forgot, I owe you something," Tim says. He leans over and takes my face in his hands and kisses me, long and deep, just as we lift off the ground, the g-force of the earth pulling us back as we fight, against all odds, to rise up.

"Michelle?" He pulls back. "Michelle, open your eyes. It's over."

Just do it, I tell myself. *Don't be scared. Just let go.*

"You can see the whole world from up here," Cass marvels.

"You're missing it!" Denny cries.

"Just breathe," Tim says.

And then my ears pop. The static breaks. I open my eyes.

I'm on my way.

ACKNOWLEDGMENTS

Thank you to my wonderful editor, Jessica Almon, whose patience, humor, and creativity saved me many times throughout the writing process—and whose glasses I covet to a degree that is possibly not healthy. The entire staff at Razorbill, most especially Ben Schrank and Casey McIntyre, also earn my undying gratitude. Your enthusiasm, support, and incredible warmth mean the world to me, and unless you tell me to stop I will continue to profess my love awkwardly every time I see you in person. Anthony Elder designed a cover that surpassed my wildest dreams, so every time you look at the front of this book, you should give him an air high five.

As always, I am indebted to my crackerjack agent (and favorite coffee date) Brettne Bloom, who is my champion by every definition of the word, and who gently encourages me to occasionally pause my *Broad City* marathons to write words down on paper.

Additional thanks go out to everyone who made the writing of this book less lonesome and/or scary: to the Hungry Ghost Coffee Bar and Café on Flatbush and 6th Avenue, whose delicious lattes and baked goods fueled many a writing session, and whose music never sucked; to the village of sitters—Willow Westwood, Phoebe Smith, Cailin Smith, my parents, and my sister Zoe—who took care of my child while I ran off to become the cliché that is the tortured writer pounding the aforementioned lattes in the aforementioned coffee shop; to PO1 Charles Horwitz of the Montgomery County Police

Department and Ilana Harwayne-Gidansky, MD, who kindly offered their professional expertise regarding police procedure and hypoglycemia, respectively (if anything is factually inaccurate, it's due to the creative license I took with their sage and patient counsel); and to my dear friends and family, who inexplicably continue to love, encourage, and feed me regardless of how disheveled and/or cranky I appear in their presence while on a deadline.

Finally, as ever, I am grateful to my husband, Jeff, for his love and support—especially his fortitude in the face of the emotional hurricane that is being married to a perfectionistic writer—and to my son, Sam, who is quite simply the best person I know. In the immortal words of '90s Canadian heartthrob Bryan Adams, everything I do, I do it for you.